T0285424

The Melancholy of Untold History

ALSO BY MINSOO KANG

Fiction

Of Tales and Enigmas: Stories

Nonfiction

Invincible and Righteous Outlaw: The Korean Hero Hong Gildong in Literature, History, and Culture

Sublime Dreams of Living Machines: The Automaton in the European Imagination

Visions of the Industrial Age, 1830–1914: Modernity and the Anxiety of Representation in Europe (co-editor)

Translation

The Story of Hong Gildong (Penguin Classic)

The Melancholy of Untold History

A NOVEL

MINSOO KANG

wm
WILLIAM MORROW
An Imprint of HarperCollins*Publishers*

This is a work of fiction. Names, characters, places, and incidents are products of the author's imagination or are used fictitiously and are not to be construed as real. Any resemblance to actual events, locales, organizations, or persons, living or dead, is entirely coincidental.

FIRST EDITION

Designed by Leah Carlson-Stanisic

Library of Congress Cataloging-in-Publication Data has been applied for.

ISBN 978-0-06-333750-3

24 25 26 27 28 LBC 5 4 3 2 1

To my mother,

for her gifts of

literature 문학

kindness 자애

and

love 사랑

The Melancholy of Untold History

THE REALM OF THE GRAND CIRCLE

Early Dragon Child State

Autumn Bird State

Summer and Winter Period

Supreme Dynasty

Lofty Dynasty–Immaculate State (?)

Immaculate Dynasty

Seven Dynasties Period

Radiant Dynasty

Tranquil Dynasty of the Grand Circle

Three Dynasties Period

Celestial Dynasty of the Grand Circle

Amity League of Autonomous States

Prologue

The storyteller knew that he was doomed.

His body shivered in the cold grip of terror as he sat hunched in a corner of a cramped cell with a tightly packed crowd of people who were as frightened, filthy, and starving as he was. The enclosure was one of countless rows of them in a massive underground complex with stiflingly poor air circulation and the precarious light of a few flickering oil lamps. Six days ago, when the storyteller and many others had been taken down there, he had been horrified by the place and equally astounded to learn of its very existence. For the last three years, he had been walking over the site, completely ignorant of the dark immensity below his feet. It had dawned on him then that this hellish dungeon must have been built before the construction of the glorious new city on the land had begun. At the break of dawn, soldiers came and forced out the people from a cell, herding them away to some unknown place from which they never returned. The prisoners were given no food and just enough water not to expire, so it was obvious that none of them were meant to be kept there for long. He wondered if the multitudes who had labored to dig out these secret prisons had met the same fate, which made him shudder anew.

The storyteller wondered at the dire situation he had fallen into, as his journey to the place had begun with what had seemed like an amazingly fortunate turn in his life. He was born into a humble family, the son of a blacksmith who was expected to follow his father in the trade. At a young age, however, he displayed a remarkable talent for telling stories. He began by amusing members of his family and their acquaintances at household gatherings. Then an uncle, a street merchant who was particularly taken by his nephew's natural skill, had an inspiration and asked the boy's father for permission to take him to the marketplace to perform. The boy delighted his audience with such animated storytelling of one tale after another that the appreciative coins they tossed before him fell like rain, enough money to feed his family for ten days. After that, his father stopped teaching him the blacksmith's craft so that his uncle could continue taking him to the marketplace.

As he grew up, his reputation as a storyteller spread throughout the province, and he became especially famous for his astounding talent in making up a new story on the spot after someone suggested a subject, a theme, or the first line. "A fair maiden walking through a forest hears the roar of a tiger," someone would suggest. The storyteller would take only a moment to think before starting a tale of the maiden who helps a tiger caught in a trap, which would go on for hours. His listeners would be astounded by his creativity as well as his ability to arouse their deepest emotions with a moving narrative of the beautiful friendship between the girl and the beast.

He also became known for taking well-known tales from venerable sources to elaborate on them. Although he lacked formal education and could not read such works as Clouded Mirror's *Miscellany of Past Events*, Empty Vessel's *Ancient Whispers*, and Turbulent River's *Sixty Luminous Dreams of Sixty Dark Nights*, he took stories from them that he had heard through oral recounting and came up with much more detailed versions that were sometimes bawdy in nature. That garnered him the attention of even learned people who rather enjoyed, as a form of guilty pleasure, his riffs on classical tales in which gods, kings, and heroes spoke and behaved like everyday people, using profanity and acting silly. He was invited to perform at the homes of wealthy landowners, scholarly gentlemen, and even government officials who paid him generously for his efforts. But he continued to appear in markets, taverns, and other humble venues, as he genuinely enjoyed the company of the common folk who were his people. By the time he became old enough to marry, to a lovely seamstress who he wooed with tales of love, he was prosperous enough to buy a nice home and a modest tract of land for his family.

Then, just after his wife gave birth to twin boys, he was visited by what appeared at the time to be an incredible fortune. Word of his talents had somehow reached the ear of the emperor himself! And the Lord of All Under Heaven had dispatched a government official to offer him a job with the promise of a great reward. As the storyteller and his entire family prostrated themselves in the courtyard of their home, humbling themselves before the grand personage from the capital city who bore the golden dragon insignia of the emperor, the official explained that the exact nature of the job was a state secret and that it required the storyteller to be away from home for a number of years. Despite the mysterious nature of the proposal, he dared not refuse such an honor, one which also promised to make him wealthy beyond his wildest imagination.

After he bade tearful farewells to his parents, his wife, and his infant sons, the storyteller went to the local government office, where a massive enclosed wagon pulled by six horses and a military escort awaited him. There were already five people inside the vehicle, and they picked up many more in the course of the long journey to the far north that followed. As the storyteller got to know the others, he discovered that they were all people of special skills, including a house builder, a potter, a poet, a calligrapher, and so on. They traveled for almost a month, during which time they were forbidden by the soldiers from interacting with people in the places where they rested, ushered into rooms at inns in the middle of the night, and then put back in the wagon before dawn.

When they finally arrived at their destination, they were astounded to find themselves in what appeared to be a brand-new city that was under construction, with great buildings of marvelous design, magnificent gardens, and wide, well-paved streets. Many thousands of laborers, artisans, and artists were busy working at different sites under the supervision of architects and officials. A functionary in charge of newcomers showed the storyteller to his lodgings, a comfortable room in a clean new dormitory on the edge of the city. It was only then that he was finally informed of what his job there entailed. He was to report in the morning to an office in the city where he would be met by scribes. He would then recite stories for them to record. He was permitted to tell any kind of narrative he could come up with, but under the strict condition that they all had to be original tales that no one had heard before. He was warned that there would be severe punishments, including flogging, mutilation, and ouster from the place with no payment and no transportation back home, if it was found out that he had given them a story that was not of his creation or one that he had told before. But if he performed the task well, he would return home a fabulously wealthy man.

For the next three years, the storyteller worked hard at the task, with ten work days followed by two rest days. Despite the uniformity of the daily schedule of going to the office, sitting before the scribes, and telling stories, he found himself enjoying the routine. All mundane tasks of everyday living were taken care of, with maids who cleaned up his room and washed his clothes and a communal eating hall where good food was served in abundance. So he could spend all his time engaged in what he liked to do best–making up stories and reciting them. Even during his free time when he socialized with friends he made there over food and wine, took walks through the city under construction, or lay down on the mattress to rest, he found himself thinking of the next story to tell and the one after that. He dearly missed his lovely wife, his adorable children, and his proud parents, but it seemed like a great blessing to spend time doing what he loved while also ensuring a comfortable life for his family in the future.

After three years of telling countless tales, when the grand city was nearing completion, it was announced that the emperor himself was coming to inspect the place and to reward them for all their hard work. In the next months, excitement mounted as workers labored extra hard to complete their tasks, and the storyteller told his final tales, which he put a great deal of effort into perfecting. He was especially proud of the last stories he told, of two gods and two goddesses who lived on the four peaks of the mountain known as Four Verdant Mothers just outside the imperial capital, how their friendship turned into enmity that unleashed a great calamity upon the world. When he finished telling it, he was certain it was the finest tale that he had ever come up with, which made him feel very proud.

On the day of the emperor's arrival, all the people who had built the grand city gathered at its outskirts, ready to welcome and pay respects to the Lord of All Under Heaven on their hands and knees. What appeared on the horizon, however, was not the ruler and his retinue but a great army of soldiers that marched toward them as if to engage them in battle. Fearsome men in full armor and bearing lofty spears surrounded the crowd in good order while cavalrymen rode into the city to make sure that no one was absent. Once they ascertained the presence of all, they herded them into the massive underground complex that none of the people had known existed beneath their feet the whole time and locked them up in cells. The next morning, the soldiers returned to take out the first group of people who never returned.

As the storyteller sat against the cold wall of the cell with his arms wound tightly around folded legs and his head bowed down on his knees, he thought of his wife and his parents waiting anxiously for his return, which made him break down in tears. When he had begun his work at the new city, he had looked forward to becoming an honored personage in his hometown, one who had the distinction of having been in the service of the Lord of All Under Heaven. But now that it appeared that he and all his stories would be consigned to oblivion for a reason that none of the terrified people in the prison could fathom, all he wanted was to lie down with his wife, hold his children, and pay respects to his parents one last time. He wondered if they would receive the reward he had been promised for his work, or if they would also meet the same fate as him.

Why? he wondered as he wept. *Why is the emperor doing this to us? What have we done to incur his wrath? All we did was work diligently at our individual tasks that he had assigned to us. So why are we sitting in this terrible place awaiting some dark fate?*

He was aroused from his mournful thoughts by the sound of people gasping in fear around him. When he looked up, he saw three soldiers walking down the corridor between the cells. Their appearance in the middle of the night was unexpected, as they had always come at dawn to take people away. They stopped outside his cell, and, to the storyteller's horror, the officer among them pointed a finger at him.

"You! Storyteller. You are coming with me."

The storyteller remained still, frozen in fear, as the soldiers unlocked the cell and approached him, the other prisoners frantically moving aside to make way for them. Without waiting for him to recover from his petrified paralysis, the soldiers roughly picked him up and pushed him out of the cell. He went along passively as they walked him through the prison complex, then up the stairs and out to the frigid night. He fell into a numb daze as his mind sought desperately to escape from the sheer terror of the moment. He was barely cognizant of being hauled into a nearby building and into a tiny room with nothing in it but a bucket of water, a small towel, a set of fresh clothing, and a bowl of rice gruel.

"Eat, clean, and get dressed," the officer commanded before they left the room and locked the door.

The bewildered storyteller stood still for a moment, but his desperate hunger presently took over as he lunged at the bowl of gruel which he swallowed in a few large gulps, hardly tasting the lukewarm thickness. After he licked the bowl clean, getting the last bits of soggy rice, he moved automatically in removing his filthy clothes, washing himself with the ice-cold water, drying himself with the towel, and getting dressed. As he began to feel a little stronger from the food and the refreshing sense of cleanness, he wondered if he could dare to hope that this was perhaps not the end for him.

The door was unlocked and the officer appeared again, waving imperiously at him to come out of the room. They took him outside again, and they walked for a long time through the wide streets of the new city, eerily empty in the late hour. In the central part of the site, they came to a large mansion that was well guarded with numerous soldiers in full battle armor and bearing glimmering halberds. Those at the main gate saluted the officer and opened the entrance for them to pass through. They proceeded across a spacious courtyard and into the main building. At the end of a long corridor, another pair of guards opened the sliding doors to reveal a vast hall lit up with many oil lamps. In the middle of the space was a long table covered in sumptuous dishes of all kinds–beef, pork, pheasant, and fish, as well as vegetables, mushrooms, and dumplings. The bowl of gruel had done little to allay the storyteller's hunger, so his mouth began to water at the sight and fragrance of the food. It took him a moment to notice the man sitting on the other side of the table, a great, bloated figure clad in a robe of red radiant fabric who was pouring liquor into a cup.

"Oh fuck," the storyteller inadvertently muttered just before the officer violently pushed him down, making him fall to his hands and knees.

"So you are the storyteller I heard so much about," said the emperor, the Lord of All Under Heaven. "I am bored. Tell me a story."

"Fuck," the storyteller could not help saying under his breath once again as the tiny flicker of hope inside him was extinguished and terror gripped his heart once more.

"WHEN A CIVILIZATION tells stories about itself," the historian told his undergraduate students in the packed lecture hall, "it starts by relating tales of gods, monsters, and heroes. As that civilization develops, even as it continues to tell fantastic stories of the divine, it also begins to narrate its history, especially about important personages of the past who achieved great things in the world. But when it enters the modern era, it becomes increasingly interested in the lives of ordinary people, including their inner thoughts and feelings. This development, from myth to history to ordinary life, can be discerned in cultures across the world, but it would be simplistic to think of the three modes of storytelling as absolutely distinct from one another. A new mode becomes dominant, but certain characteristics of the previous one persist in different degrees. So even as people tell stories of worldly events, they sometimes feature the intimation of the divine, of unseen gods affecting things from behind the scenes. Even in our time, a historian may speak of the 'spirit of the times' as an abstract concept, but it is sometimes treated like an actual being that influences the course of events. Gods and monsters may have retreated to the shadows in the face of modernity, but they still haunt us in the guises of ideas and longings. So rather than thinking of myth, history, and ordinary life as strictly discrete categories that storytellers moved through in the course of time, consider them as phases in a spectrum in which one way of making sense of a people's place in the world blends into another in a gradual evolutionary manner.

"In our next lecture, we will explore a famous example of this, comparing the myth of the founding of the Autumn Bird State to the historical account found in Grand Historian Clouded Mirror's work *True Records of Past Events*. That is all for today."

There was the sudden bustle of students putting away their notebooks and laptops before leaving the hall, a few of them coming up to the podium to ask questions. The historian dealt with them with patience, appreciating the enthusiasm and intellectual curiosity of those who wanted to find out just one more thing before the next class. So it took a while for him to get out of the hall and walk to the adjacent building that housed his office in the department of history.

As he reached the central corridor through the floor, a door opened and a colleague rushed out. She was a young woman who had been hired as an assistant professor just three years before.

"Late?" the historian asked in amusement as she struggled to lock her office door in a hurry.

"Very late," she replied with a smile. "Looking forward to tonight though."

"Good. Make sure you and your boyfriend come hungry. My wife is apparently cooking something elaborate."

"Can't wait," she said as she departed.

She had earned her undergraduate degree at the university but had gone overseas for her graduate work before returning home to teach at her alma mater. Despite the fact that the two of them were of different generations, they had hit it off right away, and he had naturally become her mentor at the department. He was one of the most eminent figures of national history, having made significant discoveries that overturned previous views of the traditional past, while she was just starting her career in cutting-edge fields of gender studies and material culture. Yet they found it easy to relate to each other as colleagues and, later, friends. In their interactions, he found her to be a brilliant scholar as well as a delightful person with an enthusiastic personality and kindly disposition. After he had her over to his house a number of times, it pleased him that his wife became fond of her as well. As he had gone through a few rather hectic days, dealing with contentious committee meetings and graduate students in dissertation crisis, he was very much looking forward to rounding off the week with a pleasant dinner with his favorite people.

He took care of some urgent matters at his office before heading home early to see if his wife needed help preparing dinner. She had to go on what promised to be a grueling three-day trip the next day, to inspect the damage done by massive flooding along the northeast coast so that she could determine how her nongovernmental aid organization could best provide help. He had offered to prepare the meal himself or pick up something from a restaurant so that she could prepare for her journey, but she had insisted on cooking as there was a new dish she was anxious to try out.

The dinner proved to be a great deal of fun, with his sociable wife and vivacious colleague doing most of the talking and him contributing every once in a while. His colleague's boyfriend, however, hardly said anything at all, though he seemed engaged in listening to the lively conversation. At the end of the evening, after the guests left, the historian insisted on cleaning up and doing the dishes so his wife could relax a bit. She kissed him in appreciation and went upstairs to take a bath.

"She's rather wonderful, isn't she?" she said as they got ready for bed.

"Yes," the historian replied. "A real breath of fresh air in a department full of old fogies like me."

"Oh, you are not old," she said with a smile. "Besides, if you are old, so am I."

"I certainly wouldn't say that," he said, returning the smile.

"She's brilliant, and so much fun as well," his wife went on. "If she hadn't been so dead set on having an academic career, I would have snatched her right up to work at my company."

"That would have been a great loss for us and great gain for you."

"She's also so beautiful, but..."

"What?"

"Oh, nothing. I had a mean thought. Never mind."

"Tell me."

"This is bad, but... why is she with that guy?"

The historian could not help laughing at that. His colleague's boyfriend was a nice enough fellow who worked as an IT engineer at a major corporation. But he was also a rather nondescript guy with very little of interest to say. He did seem mismatched with such a bright and attractive woman.

"Who knows what goes on in a relationship," he said.

"That's true."

"Besides, I bet a lot of people say that about you being with me."

"What? Why would they do that?"

"Oh, you know."

"That's ridiculous. They say, 'Look, she's with that impressive man who's a famous historian and a charismatic professor.'"

"I don't think they would use the word 'charismatic' when I'm standing next to you."

"Oh, shut up and kiss me."

Given the busy day ahead of her and an early-morning class he had to teach, they had planned on going to sleep early. But as they kissed, they found themselves becoming heated, and they ended up making slow and gentle love that pleased and relaxed them both. Afterward, they continued to kiss and stroke each other's cheeks and hair while looking into each other's eyes, until they gradually fell asleep with smiles on their faces.

All his life, the historian had never found the need for an alarm, as he possessed an internal clock that unerringly woke him at the right time. When he had to get up to go to work, he made an effort not to disturb his wife, sliding carefully out of bed and tiptoeing over to the bathroom. He took a shower before he went into the adjacent walk-in closet and got dressed for the day.

When he came out, he looked down at the sleeping figure of his wife and suddenly felt overwhelmed with emotion by the sight of her form in graceful repose. He thought of how she had come into his life at a time when he had virtually resigned himself to a solitary existence, and how she had changed everything for the better. As he was about to leave the room, he felt a sudden and strong urge to wake her and tell her how much he loved her. He wanted to see her reaction to those words on her face so that he could remember it in the following days of her absence. But then he considered that it would be selfish, as she needed her rest to face the arduous trip ahead of her. So he just mouthed "I love you" to her before quietly leaving her presence.

He would come to deeply regret not having disturbed her and saying those words, as that would be the last time he would see her alive.

Myths operate within the diagram of ritual, which presupposes total and adequate explanations of things as they are and were; it is a sequence of radically unchangeable gestures. Fictions are for finding things out, and they change as the needs of sense-making change. Myths are the agents of stability, fictions the agents of change. Myths call for absolute, fictions for conditional assent.

—Frank Kermode, *The Sense of an Ending*

CHAPTER ONE

Myth I

On Four Verdant Mothers

Three days before the emperor came to the new city, the storyteller sat cross-legged on a thick mat in a spacious office in a building of light lacquered wood. Before him was a small octagonal table with a turquoise pot of tea and a cup. Three scribes dressed in the blue robes of lower functionaries sat facing him before their own individual tables, each with a stack of paper, an ink block, and a brush. A long narrow window on the top portion of the wall behind the storyteller let in a slanted pillar of the morning light which rested in a languid diagonal across the floor.

The storyteller sat still with his eyes closed for a while, calmly banishing any mundane thoughts, concerns, and desires from his mind so that the river of narrative would flow freely down from the clouded mountain of his imagining self. When he finally opened them, the scribes picked up their brushes, ready to write down his every word.

THE MAGNIFICENT MOUNTAIN known as Four Verdant Mothers rose steeply out of the ground like four great pillars on a shared base, covered in luminous foliage of green and yellow. The grandeur of its heights was accentuated by the perfect flatness of the land around it that stretched all the way to the horizon. It was a rich place of fertile earth, clear waters, and mild weather where myriad animals and birds wandered about in peaceful harmony. Human beings had yet to disturb the tranquil land.

On the four lofty peaks, there resided two mountain gods and two mountain goddesses, each with a home on a summit. They lived on amicable terms with one another, often gathering at one of their dwellings to enjoy meals, wine, and one another's company, a great pleasure of their serene and leisurely lives. On one particular meeting at the home of one known as Red Mountain God, they sat on a veranda that was perched over a sheer cliff, affording them a magnificent, open view of the vast and colorful land below. They whiled away the spring day reclining on plush mats, drinking wine, and making remarks that were profound and humorous by turns. Their animal companions–a fire bear, an autumn bird, a radiant tiger, and a deer dragon–lazed about in a nearby garden, napping in the comfort of the sun's benevolent warmth.

One known as Green Mountain Goddess gazed upon clouds floating by the peak, and she spoke out.

"See those shapes that look like so many sheep, how they swim across the sky without a care in the world. What a fair sight it is." She then picked up her cup and finished her drink.

Red Mountain God politely poured more wine for her before he turned to look at what she beheld.

"The sight is indeed fair, my dear friend," he said. "But do you not see that it is not the clouds that are moving? They are still, hanging motionless in the sky like lotus flowers on calm water. It is the world that is moving around them, giving the clouds the mere appearance of motion." He took up his own cup and finished the drink.

One called Yellow Mountain Goddess poured for him before taking her turn to express her thought.

"Ah, my most respected friends, how it mortifies me to disagree with both of you. It is neither the clouds nor the world that moves, for they are but phantoms of our imagination. And how can such insubstantial things be said to do anything at all? What is moving is our minds." She finished her drink.

"What are you all babbling about?" one known as Blue Mountain God said, pouring for Yellow Mountain Goddess. "You think you are saying something profound when you are only farting out of your mouths. Shut up with your nonsense and have more wine, you drunken donkeys."

They all laughed uproariously at that, which woke up their animal companions, who looked at them with annoyed expressions before returning to sleep.

"Speaking of wine," Blue Mountain God said, "it looks like our host did not think well enough of us to prepare a sufficient amount." He shook a vase over his cup but only got a few drops.

"How inexcusable of me!" Red Mountain God exclaimed. "I thought I had gathered more than ample to enjoy all day long, but I had forgotten what a bunch of gluttonous lushes you are. But no need to concern yourselves. I have a good friend who is the master of a sky orchard where he grows sublime fruit for the lofty personages of the Heavenly Realm. He also makes the most exquisite wine from the fruits. He is like a brother to me, so I am certain that he will provide me with all we need."

He jumped to his feet and rushed to the garden, where he roused his animal companion, the fire bear, before climbing onto its back. At a command from the god, the beast burst into flames and sprouted two great wings of fire. It then flew up into the sky.

The fiery creature and its divine master sped across the heavens, covering a hundred great spans in an instant and leaving a trail of fire behind them. They slowed down only when they approached a vast cloud upon which sprawled a great orchard full of trees with colorful fruits of many kinds. When they reached the place, Red Mountain God's dear friend, Heavenly Orchard Master, was already waiting for him at the edge of the cloud. They exchanged happy greetings before Red Mountain God explained his predicament to him. Heavenly Orchard Master laughed heartily before assuring him that it would be a pleasure to provide him with some of his best fruit wine. He ordered his servants to bring some in a pot before he and his old friend exchanged news of their recent activities.

The servants presently brought an enormous pot full of wine, and Red Mountain God placed it securely on the fire bear's back. He then expressed his gratitude to his friend and promised to bring him an equal amount of sweet tea leaves from Four Verdant Mothers. The god then mounted his animal companion and flew away to return home.

When they were halfway back, he noticed that they were being followed by someone on a speeding cloud. He peered at the pursuer and was astounded to see a naked sky baby approaching him.

"Uncle! Uncle!" the sky baby called out to him. "A moment ago, I was traveling to the Heavenly Realm when I caught a whiff of the delicious fragrance coming from that pot. My guess is that it contains wine made from sublime fruit."

"So? What business is that of yours?" Red Mountain God asked, annoyed that the little rascal dared to address him as "uncle" rather than call him by a proper and respectful title.

"Uncle, I have been traveling on this cloud all day, and I am so very thirsty. Could you spare me just one cup of wine?"

"What? But you are just a baby. How could someone as young as you drink wine? Why don't you go beg someone for a cup of milk?"

"I may be a baby, but I am a sky baby!" he asserted proudly. "I can fly on a cloud, rip up a mountain with my bare hands, and beat anyone in a drinking bout. I bet I can beat you, Uncle, and see your face hit the ground in a drunken stupor and break your nose. What a ridiculous sight you would be then," he said, and laughed.

"Such insolence from such a little one! Begone, child, I have no wine for you. It is for my friends who are grown-ups."

"But you have so much, Uncle! Look at the size of that pot. Surely you can part with one measly cup of it."

"I said, begone! What an obnoxious child."

"Obnoxious! Not only do you not give me any wine, you insult me as well. Very well, you stingy old bastard, you flaccid pig's dick, you donkey's dirty anus. May you pay dearly for your lack of generosity!"

The sky baby cursed him and flew off in a rage.

"What an awful baby!" Red Mountain God exclaimed. "Someone needs to give that little brat a good spanking or a switch to the calves."

He went on to Four Verdant Mothers Mountain, where he forgot about the child as he shared the delicious wine and made much merry with the other three gods throughout the day.

In the meantime, the sky baby went off fuming and still very thirsty. He then hit upon the idea that if he followed the fiery trail left by the fire bear to where it had come from, he could find the source of the wine. So he flew on his cloud until he arrived at the sky orchard. Spying the delicious fruits hanging ripe on so many trees, he snuck into the place, careful to evade the guardian spirits there. When he came across a soaring tree of countless branches that was filled with huge ripe peaches, he quickly plucked five of them and ran out of the orchard. He got back on his cloud and flew far away before he stopped to enjoy the fruits of his theft. They proved to be so delicious and juicy that they not only quenched his thirst but filled his stomach as well. After he consumed three of them, he decided to save the other two for later. He was about to be on his way when suddenly a great luminous dragon appeared out of nowhere and spoke to the sky baby.

"Sky Baby, Sky Baby, I was on my way to the southern sea when I caught a whiff of the delicious fragrance coming from those peaches. My guess is that they are sublime fruits from the sky orchard."

"So? What business is that of yours?" the sky baby asked the dragon, wary of what it might want from him.

"Sky Baby, I have been flying through the sky all day, and I am so very hungry. Please give me one or two of those peaches to eat."

The sky baby was about to refuse, but then he remembered how it felt when Red Mountain God rejected his request for a cup of wine, how humiliated and enraged he had become at his parsimony. *I should not act in the same way as that nasty old mountain god and make this dragon feel bad. Heaven has decreed that all creatures should be kind to one another, and their failure to do so is the cause of all discord in the world.*

"I was going to save these peaches to eat later," the sky baby told the dragon, "but you are hungry now, whereas I am full and content. Here, you can have them." He tossed the fruits to the dragon, who swallowed them both in one gulp.

"Thank you, Sky Baby, that was absolutely delicious," the dragon said. "You are a most generous creature. How would you like to ride on my back for a while? We can have some fun together flying about."

"That sounds good to me!" the sky baby said, and jumped on the dragon's back.

As the dragon raced through the air, doing somersaults and side rolls, the sky baby laughed out loud in delight. At some point in their play, the dragon released a fart with a thunder-like noise, sending forth a thick purple cloud with red lightning flashing inside it, which made them both laugh. The dragon then let out a tremendous burp, and a peach pit fell out of its mouth, which made them laugh again. After that, the two became the best of friends and embarked on many adventures across both the heavenly and the terrestrial realms. In fact, all the tales of their doings, if collected together, could fill one thick volume. There is a particularly amusing story of how they came to a forest where an army of nasty goblins lived. The creatures emerged from the woods at night to terrorize people who lived in nearby villages. How the dragon and the sky baby made war on the goblins is a most delightful tale, but this is not the time to tell it.

The peach pit that the dragon burped out fell from the sky and landed in the garden of Red Mountain God's home, where it buried itself in the earth. The two mountain gods and the two mountain goddesses did not notice, because all of them were fast asleep on the veranda, having fallen into a stupor after partaking of the delicious wine that Red Mountain God had brought from the sky orchard. In fact, their sleep was so deep that it is unknown whether they slept for an entire day, a month, a year, or even a hundred years. If they had slept for a hundred years, then the animal companions they would have found in the garden upon waking would not have been the ones they had known, but their descendants, as the creatures would have kept faithful watch over their masters from one generation to the next. The immortal gods, with their utterly different sense of time from mortal creatures, would hardly have noticed the difference.

The first to awake from the profound slumber was Blue Mountain God, who felt a tremendous need to empty his bladder. Still groggy from his sleep and a dream in which he was a cat wandering among piles of books in the study of a grieving historian, he slowly got to his feet and began to make his way to the outhouse. When he was only halfway there, however, he suddenly realized that he was not going to make it to the building. Wary of humiliating himself in front of his friends, he quickly ran through some bamboo trees in the garden and relieved himself there. As he did so in great profusion–in a veritable waterfall, enjoying the underrated and rarely appreciated pleasure of release–he looked up at the sky and beheld a strange sight.

The great dome above was just starting to darken with the coming of twilight. In the midst of the clear expanse of deepening blue, there was a thick purple cloud hanging ominously above the mountain with red lightning flashing inside. Blue Mountain God could not know that it was the dragon's fart cloud.

"An omen of discord," he said to himself in concern. "But surely not among us."

When he was finally done, he shook his member and put it away, feeling deeply relieved. He was about to rejoin his friends when he saw another peculiar sight. Among the tall bamboo, there was a small tree with only one branch, which carried a huge peach. He walked over and touched the fruit, mesmerized by its perfect shape and its promise of deliciousness. At that moment, he wanted nothing more than to pluck the fruit and gulp it all up.

He would have done just that too, but unbeknownst to him, just after he went in among the bamboo trees to relieve himself, Red Mountain God also woke up from the same need. His bladder was not as full as his friend's, though, so he was able to stroll leisurely over to the outhouse, where he completed his business. He was walking back to the veranda when he also saw the purple cloud with red lightning in the sky, which made him stop in wonder.

"An omen of discord," he said to himself. "But surely not among us."

He was about to return to the veranda when he noticed Blue Mountain God standing among the bamboo trees in his garden. His curiosity aroused, he went over to him.

"My esteemed friend," he called out, "what are you doing there among the trees?"

Blue Mountain God jumped in surprise and looked back at Red Mountain God with a guilty expression. The other frowned at his strange behavior, but then he noticed that, close to where Blue Mountain God was standing, there was a small tree with a peach hanging from its single branch.

"What is this?" he asked as he approached it.

"It is mine," Blue Mountain God said. "I found it, so it belongs to me."

"What are you talking about?" Red Mountain God said, incredulous, as he gazed at the fruit and saw how ripe and delicious it looked, instantly becoming mesmerized by it as well.

"It is mine, I tell you," Blue Mountain God repeated.

"How can you say that?" Red Mountain God said. "This is in my garden. You can't just point to something on my property and claim that it is yours."

"Why not? You would have never found it. If you hadn't come along, I would have just eaten it here and now. You only know about this peach because you are so annoyingly nosy."

"Annoying? Nosy? About what is in my own garden? Why should I not be nosy about it? Now, step away from that peach so I can take a better look at it."

"No! It is mine, I tell you."

"Nonsense!"

And so they argued, their voices becoming louder and louder, and their anger rising and rising.

The sound of their shouting awakened Green Mountain Goddess from her slumber. When she opened her eyes, the first thing she saw was the purple cloud with red lightning hanging in the sky above.

"An omen of discord," she said to herself. "But surely not among us."

As Red Mountain God and Blue Mountain God continued to argue, making it impossible for her to return to sleep, she got up and went over to investigate. Listening in on their words, she learned what they were so upset about, so she looked in among the trees and saw the peach, which mesmerized her as well. She wanted to eat it, but she had no basis to claim it as her own. Still...

"In the interest of our harmonious friendship," she interrupted Blue Mountain God and Red Mountain God, both of whom jumped with surprise at her unexpected appearance, "we should share it. Look how big it is. Enough to go around for all of us."

Both Red Mountain God and Blue Mountain God frowned at that.

"But why should you get a piece at all?" Blue Mountain God asked. "You didn't find it."

"And this isn't your garden," Red Mountain God said. "It's my garden. So anything that grows here belongs to me."

Then all three began to argue over the peach.

Red Mountain God, in his enraged animation, moved about while shouting, until he stepped into the puddle of Blue Mountain God's urine.

"Ah fuck!" he exclaimed, and shook his foot. "You filthy beast! Pissing in my garden like a damn animal! Disgusting!"

"Don't yell at me after blundering into my piss, you clumsy oaf."

"Kiss my ass!"

"Your fat pimply monkey's bum? Never!"

Wary of standing on urine-soaked ground, all three of them walked out from among the trees as they continued to argue.

Yellow Mountain Goddess woke up then and saw the purple cloud with red lightning in the sky.

"An omen of discord," she said to herself. "But surely not among us."

As the other three were nearby now, Yellow Mountain Goddess could clearly make out their words from the veranda. When she learned what they were arguing so vociferously about, her curiosity became aroused. She got up and, careful not to be seen by the others, snuck around the garden until she was among the bamboo trees. She saw the peach, which she found irresistible, so she quickly plucked it from the branch and hid it in the sleeve of her robe before returning stealthily to the veranda.

"Ah, I can't sleep with the three of you pecking at one another like a bunch of crazed chickens," she said, stepping down from the veranda as if she had just woken up. "What a lousy end to a nice day, ruined by your pettiness. You should all be ashamed of yourselves, acting like greedy children. I am going home."

She called her animal companion, the deer dragon, which came over and bent down for its master to mount it. When Yellow Mountain Goddess was seated comfortably on its back, the creature shook its silver antlers and the golden scales of its body and leapt into the air. With one jump, it cleared the walls of Red Mountain God's house, and it proceeded to take its master home with a series of such mighty leaps. They did not get far before Yellow Mountain Goddess could wait no longer and took out the peach to eat it. It was the most delicious thing she had ever tasted, so she consumed the entire thing in a few large bites. When she was done, she spat out the pit and sighed in deep satisfaction as the deer dragon bore her home.

In the meantime, the words of Yellow Mountain Goddess shamed the others, so they reluctantly agreed to share the peach, which would be divided into three equal pieces for them to enjoy. When they went to the tree, however, they found the fruit gone. After a moment of stupefaction, Red Mountain God and Blue Mountain God accused Green Mountain Goddess of having surreptitiously taken the peach while the two of them were distracted by their argument. Green Mountain Goddess reacted with enraged indignation at the accusation, which was all the more acute from secretly wishing she had done exactly that. After she cursed them both for their slander, she stalked off to her companion animal, the autumn bird, mounted it, and flew away.

The two remaining gods, filled with resentment at being deprived of the fruit that each had thought was rightly his, found that they had nothing more to say to each other. Blue Mountain God mounted his animal companion, the radiant tiger, and rode off. Once he was gone, Red Mountain God cursed the entire day and his unfaithful friends. He went into his house and tried to meditate, but he found that he was still too angry to empty his mind. So he decided to take a walk with his animal companion, the fire bear.

As the day came to an end with the sun sinking behind the far horizon, Red Mountain God was returning home when he came across a peach pit on the ground. It lay in the direction of the peak where Yellow Mountain Goddess lived, so he knew at once who had eaten the fruit. Filled with renewed rage, he loudly cursed Yellow Mountain Goddess for her deception, Blue Mountain God for not letting him have the fruit of his garden in the first place, and Green Mountain Goddess for trying to get a piece for herself when she had no right to any. He then resolved not to have anything to do with such false friends ever again. At the same time, Blue Mountain God and Green

Mountain Goddess made the same resolution, while Yellow Mountain Goddess decided to avoid the others from the fear that they would somehow discover that she had taken and eaten the peach all by herself.

That is how the four friends on Four Verdant Mothers became estranged, each nursing their resentment toward the others. And so harmony on the peaks was broken, giving way to enmity.

CHAPTER TWO

Life I

The Melancholy of Untold History

The lovers lay close together, their bare bodies touching and their limbs intertwined, luxuriating in the warm comfort of their intimacy.

"How does the story end?" she asked in a dreamy voice.

"I don't know," he replied. "I don't know if the ending can be known. I don't know if there can be a real ending."

"That makes me sad."

"Why?"

"All unfinished stories make me sad."

He considered her words. "Hmm . . . the sadness of unfinished stories."

"Maybe that's what drives me in my work," she said. "What drives all of us. To escape that sadness."

"Are you perhaps thinking of the oppressed women of the Radiant dynasty who could not tell their stories?"

"Oh, thanks for reminding me that I have a manuscript to finish," she said with mock sarcasm, "which I should be working on right now."

They both laughed at that.

She was in the process of revising her PhD dissertation into a manuscript for publication, the subject of her work being the history of women during the Radiant dynasty. It was a rather audacious undertaking, as the period was notorious for its particularly severe patriarchal regime, under which women were barred from playing significant roles in public, deprived of access to education, and afforded few means of self-expression. Given the paucity of documentary evidence about the lives of women even at the highest level of the society, much of her book engaged in the use of unusual sources of evidence in building a picture of those who have been relegated to the margins. The chapter she was currently working on dealt with ghost stories from the era, many of which featured the lamentations of women who died under such iniquitous circumstances that they turned into discontented spirits. She showed that a close examination of the ghosts' complaints provided insights into ill treatment that women at the time were often subjected to, for which they could find no redress in legal or political institutions. They could only resort to supernatural means to express their sorrow and rage, as well as to exact some measure of justice for themselves.

"But there should be a way to finish your story," she said.

"Not through history," he said. "There's not enough evidence in the archives, no text to analyze, no material object to examine, nothing. The story starts simply enough, then blossoms into all its glorious complexities, then . . . just fades away to nothing."

She considered the matter for a time.

"If not through history," she said, "then perhaps through other means."

"What do you mean?"

"This reminds me of Saidiya Hartman's work."

"How?"

"In her research on the transatlantic slave trade, she wanted to tell stories from the perspectives of the enslaved people. But she had to deal with the massive imbalance in the available evidence from the point of view of the traders and the owners versus that of the slaves. Given the dearth of direct accounts by the victims, she asserts that following the standard rules of historical scholarship makes one complicit in the silencing of the oppressed. In such a circumstance of extreme power disparity, one could and should utilize what she calls 'critical fabulation' to redress the situation. That includes using the historian's personal meditation and fictional imagination to describe what the experiences of the silenced must have been like, to speak for those who were prevented from speaking for themselves."

"How could one apply 'critical fabulation' in this case? I'm not dealing with the suffering undergone by real human beings. I only have fragments of mythical tales with missing endings."

She considered the question.

"Well, Hartman was approaching the topic as a historian. A historian who finds it necessary to use imaginative tools to tell the full story of her subjects. But since you are dealing with myths, what if... what if you approached it from the other direction?"

"What do you mean?"

"You start from the imaginary, say in the form of fiction, and then you use historical writing to tell the story that you otherwise could not tell, or at least fill in the gaps where things have, as you said, faded away to nothing."

"Isn't that just historical fiction?"

"No," she said, and suddenly sat up, energized by her thoughts. "Because in historical fiction, the writer tries to immerse the reader in the story that takes place in the past through the mimetic effect."

He slid up next to her as she went on.

"I'm thinking of a hybrid work that reads partly like fiction and partly like history, that deliberately points to the very disjunction between the two that historical fiction tries to hide. Just as Hartman sought to go beyond the constraints of conventional historical writing, you could go beyond the constraints of conventional literary writing. So you deliberately violate the banal rule of 'show not tell' by telling as a historian when you need to. Instead of 'critical fabulation,' you could call it . . . 'fabulist history.' With that, you can provide an ending for the story, instead of just leaving us in the lurch because of some rigid commitment to academic rules of history."

"You are talking about a whole new genre of writing," he pointed out.

"Perhaps."

The historian considered it for a long moment.

"I don't know if I could create new content wholesale without any reference to sources," he said. "My historian's instinct would go against it. It would be too much of a challenge for me."

"But would it be any more challenging than what you do as a historian? Rarefying facts from uncertain evidence, dealing with unreliable accounts, conflicting records, outright lies and forgeries. Sometimes reading between the lines, filling gaps in the sources."

"Perhaps not more challenging, but... a different set of challenges. I don't know if I have the imaginative capacity for that. Besides, I rather like being rigidly committed to academic rules of history."

They both laughed.

"You shouldn't sell yourself short," she told him. "I think you are capable of anything."

He looked down at her face, so close that they were almost touching, and appreciated how luminous she appeared in the reflected sunlight coming through the gaps in the window blinds. He kissed her on the mouth and held her even closer, silently taking in the heat of her warmth and softness. They stayed together for a while longer, but then they both began to get up at the same time, as if having agreed on the moment when they would part. They dressed in silence before taking turns in the bathroom to clean themselves up. When they were done, they got ready to go out.

At the doorway, a fluffy cat with bluish fur appeared to see them off. The woman got down on one knee and scratched the animal on the head and cheeks, much to its purring pleasure.

"Goodbye, Radiant Tiger," she said regretfully.

They left his apartment building, walked down to the café around the block, ordered their usual drinks, and sat down at a quiet corner next to a wide window. It afforded them an open view of the intersection outside, where the traffic was light in the midmorning. They maintained their silence while sipping their drinks, listening to the music playing in the establishment, the heartbreaking melody of the second movement of Adrian Leverkühn's *Die Wahlverwandtschaften* symphony. As the warmth of their previous intimacy faded, it gave way to a somber chill in their mood.

"I . . . I can't do this anymore," she said in a subdued voice while gazing out the window. "My boyfriend . . . he is coming back tomorrow, and I don't want to . . ." She stopped and bowed her head.

He felt a sharp pain in his chest from hearing her words, though he had been expecting them in the last days, perhaps during the entire time they had been together. But what truly saddened him was that it did not hurt more, that he was incapable of feeling anything more than this quick stab and then the numbness that had become his usual state. He still cared about her deeply, so he tried to make it as easy as possible for her.

"I understand," he managed to tell her in a gentle tone. "And it's all right."

"But . . . but are you going to be all right?" she asked, looking at him with a distraught expression.

"I'll be fine."

His reply sounded so perfunctory and unconvincing that tears came to her eyes.

"Oh no," she said, looking away while quickly wiping her eyes.

"No, really," he tried to assure her. "I know how it sounds, but I promise I will be fine. Besides, it's not your responsibility to take care of me. You have your own life to live. I'll miss your company very much, but . . . I do understand. And I am . . . grateful."

She sat back and looked out the window again.

They remained silent for a long while.

"I think . . . I think I'd better go," she finally said.

"I can drive you . . ."

"No, thank you. I'll take the subway. I . . . I'm going to go, okay?"

"All right."

He began to get up to embrace her, but she turned away as soon as she got to her feet.

"Please take care," she said, and hurried out of the café.

From the window, he watched intently as she walked quickly out to the street, to a nearby crosswalk where half a dozen people were gathered. After a moment of the world appearing to be in suspended animation, the green light came on, and she joined the others in crossing the street. He followed the sight of her bright yellow coat as she made her way to a subway entrance and disappeared into it. Once she was gone from his sight, he sat back in his chair, feeling completely empty. *I'm a straw man*, he thought, *put together by myself*. He smiled bitterly at the idea before he sipped his drink.

A little over six months had passed since he had lost his wife. She had been returning from a tour of the coastal area devastated by a flood when the helicopter she had been on crashed. The overwhelming sense of numb emptiness that had fallen over him at receiving the news of her death had not abated at all since that time. And he had the distinct sense that he was condemned to remain in that state, of feeling removed from the world as well as his feelings, for the rest of his life. He knew that the people who cared about him would be less worried if they saw him break down in grief rather than appear so distant and distracted all the time, but he felt no compulsion to change his behavior to ease others' minds and could not force himself to feel what just was not there.

He thought of his young colleague who had just left him, considering the unexpected turn in their relationship. She was a naturally kind and generous person, a popular professor to the students for the active interest and support she showed them. On a number of occasions, she had gone out of her way to look after students who were in crisis, not only being attentive to their needs but also finding both campus and external resources to help them. When his wife died, she characteristically spent a significant amount of time taking care of him. Even as he appreciated her attention, he could not help speculating that she was moved to do so by the experience of a similar tragedy she had suffered in her past. After they had become friends, he had learned that when she had been in middle school, she had lost her beloved older brother in a fatal accident. So she was familiar with the devastating impact of such a loss on the living. He retained very little memory of his wife's funeral, which he had attended in a state of confused daze, but for some reason he clearly remembered seeing his colleague cry freely, almost breaking down completely, when he himself could not shed a single tear.

In the days that followed, he had found that he could not bear to be in his house that was filled with reminders of his wife. So he asked his brother-in-law, who owned a real estate company, if he could handle selling the place for him. He was very understanding and helpful on the matter, which allowed the historian to move right away into a small apartment that was within walking distance to the university. It was only after he signed the lease agreement that he wondered why he had chosen the locale, since he had been granted a leave of absence and he frankly did not know when or if he would return to his job. He could afford to quit, as he was financially well-off, not only through his professional successes but by inheriting his wife's immense wealth. He was aware that isolating himself in his grief was not a good idea, but he felt such an aversion to interacting with people that he could not imagine going back to the classroom to lecture and deal with students anytime soon.

When his colleague started visiting him at his new place, he found that hers was the only company he could stand. She provided him with a modicum of social interaction, keeping the talk mostly to mundane scholarly matters, the progress of her work, and the goings-on at the university and in the history department. He hardly cared about such things anymore, but he was grateful that she did not ask him about his feelings or try to change his behavior. She started coming around with increasing frequency, claiming that she had time on her hands because she needed to take a bit of a break from her manuscript to clear her head and her boyfriend was away on an extended business trip abroad. It was also good that Radiant Tiger, his wife's cat, who was generally a solitary creature that was shy of strangers, was fond of her and readily went to her for affection. It pained him greatly to see that the cat missed his wife, often wandering around the apartment looking for her and then staring at him with an expression of resentful accusation. His colleague's presence seemed to alleviate something for Radiant Tiger.

One day, as if he needed another misfortune, he twisted his ankle while going down the stairs of the apartment complex. He found it difficult to move around, so his place became messy from the neglect of basic housework, a task that he had become indifferent to even in the best of health. When she visited him, she looked around the space and insisted on cleaning it up. He protested vigorously, but she ignored him and went ahead, taking the vacuum and cleaning supplies out of the closet. Feeling guilty that he could not help because of his injury, and that he needed such help in the first place, he withdrew into his study to get out of her way at least. At his desk, he tried to get some work done, but he soon found himself gazing emptily out the window, at the faraway peaks of Four Verdant Mothers that soared over the gray cityscape. The green and yellow foliage of the mountain shimmered brightly under the afternoon sun, giving the place the appearance of a marvelous jewel that was also a colossal living being. But its grand beauty hardly registered in his mind as he beheld the view without a thought in his head or a feeling in his heart.

He was still looking out when she came in to tell him that she had finished and was going home. He thanked her and said goodbye before he resumed his blank staring. Some time passed during which he assumed that she had left, but when he finally turned a little, he was startled to see her at the doorway observing him. He was surprised again when she came over and sat on his lap. She then put an arm around his shoulder and laid her head on his chest to hold him tightly. It took a while, but he finally found himself relaxing into the comfort of her embrace with a sense of fatigued capitulation. He still could not bring himself to let out his grief, but he held her tightly like his life depended on it, like a drowning man on a buoy. After some time of the silent closeness, they looked at each other, and after another passage of time, they kissed. They stayed in each other's embrace for a while, until they wordlessly agreed to get up and go to the bedroom, where they made love for the first time. Afterward, he could remember little of what it was like, whether sweet or frantic or messy or beautiful, but he recalled a great sense of relief in the end. It felt like a temporary escape from the heaviness of his mourning, an all too brief time in which he felt somewhat human again.

She got dressed and left the apartment in such a hurry, as if in a panic, that he thought that she considered what had happened to be a terrible, embarrassing mistake, and that she would never return. But three days later, when his ankle felt much better, she appeared with some food in plastic containers. They talked as if nothing unusual had happened between them, so he thought that maybe it was to be a one-time thing that they would not speak of.

As they helped each other with the dishes after dinner, their conversation turned to a news report about the environmental state of Divine Bird River, which flowed through the northern part of the city. He was telling her about something he had seen on the waterway while he was on a boating trip there, when he suddenly recalled a moment with his wife from that time. As she had gazed out at the view of the river that glistened in the deep afternoon light, the sun had illuminated her in such a way that the reflection from the elegant green dress she had been wearing had created an emerald glow around her form. He had been staring enraptured at her when she had turned, noticed his look, and flashed him a smile that had been so radiant in its affection that he had found it hard to breathe. He remembered it as a rare moment of pristine perfection that affected him in a powerful way, making it certain that he would carry it with him always.

As he became overwhelmed by the memory, he stopped speaking in the middle of a sentence and froze, the water from the faucet running down the dish in his hand. He remained standing still, until his colleague took the dish, put it in the sink, and turned the water off. She then embraced him tightly. Just like before, they held each other for a time before they kissed, and then they went to the bedroom. If he had been in a normal state of mind, he might have obsessed over the unexpected development, worrying over its propriety and consequences, especially for his colleague. But even the affair felt like something that was taking place at a great distance from him, like he was sitting in some dark, lonely place, watching a movie about his life in ruins. It was not that he did not care about what was happening, or care for her, but it all felt somehow unreal to him.

As for her, when she pondered her actions afterward, she suddenly thought of a recurring dream that had haunted her for years after her brother's death. It was of her jumping into a dark pool of water, almost oily in its thick blackness, which he had fallen into. She tried desperately to pull him out, but he was too heavy and lifeless, and the water was so cold and suffocating. She would wake up terrified and heartbroken, falling into a fit of weeping. It naturally occurred to her that as the historian seemed to slip into the silent abyss of his grief before her, she felt compelled to pull him back from the brink, to make him want to remain in the world, which she kept failing in her dream to do for her brother.

After they made love, they stayed in bed talking for a long time while holding each other close, sometimes joined by Radiant Tiger, who scratched at the door to be let in and then sat at the foot of the bed to watch them with a judgmental expression. In the beginning, they studiously avoided talking about their new relationship, sticking to their usual scholarly interests in conversations that could have taken place in his office within the earshot of people passing by in the hallway. But they were naked and in each other's arms, periodically touching each other with gentle, unconscious strokes. It was a paradise of sorts for him, but one he knew to be fragile and transient in the midst of the vast and frigid wasteland inside him.

One night, they were watching a movie on the living room couch, becoming increasingly bored with a much-lauded fantasy epic that consisted mostly of one tedious battle scene after another, fought between armies of creatures marked simplistically as good and evil. He looked over at her to see if she felt the same way about the film, but he ended up staring fixedly at her face as he suddenly felt deeply moved by gratitude for her presence.

"It's so kind of you to be here with me," he told her. "You are very kind."

She looked at him and smiled. But then she turned away, her expression suddenly darkening.

"That's . . . that's not how I am."

"What do you mean?"

"I'm not such a kind person," she said with a distant look. "Not really."

"Why do you say that?" he asked. "After everything you've done for me, for your students . . ."

"I try to be . . . helpful to people, but . . . maybe it's to make up for knowing what a terribly callous person I truly am."

"Callous? What do you mean?" he asked as he grabbed the remote and turned off the movie that was annoying him.

She stopped to think for a while before answering him.

"Everybody loved my older brother," she said. "My parents, our relatives, the people at school. He was so smart and handsome, and he was genuinely nice to everyone. Won awards for academic excellence and trophies at track and swimming competitions. He also defended weak kids at school from bullies. That's the kind of boy he was. I loved him too, of course. He was such a great older brother when I was growing up. He always made time to play with me and was very patient. I don't remember him getting annoyed or losing his temper even once, even when I knew I was bugging him, being a needy younger sister. So when he died in the hiking accident, everyone was devastated. Especially since . . . since there were circumstances surrounding his fall that left open the possibility of suicide."

"Really? What circumstances?"

"I don't want to talk about that."

"All right," he said, understanding her reluctance.

"There was so much expectation placed on him, from my parents of course, but also from a lot of other people. He was studying for the college entrance examination that year, and everyone expected him to do well on it. After he was gone, some of his closest friends told me that he was feeling really stressed and depressed from the burden of all that pressure, all the hope for his future success. Yet he never showed any sign of that at home. He couldn't talk about it with my parents because they are old-fashioned people from the provinces who don't really know how to talk about feelings. And he had to be the strong, protective older brother to me. He asked how I was doing almost every day, and he listened attentively to everything I had to say, even if it was just trivial stuff. I realized after his death that I never asked him back, not once. I wondered if anyone did, everyone thinking that he must be doing fine with his intelligence and popularity and just being naturally good at everything he did. Maybe he killed himself because nobody asked him how he was doing. Maybe if it had occurred to me to ask . . ."

She had to pause to gather herself.

"Anyway," she continued, "I don't know if he killed himself. That's not for certain. And I really hope he didn't."

She fell silent again, lost in her thoughts.

"As I said," she went on after a while, "my parents are very traditional people, from the same little village where their people were small farmers, growing sorghum and raising pigs. They were the first in both of their extended families to get a proper education and move to the city for office jobs, but they remained conservative rural people inside. And they frankly had no idea know to deal with the grief of losing their beloved son. After he was gone, they became . . . angry. They became such angry people. My father began to drink a lot and sometimes got into fights with random people in liquor joints, and my mother became irritable all the time, criticizing and yelling at every little thing.

"I was going through my own mourning, but I tried to do what I could to make the situation at home a little better. I went out of my way to be helpful to my parents, taking on the chores and errands my brother had done, keeping up a cheerful front. It was exhausting really, especially with them being so upset all the time. Then one day, when my mother started yelling at me for not doing the laundry properly, I kind of lost it. I yelled back at her, and she blew her top, and then . . ." She trailed off.

"What happened?" he asked.

"I don't remember what she said. Not the exact words. I think I may have blocked it out because it was too painful, but the gist of it was that I should be the one who's dead, not my brother."

"Oh . . ." He couldn't think of what else to say.

"I . . . I couldn't believe what I'd heard, so I just stood there stunned. Then I went to my room and cried harder than I had ever done before, even harder than at the funeral. I think I heard my mother outside my door, but she never came in to talk to me. Didn't even knock on my door. Anyway, after that I stopped trying, and I pretty much stopped interacting with my parents. I didn't become a wayward rebellious daughter like some might have, though. On the contrary, I actually socialized less with my friends and studied more, spending all my free time doing extra schoolwork and reading books. I did my chores and sat down for meals with my parents, but other than that I pretty much stopped talking to them. I decided that since they didn't care about me at all, I should just act as if I were a boarder at the house. It was like that all throughout high school.

"Then I took the college entrance exam and got into Dragon Child National University with a scholarship, which was something that had been expected of my brother. I didn't even tell my parents about it. They only found out because the school principal called home to congratulate them. That night, when I was studying in my room, my father came in and sat down on the bed. His drinking had gotten better in the last year, but he remained a pretty angry guy. He asked me if I really got into Dragon Child on a scholarship, and when I said yes, he asked some questions about starting school and what I needed and so on. After I responded to all his questions with brief answers, he just sat there, trying to say something. I knew it was very difficult for him, being a naturally reticent guy who had a hard time articulating anything having to do with feelings. But after a while, he managed to say, 'Mother told me what she said to you years ago, after your older brother died. She didn't mean it.' He then abruptly left the room.

"This may sound strange, but that infuriated me. I wanted to scream and punch the walls and then leave the house and never come back. It really upset me that Mother did not have the decency to tell me that herself, that she had to put Father up to it. And it wasn't even an apology. So, in addition to being reminded of what she had said, her cowardice made me hate her even more. As for Father, I knew that he was trying to tell me that I did a good job and that he was proud of me, but he couldn't bring himself to say the actual words. Which reminded me that after my brother died, they didn't look after me at all, even though I was as devastated as they were. I was their child too, and they were supposed to take care of me. Instead, I took care of them while they just ignored me to nurse their own rage over what had happened. But... what upset me the most... what still upsets me..."

She had to stop to calm herself before she could go on.

"What Father said ... it wasn't true. Mother *did* mean what she'd said. If he had been completely honest, he would have told me that she shouldn't have said it out loud. The truth is... if they could have chosen which one of their children to lose ... there was no question that they would have sacrificed their daughter over their superstar son. Knowing that . . . I just can't . . ."

She had to stop again.

"Anyway," she went on after a while, "in my first week at the university, I met these three girls from the provinces who were going to live together in a small two-bedroom apartment. There was supposed to be a fourth girl living with them, but she had to drop out for some reason, and they were desperate for another roommate. Without considering it, I volunteered. I got a job at the university library so I could pay my share of the rent, and I moved out of the house without giving much notice to my parents. I could tell that they were surprised and saddened, but not so much and not enough to try to dissuade me. I went through my undergraduate years living with those girls, who are still my close friends, and in my senior year I got that government grant to do my graduate work abroad. When I was away, I called my parents only a few times a year, on Lunar New Year's Day, on their birthdays, and so on. And they called me on my birthday. But we never had much to say to one another, and we always hung up claiming the call was too expensive to stay on for long.

"Even after I returned, when I visited them, I always left fairly quickly after finishing a meal. I know . . . I know that if I were a better person, a better daughter, I would sympathize with what they've gone through. Given the kind of upbringing they had, they really didn't know how to go on after losing their son. But I'm still so angry at Mother for what she said and so resentful of their neglect that I can't bring myself to forgive them. And I know I am punishing them by depriving them of a relationship with their remaining child, but I still feel that they don't deserve to have me in their lives. I'm not even sure they want me in their lives. When I try to be helpful to the people in my life, perhaps it's to make myself feel that I am not such a terrible person. I may even overdo it sometimes. But deep down inside, I know that I'm not good."

She turned to look at him. "How could I be when I've basically cut myself off from my own parents?

"When I met my boyfriend and we went out on our first date, I really liked that his life experience was so different from mine. His past was untouched by the shadow of death. His parents, grandparents, younger brother, and older sisters are all alive and doing well. And they are all such content and easygoing people who are simply decent to one another, just as he is always nice to me. It felt good to be around someone like that."

As she fell silent with a downcast expression, he took her hand and gently grasped it.

"I'm so sorry all that happened to you," he said. "But none of it means that you are a bad person. What your mother said, it was a wound inflicted on you at the worst possible time in your life. And you are still recovering from it. Just because that takes time and you need to be away from your parents to heal, that doesn't mean that you are doing anything wrong. You *are* a good person. And I am so grateful that you are in my life."

They looked into each other's eyes for a moment before they kissed, and then held each other close. They sat in silence for a time.

"What are you thinking about?" she asked, seeing a searching expression on his face.

"Forgive me, but I don't remember you as an undergraduate at the university."

She laughed briefly.

"That's okay," she assured him. "I wasn't around the department much because I was a prelaw major then. It took me two years to realize that I hated the subject and had no interest in becoming a lawyer. I took two of your big lecture courses though. That's when I realized that history was going to be my real passion. But there were forty or fifty students in those classes, and the TAs did all the grading, so there's no reason you'd remember me."

"You didn't think about coming to see me once you decided to go to graduate school in history?"

"I thought about it, but..." She laughed at what she was about to confess. "I was so intimidated by you. I mean, you were the historian who proved that an entire period of our history was a complete fabrication! And your lectures were so amazing. I was always excited to go to class, even the one that met so early in the morning. There was one thing you said that I found particularly fascinating, something that I thought about a lot over the years. You said that when a civilization tells stories about itself, it starts with myths, dealing with gods and monsters. Then, when that civilization develops, it moves on to history, telling stories of important personages who achieved great things. When it moves into the modern era, it becomes increasingly interested in the lives of regular people, their thoughts and feelings. You described it as the movement from myth to history to life. During the summer vacation before my senior year, I read all your books and all the articles I could find. You should know that it was your lectures and writings that made me want to become a historian."

"I'm sure you would have found your path to history anyway, but it makes me happy to hear that. And you will be a great historian. I have no doubt in my mind about that."

"Thank you."

They smiled at each other.

"The way..." he began to say but stopped, looking concerned.

"What is it?" she asked.

"The way... the way I'm dealing with... my situation," he said in an uncertain tone, "does it remind you of how your parents dealt with your brother's death?"

"Oh no," she said. "Not at all. Really, no. You are not angry. You never got angry like my parents did. If you had gotten angry, that might have made me feel uncomfortable. But you are not like that. You are a gentle person. So you are okay. I mean, the way you are dealing with it... it's okay with me."

"All right."

"You don't sound convinced. Do you want to talk about it?"

"No," he said quickly. "Not really."

"All right."

He kissed her on the top of her head.

Radiant Tiger startled them by jumping on top of the couch and just as quickly running off again, which made them laugh. The cat went into one of the rooms and let out a plaintive meow for some reason.

CHAPTER THREE

Myth II

Beyond Four Verdant Mothers

Two days before the emperor arrived at the new city, the storyteller sat before the scribes to continue his story of the two mountain gods and the two mountain goddesses who lived on the peaks of Four Verdant Mothers.

AFTER THE INCIDENT of the peach that broke up the friendship among the four gods, they stayed away from one another through enmity, depriving themselves of the pleasure of their mutual company. Consequently, each of them had to find other ways of filling the extra time in the endless expanse of their immortal lives. For Yellow Mountain Goddess, she took to making frequent trips away from the mountain, bounding across the world on her animal companion, the deer dragon, to enjoy the scenery of different lands, rivers, and mountains.

One day, in the midst of one of her outings, she came across a group of humans traveling in a tight group like a herd of fearful animals. They were a primitive people dressed in furs, some armed with sharpened sticks, all of them looking dirty, exhausted, and demoralized. Her curiosity aroused, Yellow Mountain Goddess rode the deer dragon up to them. When the humans saw the goddess clad in a radiant robe of yellow, sitting on a great beast with silver antlers and a body covered in golden scales, they fell to their hands and knees in terror and awe. They bowed their heads down low, afraid to gaze upon the divine being.

"Who are you people, and what are you doing here?" Yellow Mountain Goddess asked them.

Their leader, an elderly man with a long white beard, managed to overcome his terror and approached the goddess by crawling on his hands and knees.

"Oh great goddess, we are but a simple and humble people searching for a new home," he told her in a trembling voice. "We come from a place that was once fertile and safe, but due to some curse laid upon us for an unknown trespass, our crops died in the fields, our water source turned foul, and marauders came to plunder our village. So we had no choice but to leave and search for a new land to live in. We have been traveling for a very long time but have found no suitable place in this great and vast world under heaven. And so we are on the verge of starvation and despair. Oh great goddess, if we have inadvertently offended you by coming here, please have mercy on us poor people. Yet another misfortune will destroy us for sure, when all we want is to live somewhere in peace."

"You have done nothing to offend me. And if you are looking for a good land to live on, I know such a place that is not occupied by people. Would you like me to show you the way?"

"Oh great goddess, what a blessing you would be bestowing upon us if you did so! Our gratitude toward you would know no bounds."

"Very well, then, follow me."

She rode her deer dragon at an easy pace, leading the destitute people to the land beneath Four Verdant Mothers. There, she not only showed them the best place to make their home, near fertile fields and a clear river full of fish, but it amused her to teach them new things as well. Seeing that they dwelled in simple tents that provided little protection from the environment, she taught them how to build houses with wood and mud. Their farming techniques were rudimentary, so she demonstrated better ways that would yield much more food for the people. She also instructed them on domesticating local animals, including sheep that provided them with wool to make clothes and blankets, the knitting and sewing of which she taught them as well.

Within just a few years, the people thrived at the place with comfortable homes and plenty to eat. At first, Yellow Mountain Goddess visited them regularly to remind them of the knowledge she had bestowed on them, correct their mistakes, and instruct them on new skills. But after a while, they proved to be a resilient and resourceful people who could manage and figure things out on their own, which pleased her a great deal to see. As she watched one generation of the people after another, they grew healthy, prosperous, and numerous, their village increasing in size decade after decade.

As time flowed on, new people began to arrive at the place, many of them following rumors of a land of plenty. The villagers welcomed the strangers and, remembering Yellow Mountain Goddess's kindness to them, passed on what they had learned from her. Eventually, another village was formed, then another, and yet another, until the land below Four Verdant Mothers became filled with people farming, fishing, hunting, building, and raising families. There was hardly any conflict among them, as there were more than enough fields, animals, and living spaces for everyone. And they were also united by their common love of Yellow Mountain Goddess, whom they worshipped as their deity, abandoning their traditional gods, who had done them no good. In their awe of the goddess, they dared not represent her directly in images, so they made statues of her animal companion, the deer dragon with silver antlers and golden-scaled body, through which they paid homage to her. On a certain day of each month that they set aside for her, they did no work but sang and danced before the statues and made offerings, all to express their gratitude and love for their divine patroness. They even took to calling themselves the Deer Dragon People. All of that delighted Yellow Mountain Goddess to no end.

Meanwhile, on Four Verdant Mothers, Red Mountain God was meditating on the veranda that hung over a cliff when he was disturbed by noises coming from the land below. When he looked down, he was surprised to see so many human beings gathered there, chanting in joy while dancing hand in hand. Ever since he had stopped socializing with the other mountain deities, he had spent much of his time with acquaintances in the sky, like his friend Heavenly Orchard Master. He had also visited the Heavenly Realm quite often to stay with important personages there. Given his frequent and extended absences from his home on Four Verdant Mothers, he had been completely oblivious to the developments in the world below, in particular the influx of humans in the area. But now, as he watched all the vibrant activities in the land, he became curious and decided to investigate. At first, he intended to ride his animal companion, the fire bear, down from the mountain, but it occurred to him that the people would become terrified by the creature. So he disguised himself as a humble traveler in a straw coat and a bamboo hat and strolled down to the villages, where he discreetly insinuated himself among the celebrating humans.

He found everything there to be of interest, including the large dwellings the humans had built, the great feasts they had prepared for everyone to enjoy, the melodious songs they sang, and the graceful dances they moved to. He was so entertained by all the sights and sounds that he even thought of bestowing some gift or blessing upon these peaceful and joyous people. But then he came across a large stone statue of a deer dragon. As he watched the villagers pile up all manner of food and other goods on an altar before the image as offerings, he suddenly understood how they came to thrive at the place.

He realized that all this was the doing of Yellow Mountain Goddess, the same goddess who had stolen the peach that had rightly been his.

Hundreds of years had passed since the incident at his home when he had come to break off his friendship with the other mountain deities. But when he was reminded of what had happened, he became filled with renewed rage.

And he resolved to get his revenge by destroying the humans under the care of the goddess.

He was going to summon his fire bear and command it to wreak havoc on all the villages by burning everything down with its flames. But then he thought of a subtler strategy, one that would hide his hand in it, in the same way that she had tried to hide her theft of the peach from him. Yes, he thought, he would see these people brought down low, but apparently at the hands of other humans.

He left the village and returned home, where he mounted the fire bear and flew up into the air. He traveled to the sky orchard, met with Heavenly Orchard Master, and told him what he needed. His friend listened before addressing him seriously.

"You are like a brother to me," he said to Red Mountain God, "and I would do anything for you. But I think you should reconsider the course you are taking. Why are you so angry about something so trivial that happened so long ago? Why not forget it and reconcile with your former friends? You used to be so close to them. I fear that what you mean to do will bring much suffering to the innocent, and it will lead to a terrible fate for you as well."

"I was close to them because I did not know what a bunch of deceitful, selfish, and greedy villains they were," Red Mountain God replied. "Once I found out, I could no longer stand the sight of them, never mind remain friends with them. You may be right, my true friend, I may have to face the consequences of my enmity toward them sooner or later, and it may not turn out well for me. But right now, I need to see this through. I need satisfaction for the wrong that was done to me."

When Heavenly Orchard Master realized that he could not dissuade his friend from carrying out his plan, he sighed in resignation before going to his house and bringing back a small bottle of liquor.

"This is the most potent thing I have ever made," he told Red Mountain God, "so it should serve your purpose."

Red Mountain God took the bottle, thanked his friend, and mounted the fire bear to return to Four Verdant Mothers. At the mountain, he spied on the home of Yellow Mountain Goddess until he saw her leave on the deer dragon. He hurried over to the dwelling's well and poured the liquor into the water. Once that was done, he got back on the fire bear and flew away from the mountain once more.

That evening, Yellow Mountain Goddess returned home after happily observing the religious festivity in her honor at the village. She made some tea with water from the well and drank it leisurely while appreciating the beauteous sight of the night's full moon. When she was done with the drink, however, she was suddenly overcome with such a heavy fatigue that she lay down and fell into a deep, dreamless sleep.

Meanwhile, Red Mountain God flew for many days until he came across a group of humans, fierce nomadic marauders who engaged in raiding and pillaging the villages of settled people. The god and the fire bear descended before them in all their glory, which made the humans fall to their hands and knees in terror and awe.

"I have been watching you for a long time," Red Mountain God lied to them. "Because I have become impressed with your strength, prowess, and courage, I decided to become your divine protector. It is my purpose to elevate you to a great and powerful people. The first thing you need to do to become great and powerful is abandon your nomadic way of life and settle down in a land where you can build the base of your greatness and power. I know a place that is fit for the purpose. It is already occupied by people, but they are weak and lowly, fit only to be your slaves. I will lead you to the land, where you will defeat and subjugate them. They are more numerous than you, so in order to overcome them, you need strong weapons. Much stronger than the simple spears and bows you have. I will show you how to make such arms."

Just as Yellow Mountain Goddess had taught her people how to farm, build dwellings, and make clothes, Red Mountain God taught the nomads how to extract metal from the earth and shape it into swords, axes, and armor. He also instructed them in martial arts and war strategy, making them drill until they learned to fight as one.

When they were ready, Red Mountain God rode his fire bear and led them to the land before Four Verdant Mothers. At a distance where they could not be detected by the Deer Dragon People, the nomads rested during the day but got ready to move once the sun went down. They picked up their fearsome weapons, put on their armor, and marched forth, carrying lofty banners that were red with the symbol of the fire bear on them. Red Mountain God's instruction to them was simple:

"Slaughter those who resist; subjugate those who surrender."

After the passage of some time, Yellow Mountain Goddess suddenly woke up from her deep slumber and immediately sensed that something was wrong. With trepidation mounting inside her, she called out to her deer dragon, who came to her looking old and dispirited. She worried at that even as she mounted the creature and bounded down from the mountain to see an astonishing sight on the land below.

The small villages that had stood apart from one another among wide, fertile fields were all gone, replaced by a massive walled city with stone buildings and labyrinthine streets. Even from a distance, she could tell that the place was packed with tens of thousands of people. She also saw lines of heavily armed and armored soldiers marching about and countless dispirited-looking people working at erecting new structures.

When she managed to recover from the shock of what she beheld, she turned herself into a dragonfly and flew down to find out what had happened. From what she saw and heard in the conversations among the people, she learned that some sixty years had passed since she had fallen asleep. During that time, a warlike people had come to the land and slaughtered and subjugated her people, reducing the survivors to slavery. The newcomers had destroyed their villages and forced them to build the city, first the walls, then a lofty palace where the rulers lived, and finally a great temple to their god. The Deer Dragon People toiled as laborers in the city and peasants in the fields, all of them under the constant threat of the whip for those who did not work hard enough and the sword for those who dared to disobey. There were rotting bodies hung up on the walls, the remains of those who had been executed for resistance, displayed as a warning to others.

The new people were apparently not content just to be lords over the original inhabitants of the land. Yellow Mountain Goddess saw them send out large groups of warriors to find people in other lands and bring them back as either slaves or conscripts for their army. As a result, despite the fact that the city was a place of utter misery and oppression for the vast majority of its denizens, its population was growing every day, as were the ranks of its military.

When Yellow Mountain Goddess flew into the city's temple, she found in its main hall an enormous stone statue of a bear with flames coming out of its body. Lines of people were bowing before it and making offerings of food, goods, and coins on an altar. Seeing the image, Yellow Mountain Goddess understood who was responsible for all the cataclysmic changes that had occurred during her long sleep. It was confirmed when she heard the newcomers refer to themselves as the Fire Bear People.

As Yellow Mountain Goddess watched the sufferings of those she had once nurtured, she became filled with grief and rage. She became especially emotional when she came across a group of people gathered at a house late at night to secretly worship before the image of a deer dragon. They were taking an enormous risk in doing so, as the practice was now forbidden by law under the penalty of death. A priest explained to the faithful that while the goddess had ignored their countless prayers for deliverance from their subjugation, she would return one day to free them, drive their oppressors from the land, and return things to the idyllic state that existed before the coming of the Fire Bear People.

Yellow Mountain Goddess wanted nothing more than to summon her deer dragon and go on a rampage to destroy the palace, the temple, and the walls of the city, all the while slaughtering every Fire Bear person she came across. But she considered that if she did so, Red Mountain God would surely come to fight her. And while they fought, the Fire Bear People, with their mighty army, would massacre the Deer Dragon People. No, she thought. To effectively avenge her people, she had to adopt a more subtle strategy.

What she needed were allies.

She flew back home, where she returned to her true shape and set out to visit Blue Mountain God and Green Mountain Goddess. The two were not on speaking terms with each other because Blue Mountain God still thought that Green Mountain Goddess had eaten the peach behind his back, while Green Mountain Goddess was still angry at him for falsely accusing her of having done so. But neither of them had any ill will toward Yellow Mountain Goddess, as they were unaware that she was the one who had taken the peach. Knowing that, and suppressing any guilt she felt, she visited them separately to explain what had gone on in the land below Four Verdant Mothers. She shed bitter tears as she described the sufferings of her people, which enraged the others, who already despised Red Mountain God. At the end of the meetings, they resolved to work together to punish the god for his cruelty and arrogance.

Once Yellow Mountain Goddess returned home, she made a momentous decision. In order to undermine Red Mountain God and the civilization he had built without revealing her hand in it, she decided to give up her status as a mountain deity and be reborn as a human among the Deer Dragon People, albeit one with extraordinary powers. She bid farewell to her animal companion, the deer dragon, tearfully explaining what she must do to allay her guilt over having allowed her people to fall into their sorry state. And then she set the creature free.

After the deer dragon bade farewell to its master, it bounded about the world, meeting interesting beings who became its friends, encountering others who became its enemies, and embarked on many adventures which could fill at least three volumes, perhaps four. There is a particularly moving tale of it meeting a scholarly magician who transformed it into a beautiful woman, and they lived together as husband and wife for a time. For a complicated reason I cannot get into right now, she ultimately asked to be turned back into a deer dragon so that she could resume her adventures. Before her departure, however, she left him with a child who would go on to become a truly great hero whose deeds could fill many volumes, at least six.

But this is not the time to tell those tales.

Yellow Mountain Goddess returned to the city in the guise of a dragonfly once more and searched among her people until she found a slave woman who had recently become pregnant with a child that was not yet endowed with a soul. The goddess shed her dragonfly form and went into the woman's belly to take possession of her baby's body. At the same time, Blue Mountain God went forth from Four Verdant Mothers, riding his radiant tiger until he found yet another group of humans, a band of horsemen. As Yellow Mountain Goddess and Red Mountain God had done before him, he appeared before them and promised to take them to a land of plenty. As for Green Mountain Goddess, she also relinquished her status as a mountain deity, but not to be reborn as a human being. She instead turned herself into a giant water snake and slipped into the river that flowed just north of the city of the Fire Bear People. And so Blue Mountain God led his newly adopted people to the land and Green Mountain Goddess waited in the river, while Yellow Mountain Goddess was born as a slave girl among the Deer Dragon People.

As for Red Mountain God, once he had seen that his people had everything under control in the land below, he had grown tired of watching them carry on through the generations. He left them at the height of their power to spend much of his time among his acquaintances in the Heavenly Realm. After a particularly long period of absence from Four Verdant Mothers, he finally returned, only to find the city below Four Verdant Mountains in great disarray.

A slave revolt had broken out among the Deer Dragon People, many of them rising up to kill their masters, set fire to the fields, and destroy buildings. Soldiers were sent out to crush them, but the rebels somehow managed to evade them at every turn while harassing them in hit-and-run attacks. It was rumored that they were led by a young woman with magical powers who could turn herself and her followers invisible. She was known among her people as Yellow Vengeance. At the same time, a new people appeared on the edge of the Fire Bear People's territory, fast-moving horsemen who raided outposts without venturing deep into the land. Every time a large force was about to be sent out to confront them, the slave rebels struck again, making the rulers wary of sending many soldiers away from the city. As if that was not enough, the river north of the city began to swell and flood, destroying great swathes of fields and drowning many people and animals. Fishermen claimed to have seen a great green snake in the water that was shaking its enormous body, causing the calamity.

Red Mountain God found it suspicious that the place was beset with so many problems all at the same time. As he investigated further, he discovered that the situation was exacerbated by the fact that the Fire Bear People were led by an incompetent and indecisive king who was floundering in the face of multiple crises. As it appeared inevitable that the rule of his people would fall under such pressure, he decided to intervene directly, if for no other reason than to preserve his pride by thwarting those who were behind the troubles.

Especially since he naturally suspected the hand of one or more of the other mountain deities.

He rode his fire bear to an isolated spot near the city where there was no one around. There, he split his animal companion into three pieces and turned them into powerful weapons of magic—a Seeker Whip, a Fire Sword, and a Hundred-Great-Span Bow. He hid the arms under some rocks before he transformed himself into a mosquito. He flew into the city, then into the royal palace, and finally into the private chamber of the king, where he found the fat, useless monarch taking a nap. With a sting to the back of his neck, Red Mountain God entered his body, ousted the king's soul—sending it out to wander the world as a confused and forlorn ghost—and took over his identity.

The next day, he immediately got to work, first by picking the fastest horse in the royal stable to ride over to the spot where he had hidden the magical weapons. Just when he was done arming himself with them, a messenger came rushing to inform him that slave rebels had launched another attack. He immediately got on his horse and raced back. By the time he arrived, the rebels had already killed numerous soldiers and set fire to a military station. With the raid conducted successfully, they were now disappearing one by one into thin air, their leader Yellow Vengeance using her magical powers to render them invisible. The King of the Fire Bear People came riding forth and unfurled his Seeker Whip, which he sent flying through the air. It caught the rebel leader by the neck and brought her down to the ground, which broke her spell. His soldiers arrived then and slaughtered the now-visible rebels, but the king kept Yellow Vengeance alive. He bound the woman tightly with the whip to prevent her from using her magic again and ordered her to be imprisoned in a dungeon. He meant to torture her to death in public to make an example of her.

He was supervising the hunting down of the last remaining rebels when another messenger came riding up to inform him that the river was flooding again, threatening to inundate the entire city. The king raced over to the water and unsheathed the Fire Sword. Without displaying any concern over the raging flow, he strode into the river until he was waist-deep in it. He then raised the sword, which burst into flames, and stabbed it into the water with all his strength. All around him, the river began to boil, killing the creatures in it. As the cooked bodies of so many fish, eels, and turtles came up to the surface, a piercing scream issued from its depth. A giant green water snake rose out of the water, its body disintegrating in the heat. Just as the creature was about to be destroyed completely, an autumn bird came flying out of the sky. It sacrificed itself by allowing the spirit of the water snake to enter its body while its soul left to move on to its next existence. The bird then fled the scene, screeching in rage.

Much to the awe of the Fire Bear People, their king emerged from the boiling river unscathed, the water retreating to its normal level. He barely had time to dry himself when yet another messenger came rushing to tell him that the marauding horsemen were attacking an outpost. As he no longer had to worry about the rebels, he gathered his army and marched out of the city, leaving behind only a small number of soldiers to guard the place.

When the invading horsemen, who called themselves the Radiant Tiger People, learned that the King of the Fire Bear People and his army were coming to them in full force, they prepared for battle. Their leader, known among his people as Blue Chieftain, was Blue Mountain God incarnated in human form. He rode a horse that struck everyone with awe, as it was not only the biggest stallion they had ever seen but its coat was blue with black stripes. The animal was actually Blue Mountain God's animal companion, the radiant tiger, in disguise.

The armies of the Fire Bear People and the Radiant Tiger People faced each other on an open field, arrayed in battle formation, red banners flying on one side, blue banners on the other. The King of the Fire Bear People rode out by himself into the middle of the field and took up his Hundred-Great-Span Bow. But when he nocked an arrow, he found that the side of his helmet was in the way of his drawing arm. So he took it off and put it on his lap before he raised the bow again and loosed the arrow, which flew so fast that no one could mark its trajectory except the radiant tiger disguised as a giant striped horse. When the animal saw that the arrow was headed straight for its master, it sacrificed itself by standing on its hind legs and taking the projectile in its chest. The blow shattered the animal into thousands of shiny blue marbles which flew all over the place, raining down on the lines of the astonished Radiant Tiger horsemen. The animal's demise also sent Blue Chieftain flying through the air, until he fell rolling on the ground at the back of his army. The sight shocked his soldiers, and they did not know what to do.

The King of the Fire Bear People became furious that he had managed to kill only the radiant tiger and not its master, but he knew that this was the perfect time to attack the confused and demoralized enemy. He had raised his arm to order an all-out charge of his army when an autumn bird came flying out of the sky, bearing a heavy rock in its talons. When it reached the king, it dropped the rock on his head, which was unprotected, as he had taken off his helmet. A sharp edge hit him on his top, opening a crack in the skull. The king looked up and sighted the autumn bird, so he quickly nocked another arrow on his bow and let it loose. The blow shattered the bird into thousands of shiny green marbles which rained down all over the field.

The king, however, could not feel any satisfaction at the killing, because the sheer effort that he had put into drawing the massive bow caused the crack in his skull to widen. When he touched the wound, he realized that it was a matter of moments before his head would split open. With very little time left to him, he followed an impulse and took out a piece of paper and wrote a note on it with his own blood. He then took a small object out from his belt and wrapped it in the note, which he attached to another arrow. With blood pouring down all over his head, he raised his bow and sent the arrow flying. The strain from the effort not only shattered the bow into small pieces, it caused the king's skull to split open and his brain to fall out.

Just as Blue Chieftain was getting to his feet, an arrow landed in front of him. He first thought that it was a missed shot, but then he saw something small wrapped in a piece of paper attached to it. He picked it up, but he had no time to open it, as he had to lead his soldiers into battle. So he put it away and found another horse to ride. As he raced to the front of the army, his men saw that he was alive and well, which caused them to regain their courage.

On the other side, the soldiers of the Fire Bear army stared aghast at the sight of their king lying on the ground with his skull split open and his brain rolling on the ground. When Blue Chieftain saw what had happened, he immediately ordered an all-out attack to take advantage of the situation. Deprived of their invincible king with his magical weapons, the Fire Bear soldiers lost heart and began to run even before the horsemen reached them. In the chaotic rout that followed, they were massacred on the field.

When news reached the city of the death of the King of the Fire Bear People and the destruction of his army, there was a general uprising of the Deer Dragon People, the mob killing every Fire Bear person they could find. They also found the dungeon where Yellow Vengeance was imprisoned and released her from the Seeker Whip. As soon as she was free, she took a dagger and furiously cut the whip into small pieces before using a torch to set them on fire. She then gathered the remains of her rebel soldiers and marched to the royal palace. The first thing she did there was to send a messenger to the leader of the Radiant Tiger People so she could arrange a meeting with him.

As for Blue Chieftain himself, after the battle was over, he stood before the body of the King of the Fire Bear People, having claimed as his prize the Fire Sword, the last of the magical weapons of the slain ruler. He then remembered the object wrapped in a piece of paper on the arrow that was shot toward him. He opened it and found a peach pit inside. The note, written in the blood of the deceased king, simply read: "Yellow Mountain Goddess ate it."

Just then, the messenger from the leader of the Deer Dragon People arrived to deliver her invitation to a meeting. Blue Chieftain realized then that the deceptive Yellow Mountain Goddess had manipulated him into fighting against Red Mountain God, for which he had given up his divinity to assume human form. He also had lost his beloved radiant tiger. He flew into a rage and screamed at the messenger, telling him to go and tell his leader that he was coming for her next, that he would be the one to finally punish her for her deceit.

When the messenger returned to the city and relayed Blue Chieftain's words to Yellow Vengeance, she guessed what had made him react that way. She hurriedly gathered her people and told them that the Radiant Tiger People were coming to subjugate them just as the Fire Bear People had done, and that they had to prepare the city for a siege. They became despondent to learn that just when they had regained their freedom, they had to continue fighting to preserve it. But they did as she commanded, shutting the gates of the city and shoring up its defenses.

The Radiant Tiger People were superb mounted warriors, but they knew nothing of conducting a siege, so all they could do was stand guard at the gates and try to starve out the people of the city. As a result, the stalemate between the besiegers and the defenders went on day after day, month after month. It turned into a deeply frustrating and debilitating situation for both sides, with their leaders unwilling to negotiate a way out of it.

Among the Deer Dragon People, there was a group who had lost their faith in Yellow Mountain Goddess a long time ago. They thought it foolish to continue worshipping a being who had abandoned them to their oppressors. When the slave rebellion had started, they had refused to join, regarding its young female leader's claim to be the goddess incarnate with skepticism. As the siege went on and on with no end in sight, they came to believe that the very land that they lived on had become a cursed place for them. After such a long period of subjugation, followed by a war that had brought about the current situation, they decided that the only path of survival for their people lay in leaving the place to settle somewhere far away. After a long and serious discussion, the leaders of the group decided to send a message out to Blue Chieftain. They offered to open a gate for him if he promised to let them leave the city through another gate and depart from the land without being harassed. When the general received the missive, he readily agreed to it, as he had no animosity toward anyone other than their leader.

In the deepest hour of the night, the disillusioned group of Deer Dragon People killed the guards at the West Gate of the city and opened it up before they proceeded quickly to the South Gate, through which they left the city and the land. They would travel south for a long time until they would ultimately find a tranquil place where they would settle down and eventually found their own kingdom. But they would never worship Yellow Mountain Goddess again, losing the very memory of the deity who had failed them in their direst time of need.

The Radiant Tiger horsemen rode into the city and slaughtered the defenders in the course of the night. Blue Chieftain was concerned only with confronting Yellow Vengeance, but his soldiers reported that she was nowhere to be found. When the new day dawned, the leaders of the triumphant army entered the royal palace, where Blue Chieftain sat on the throne. He was acclaimed by his men as their king, but he only had a brief moment to enjoy his royalty. Even as he welcomed his soldiers' adulation, Yellow Vengeance suddenly appeared behind the throne, emerging from her magical invisibility, and cut off the new king's head with an axe. Before his men could recover from shock, she made herself invisible again and began to kill them, one after another. A young soldier among them, a lowly adjutant to an officer, was about to flee for his life when he happened to look down on the magical Fire Sword that lay on top of the decapitated body of Blue Chieftain. On the surface of its blade, he could see the reflection of Yellow Vengeance. When he saw her coming for him with her bloody axe, he picked up the weapon and swung it at her. She tried to use her magic to defend herself against the power of the sword, but that only resulted in the clashing of the two magical forces, causing a fiery explosion that annihilated her, destroyed the weapon, and also ripped off the sword-wielding arm of the soldier.

And so ended the terrestrial lives of the beings that the two mountain gods and the two mountain goddesses of Four Verdant Mothers had become.

Upon the passing of the last of them, the people of the city witnessed a wondrous sight in the sky—a luminous dragon flying through the air with a naked baby on its back. Despite the great distance, they could clearly hear the child laughing in unrestrained delight. They were followed by a thick cloud of dark purple with red lightning flashing inside it that hung in the middle of an otherwise clear sky. Once they were gone, the place, which was known simply as "the city" before then, came to be called Luminous Dragon and Laughing Child.

CHAPTER FOUR

Life II

Of Betrayal and Remembrance

The historian and his colleague drank quite a bit of wine over dinner, so they ended up going to bed early. But she set the alarm on her smartphone to wake her up in a few hours. When the quiet, melodious tone sounded, she quickly turned it off to avoid disturbing him and slipped out of the bedroom. She took her laptop out of her backpack, went into his study, and closed the door. Because of the time difference at the place where her boyfriend was, it was the only convenient hour for both of them to connect online.

As soon as the video feed came on and her boyfriend's face appeared on the screen, she could make out a distraught expression on his face.

"Hey, what's wrong?" she asked him.

He looked down and tried to maintain control over himself, but he burst into tears, hiding his eyes in his hands.

"Oh no, what happened?" she asked in concern.

He managed to calm himself enough to speak but could not look at her.

"I have to . . . I have to tell you something. Last night, I went out with some people from work," he told her. "We did karaoke and I had a lot to drink. I got drunk. And then . . . then . . ." He could not finish.

"What happened?"

"We were all pretty much drunk, so we went to a coworker's apartment that was nearby. People went to sleep all over the place, but I stayed up a while longer with this girl from the local office. I'm so sorry . . . I'm so so sorry . . . we ended up making out. And . . . and . . ."

"Did you sleep with her?"

"No, I mean, we made out and then I fell asleep. When I woke up in the morning, I remembered what I had done and went home right away. I'm sorry. Please . . . please don't break up with me." He broke down into tears again.

She let him cry for a time before addressing him again.

"Listen, I'm not happy about this, but I'm not going to break up with you."

"Really? I'm really sorry. I . . . this is not an excuse, not at all, but I miss you so much and I was so lonely, and I made a mistake."

"Okay."

"If you can really forgive me . . . I just talked to my boss. I told him that I needed to go home. Since the work here's almost done and the other guys can finish it up, he said okay. I'm going to book a plane ticket as soon as we are done here and hopefully I'll be home by tomorrow night."

"You don't have to do that."

"But I want to. I can't stand being away from you. And I can't believe what I did. It's so stupid when I . . . when I love you so much."

"I love you too."

"God, I'm so relieved you won't break up with me, but I still feel so bad. I'm so disappointed in myself."

"It's all right. We can work this out."

"I shouldn't be surprised that you are so great about this. But part of me kind of wishes you weren't. I feel like I need to pay for what I did."

She ignored that. "Your mind's set on coming home early?"

"Yeah, I don't want to be here anymore. I want to be with you."

"Then we'll talk when you get back."

"Oh God, I hope you don't change your mind about breaking up with me."

"I won't. Really, I won't."

They talked for a while longer, him continuing to apologize and her reassuring him. When they were finished, she shut her laptop, sat back in the historian's plush leather chair, and let out a sigh. She looked down at his desk, where there were a few books and a new notebook that was open to a blank page. She knew that he had a contract to write a book about the rise and fall of the Near Western empire known as the Grand Hegemony, but he understandably had done no work since his wife's death.

As she sat still in the lonely space with nothing but a table, a chair, and three shelves filled with books, she considered what a terrible person she was. It was not just that she was unfaithful to her boyfriend, listening to his tearful confession of a much lesser transgression while sitting in the apartment of the man she was cheating on him with. As terrible as that was, she wondered at how she herself felt no compulsion to tell him about it. When she considered it further, she realized that it was because she was not with her colleague for sexual gratification or out of real passion. She did love him, but not in a way in which she could envision having an actual relationship with him, as she could and still hoped to have with her boyfriend. Instead, being with the historian at this time, when he obviously needed someone to provide him with some intimate comfort, felt like something she just had to do. In fact, it was such a natural role for her to play that the question of its propriety and ethics seemed irrelevant. But she was under no illusion about what she was doing behind her boyfriend's back, so she in a sense felt guilty about not feeling more guilty about it.

Am I really this awful? she wondered. *Will I keep doing this to him in the future? Cheating on him and who knows what else, because I just felt that it's something I had to do? Am I going to be someone who constantly lies to the person I love and keeps secrets from him?*

Since she already thought of herself as a callous person incapable of natural empathy toward her own parents, this felt like a confirmation of her low view of herself.

She sat in the study for a long while, wallowing in self-loathing, until she heard the bedroom door open and the historian going to the kitchen. She remained still for a moment longer before she finally got up and walked out of the room. He was leaning over the kitchen countertop, having just put the kettle on the range.

"Did I wake you?" she asked, putting her laptop in her backpack.

"No," he said, looking at her with a tired smile. "I, uhm . . . I had a dream. It woke me up."

"Oh," she said, sitting on a stool by the counter. "Do you remember what it was about?"

"My wife was in it," he said.

"Oh."

He stayed silent, waiting for the water to boil.

"We were in the ruins of an ancient city," he told her after a while, in a faraway voice. "The place may have been Purple Cloud. We were walking through the empty streets when she suddenly turned to me and said 'I've been fired' with an embarrassed smile. But I knew that she didn't get fired, but resigned of her own volition after selling her company so that she could do something that was more meaningful to her. And I told her that, which seemed to reassure her. I also wanted to tell her that she had done the right thing, that I was proud of her. But before I could, she disappeared among the ruins. I looked for her . . . desperately . . . running through the streets and the broken buildings, for such a long time . . . but she was gone."

The kettle began to whistle.

"I'm going to make some tea," he said. "Do you want some?"

"Yes."

After he made the tea and poured it into two cups, he took them to the dining room table, where they sat down next to each other to slowly sip the drink. The cat appeared and jumped onto the table before sniffing at the liquid.

"Hey, Radiant Tiger," she said, and lightly scratched him on top of his head and on the cheeks, making him purr with his eyes closed.

"Part of me wasn't surprised," the historian said out of nowhere, looking down at his cup with an empty expression. "When she died, part of me thought, 'Of course.'"

"What? Why?"

"Uhm . . . the years I had with her, it felt too good to be real. I always carried that feeling with me during our relationship. Meeting a woman like her, falling in love, finding out that she loved me as well, then actually having a happy life together, it all seemed fantastic somehow, like that kind of fortune wasn't something I deserved."

"Why not?"

He did not answer her.

"Do you feel that way about other things in your life?" she asked. "Like your professional success. Do you feel you don't deserve it?"

He thought about the question.

"I don't know," he told her. "I mean, the public attention–that I did not expect at all. It seems bizarre to me even now. When I finished the book on the Immaculate State, I did feel that I had achieved something significant. But when my findings got reported in the national media, I didn't know what to make of it. Besides, I don't know if anyone actually deserves the kind of success that's utterly dependent on the unpredictable whim of the public's interest rather than the quality of the work. You know, I always suspected that my thesis resonated with a lot of people because they hated studying history when they were in school, having to memorize all those dates and facts. So they relished the idea of a historian saying that their teachers didn't know what they were talking about. That might be why they kept exaggerating my findings, saying I showed that all of our national history is a bunch of lies."

She smiled at that. “I can see that.”

He smiled also and sipped his tea.

“Perhaps it’s not that I didn’t think I deserved to be with my wife,” he said. “It just seemed out of place in the life I had gotten used to.”

“Out of place?”

“My older relatives used to tell me that I was a very expressive and affectionate child. But that changed when I lost my mother. I know that I became a rather distant person after that.”

“How old were you when she passed?”

“She first got sick with cancer when I was nine. She held on for almost three years, there were ups and downs, but she finally succumbed when I was eleven. My father was devastated. I could tell, despite his attempt to hide his grief from me as much as possible. He did his best for me, but then he had his stroke when I was fourteen and died pretty quickly from it.”

“That’s awful. Both parents, gone so soon. Who took care of you then?”

“I moved in with my uncle’s family, my father’s younger brother.”

“Were you okay there?”

“My uncle is a good man, and he was always nice to me. So it was fine, although...”

“What is it?”

“Well, his wife, for some reason, she really resented me being in her house.”

“Your aunt? Why?”

“I don’t really know. It’s a bit of mystery, but I think it had something to do with her son, who was my age. She put a lot of hope in him, convinced that he was an absolutely brilliant boy who was destined to do great things. It was somewhat delusional because my cousin... Look, we were never that close, but I was always rather fond of him, so it feels a bit mean to say this, but... Well, he was an okay kid, but just not on the bright side. Got bad grades, didn’t have the discipline to study properly for the college entrance examination. There were many times when we left the house together to attend an evening study class, but then he went off to play around with his friends. I didn't look down on him for it because I thought he was just being who he was. But his mother was sure that he would somehow pull it off and get into a top university.

"I was accepted to Dragon Child National University, but my cousin didn't get a spot in any college in the city, so he had to take another year to study for the examination again. My aunt was convinced that I was to blame for that. I heard her arguing with my uncle, telling him that if he had paid more attention to his own son rather than his nephew, their son would be the one going to Dragon Child National University. It was all very strange."

"Was it that strange, though?"

"What do you mean?"

"Just . . . she was his mother. Parents do that, don't they? Want the best for their children, expect more than they should from them?" She noticed a trace of bitterness in her own words, which came perhaps from the fact that her parents never expected anything from her.

He considered it. "Sure. Her having high expectations of her son, that I understand. But to blame his failure on me, that was unfair. I do feel sorry for her, though."

"In what way?"

"She had a dream that could never be realized—becoming the proud mother of a successful son. I think she's a deeply unhappy woman who convinced herself that her son's achievements would make everything right. But she had such an unrealistic view of his abilities that every time things went wrong for him she had to blame it on other people. So, in her mind, I was somehow responsible for him not getting into a good college. My cousin had one true passion, which was golf. He really loved playing golf, which he picked up in middle school. But when he was in high school, his coach told his mother that he was good, but not good enough to become a pro, so she made him quit and concentrate on his studies. I actually think that he could have been happy as a golf instructor or a coach at a school. But my aunt would never have allowed that.

"A few years after I started teaching at the university, my cousin came to see me and asked if there was a position I could set him up with. He had ended up going to a small college in the provinces, studying agriculture, not because he had any interest in the subject but because that was the only major available to him with his poor grades and test scores. After he graduated, he went from job to job, never finding his place. Now he was married and his wife was expecting their second child, but they were still living with his parents, with his mother on his case all the time. So he was getting desperate. I felt sorry for him, so I asked around until I found an administrative position for him. He lasted about three months before they had to let him go because he kept messing up at the job, even showing up drunk after lunch one time. I later found out that my aunt was convinced I was responsible for his dismissal."

"But that makes no sense."

He shrugged in agreement. "It *was* senseless, because why would I find him a job only to get him fired? The whole thing made me look bad for recommending him for the position in the first place. Anyway, after that fiasco, whenever I went over to their place to see my uncle, she would shoot me dirty looks and avoid me. I also found out that it infuriated her to see me in the media during the whole Immaculate State thing. In her mind, it was her son who should have become a famous professor, her son who should be doing interviews on television about his groundbreaking research, her son with the fame and what she probably imagines to be a fortune I made. She apparently felt that I had somehow taken all that away from him."

He shook his head. "The last time I talked to my cousin, about two years ago, he was still living at his parents' home with his wife and now three kids. My uncle had to buy him a convenience store in the neighborhood so he could work there. He actually seemed pretty content, even if his mother wasn't. I hope she isn't putting undue pressure on her grandchildren now."

"Did she make your life difficult when you were living with them?"

"She was cold to me and would make snide comments, but I didn't care that much, especially since my uncle treated me well. And it was only for a few years. After I started at the university, I reached my majority and got full control of my inheritance money, so I got my own place."

"Did you find someone to be with when you were an undergraduate?"

"Like a roommate?"

"No," she said with a laugh. "I meant, like a girlfriend."

"I dated a few girls, but I discovered that I was really bad at it," he said with a rueful smile.

"What do you mean by that?"

"Uhm... I think they sensed the distance in me. Even with women I really cared about, I found it difficult to get close. They interpreted that as lack of interest or unwillingness to commit to something serious, which probably wasn't too far off the mark. They usually ended up leaving me, thinking that I didn't love them or was incapable of loving anyone."

"Was that because you thought that people you loved were bound to leave you, like your parents did?" She put a hand on his arm, looking a little concerned. "I'm sorry. Am I prying too much?"

"No, it's fine. And you are right. I know now that I was deeply afraid of falling in love. I couldn't reveal that to my girlfriends, how scared I was of truly caring about them. I wanted to be with them... yet part of me was constantly pulling away as well. Does that make sense?"

She considered their relationship now, from both his perspective and hers, and simply nodded.

"What I went through when my mother was dying..." He had to stop.

Radiant Tiger came over to him, and he scratched the cat's ears absently as he took a sip of tea.

"After that," he continued after a while, "I kind of gave up. I went out on dates every once in a while, when someone showed interest, but I didn't put much effort into it, so I never got into a real relationship."

"But I thought... oh, never mind."

"What is it?"

"This may have been just a campus rumor but... uhm, when I was an undergrad, I heard that you were dating that really cool professor in the art department, the one with blue streaks in her hair and tattoos."

"Oh," he said with a wry smile. "No. We never dated. Not really. We were hired by the university in the same year, so we became friends after attending new faculty events. She was married at the time, but when she got divorced a few years later, she showed interest in me, so we went out a few times."

"But it didn't work out?"

"I liked her, and we had a lot in common, so I think we might have been a good match, but... After we started spending time together, we were supposed to meet at the college end-of-the-year party. When I got there, she was talking to this handsome administrator who had a reputation for being a ladies' man. He was obviously flirting with her, and she was letting him despite knowing that I was there. It wasn't that she was interested in him, but... I could tell what she was doing. We were moving toward a relationship, so she was letting me know that she was a desirable woman who had options, and that I would have to put more effort into being with her. More than I was apparently showing her. Maybe she felt that she had to send me that message because of my distant nature. She probably expected me to come over and compete for her attention. But in that moment I found myself tired of playing the game. And I realized that I actually didn't want to put in the effort. So I walked away, talked to a few colleagues, and then left early."

"How did she react to that?"

"After not hearing from me for a few days, she sent me an email apologizing for her behavior at the party. She apparently thought that she may have overplayed her hand and ruined things between us. I assured her that she didn't do anything wrong, but I didn't ask to see her again, so that was that. She left a year later, after she got a prestigious endowed position at another university. And I just concentrated on my work, thinking that perhaps I was meant to have a solitary life."

"Didn't it get lonely?"

"Sometimes, but I was used to lonely. And I was busy doing what I loved, working on projects and teaching."

"Then you met your wife."

"Yes."

"It must have felt really different with her."

"It did."

He paused to drink his tea.

"Actually, it's not that I was completely resigned to being alone for the rest of my life," he said. "At least, I don't think I was. I was open to the possibility of meeting someone. It's just . . . because of the kind of life I had made for myself, I thought it likely that it would be someone scholarly like me. But my wife . . . she was nothing like what I expected. It still boggles my mind that someone like her came into my life.

"She was . . . magnificent really. A self-made millionaire who started her own NGO to do good in the world. She was such a glamorous and charismatic person, one of those natural extroverts who're so good with people. A true leader. I always thought how mismatched we must have appeared to others. You know that she once dated that famous movie actor."

She nodded, vaguely remembering reading about it online.

"She was different from you," she said. "But I always thought you were right for each other. And you have your own charisma, you know. More of a subtle kind than hers, but your students were really inspired by your teaching. And I know she respected you as much as you respected her. She told me something like that when I was over at the house for dinner."

"You two talked about me?"

"Of course we did."

"What did she say?"

"Are you nervous?"

He laughed, but with a trace of worry.

She smiled, touching him on the arm again. "That you were not like anyone she had ever dated before. That she had never been with someone of such depth. So yes, you were different, but I think that's part of what made you such a great couple."

He nodded and looked down.

"After a while we began to consider marriage," he told her. "Neither of us was given to romantic gestures, so we just talked about it. She told me that she did want to marry me, but there was something I had to do for her first."

"Which was?"

"That we had to go to therapy together. She needed to hear me talk about my past, my losses, and my fears. All the stuff I had such difficulty revealing to her."

"How did that go?"

"It was . . . it was extremely hard for me. It was one of the hardest things I ever had to do. But I committed myself to the process because I really wanted to make it work with her. It took some time, but eventually it began to help. I started to understand things about myself that allowed me to become more engaged with the people in my life, especially her. There was a session in which I was finally able to talk about my mother—how much I loved her, and how it affected me to see her get sick and die. I only realized then that I'd become such a distant person because I needed to protect myself from what was happening to me. I had to make myself feel less because it hurt too much to feel at all."

She nodded in understanding. His take on his condition made her consider that her being helpful to others was a similar way of coping with pain and loss.

"After that session," he went on, "we were driving home when my wife suddenly burst out crying. I was surprised because I had never seen her do that before, she being such a strong person who was in control all the time. I pulled over and asked what was wrong, and she said she felt so sad for me, for the child I was at the time. After those words, she just couldn't stop crying. I was so moved by her sympathy toward me, I became lost for words. So I just pulled her into my arms and held her close. We stayed like that for a long time, until she finally calmed down. She then told me that she loved me, and I told her that I loved her, and that's when I knew that I could trust her to stay with me."

He stopped to look up with a distant expression.

"Well," he said quietly, under his breath, "I was wrong about that."

"But she didn't leave you on purpose," she said, sniffing and wiping away the tears that welled up in her eyes.

"I know. I know. I'm not blaming her for what happened, like it's something she did deliberately to hurt me. But that morning... after I went to work, she got up and left our house, and never came back."

Radiant Tiger got up on all fours, stretched out his back in an arch, and jumped off the table.

They sat in heavy silence for a while.

"You said that part of you wasn't surprised by what happened," she said. "But you know that it didn't have to, right? As terrible as it was, there was nothing inevitable about it."

"Of course, rationally I know this. But I still can't help feeling that way. Like I've returned to my natural state of solitude after what increasingly feels like a wonderful dream I once had."

"It doesn't have to be like that."

"I can't imagine otherwise."

After a while, she got up and went to him, putting her arms around his shoulders and bending over him. He hesitated for a moment, but then he rested his face on her chest and let out a deep, mournful sigh. She stroked his hair and held him tight.

At some point, they silently went to the bedroom, where they took their clothes off, lay down on the bed, and began to make love. They moved slowly and gently, as they sought comfort more than the satisfaction of desire. Sometimes they stopped just to hold on to each other to fully take in the warmth of their closeness. When they were finished, they remained locked together, him leaning over her to look at her face. After he took his time appreciating her every engaging feature, he kissed her on the bridge of her nose, then her brow, beneath her eye, on her cheekbone, and on and on, demonstrating his gratitude toward her with every touch of his lips.

When he stopped to look at her once more, he wondered if his feelings toward her could go beyond affection and appreciation, if he could have a new life with her that would allow him to escape his lonely fate. She looked back at him and read the expression on his face, which made her eyes fill with tears. He knew then that despite the real depth of her feelings for him, she was there out of sympathy and care, and that it could never go beyond that. That understanding brought a new pain to his already broken heart, but that too felt inevitable in the life he was destined to lead.

"It's all right," he whispered in her ear before holding her even closer, wishing to melt into her so that the moment would last and last.

CHAPTER FIVE

Myth III

The Autumn Bird State

On the day before the emperor came to the new city, the storyteller sat before the scribes and narrated the conclusion to the story of the two mountain gods and the two mountain goddesses of Four Verdant Mothers.

THE FIRST WAR of the first civilization in the land ended not in jubilant triumph or utter devastation but in a kind of dazed confusion. The surviving members of the Deer Dragon People, the Radiant Tiger People, and the Fire Bear People looked at one another with wonder, unable to comprehend the source of their mutual enmity. The Deer Dragon People remembered, of course, how the Fire Bear People had come to the land and enslaved them, but the Fire Bear People were at a loss to understand why they had treated the others so badly in the first place. And once the Deer Dragon People were free, after killing many of their former oppressors, they saw no point in carrying on the fight. The Radiant Tiger People were the most confused of them all, hardly knowing why they had come to the place to make war first on the Fire Bear People and then on the Deer Dragon People. So they stood around looking at one another for some time, not knowing what to do next.

Eventually, due to the lack of any alternative, the lowly soldier who had slain the leader of the Deer Dragon People, losing his arm in the process, was acclaimed king and sat upon the throne. As neither he nor anyone else had a reason or the appetite for further conflict, he summoned whoever emerged as the representatives of the Deer Dragon People and the Fire Bear People and assured them that he had no intention of subjugating them. From now on, they would all just be the people of the city of Luminous Dragon and Laughing Child and its surrounding lands. And he asked for their cooperation in building a society of peaceful coexistence, which they all pledged to do.

The King of Luminous Dragon and Laughing Child had no experience ruling over anything, never mind a whole city, so he sought the services of the Fire Bear People who had been administrators in the previous regime. They helped him set up a new government with laws designed to uphold the monarch's promise of harmony. As time passed, however, general divisions reappeared among the people.

The Radiant Tiger People, as the ultimate winners of the war, dominated the military that remained the backbone of royal authority. The day-to-day running of the state, however, became the responsibility of experienced officials of the Fire Bear People. The vast majority of the Deer Dragon People held no positions of power, and they returned to their former occupations as farmers, laborers, and artisans. As more time passed, the distinctions among the groups became ever more pronounced. Those of the ruling military families lived modestly, as they were proud of their martial tradition, which dictated a simple and disciplined existence of constant training in the fighting arts and following a strict code of honor. Despite their humble lifestyle, everyone knew that they were the true power holders and could mobilize their armed forces at any time. Below them, the families of officials used their positions in the government to become increasingly wealthy. Unlike the military rulers, they proudly displayed their riches, oftentimes in competition with one another.

For those at the bottom of the society, who toiled under the soldier and the administrator, the greatest source of discontentment came from wealthy officials buying up property and reducing the people who labored there to dependents. Farmers who worked on lands that had once belonged to them became peasants who had to pay rent to managers who, in turn, worked for the owners, who lived in the city. The workshops of artisans were also taken over by the wealthy, turning skilled workers into wage employees. All these developments were made possible through the adoption of laws of commerce that were written by officials who persuaded the military rulers to enforce them as the best means of maintaining stability and generating wealth for the entire society. But the lives of the vast majority became increasingly miserable, while the few who lived "below the sword but above the scythe," as the saying went, built luxurious mansions filled with precious objects and spent their leisure time in sumptuous establishments of feasting and entertainment. Many who became too poor to work even as farmers and artisans found themselves with little choice but to become household servants to the very people who were responsible for their poverty.

The military rulers became concerned when incidents of protest broke out among peasants and workers, but the officials convinced them that they were the acts of a few malcontented criminals who needed to be dealt with harshly. Consequently, the protestors were made examples of through horrific public punishments. After a time, the officials began to manipulate the soldiers even further, seducing them with the trappings of wealth, often in the form of outright bribes. As a result, the ruling class began to lose its martial spirit, spending less time training and more on gathering riches through their political authority. In just a few generations, they became warriors in name and tradition only, leading lives of luxury indistinguishable from those of the officials. Under those developments, the discontent among the working people grew by the day, heading toward a calamity.

But then a more immediate problem arose for the city and its leadership.

A new group of people appeared in the north, large in number and with a significant force of armed men who appeared to be fierce and disciplined. As the people of Luminous Dragon and Laughing Child had not fought a war in almost a hundred years, the arrival of the newcomers brought them to the verge of panic. The rulers hurriedly sent out the army to defend the single bridge over the river that flowed north of the city. But scouts who observed the newcomers returned to report that they did not appear to be preparing for an invasion. Instead, they dispatched envoys, asking to speak to the rulers of Luminous Dragon and Laughing Child.

They identified themselves as the Autumn Bird People, who worshipped a goddess who was thought to have originated from the river. They claimed that they had no desire to cross the water into the city's territory, but they wished to settle down nearby to be close to the home of their divinity. The rulers of Luminous Dragon and Laughing Child were so relieved that they would not have to fight that they readily gave them permission to do so, thinking it best that they gradually assimilate the newcomers into their society.

The Autumn Bird People settled down, built a town, and worked the earth to create farms. They erected a temple to their goddess on the shores of the water, which served as the residence of their leader as well, a queen who was also the chief priestess of their religion. They proved true to their word in not venturing into the territory of Luminous Dragon and Laughing Child. When it became necessary for someone to cross the bridge to conduct business, they did so only with the explicit permission of the city's authorities. In this way the two peoples lived without conflict for a time.

The trouble began when the officials of Luminous Dragon and Laughing Child saw an opportunity to take advantage of the newcomers for financial gain. The rulers of the city had been so anxious to avoid fighting the Autumn Bird People because they, in all honesty, did not know if they would prevail against the hardy and determined-looking people. So they had allowed them to settle down without considering all the issues that may rise between the two peoples in such close proximity. The most serious had to do with the use of the river itself. While it was agreed that the water would serve as the border between their territories, they had not articulated who actually had authority over it. The river was not only a place of abundant fishing, but it also provided water for irrigation and the city's needs. For the Autumn Bird People, it was a sacred site where they worshipped their goddess.

The officials of Luminous Dragon and Laughing Child thought that by firmly establishing that the river itself belonged to the city, they could extract wealth from the newcomers for the privilege of using it for fishing, farming, and conducting religious rituals. When they first informed the Autumn Bird People of this, the newcomers willingly paid what they demanded. It was a reasonable amount initially, but then the officials got greedy and started to raise the price until it became exorbitant. Fishermen, for instance, who had to hand over a tenth of their catch in the beginning, were now forced to give up half. Finally, the Queen of the Autumn Bird People sent representatives to the city to complain to the king about the situation.

The rulers of Luminous Dragon and Laughing Child wanted to maintain peaceful relations with their new neighbors, but they were also increasingly beholden to their officials, who urged them to take a strong stance on the matter. After a protracted negotiation, the leadership on both sides decided on a compromise. The king announced that rather than collecting money from individual fishermen and on each religious occasion, the Autumn Bird People would pay a flat tax twice a year, its total coming to about half of what they were paying now. Any increase in the tax would have to be approved by the king and his ruling council, and the Autumn Bird People would be given notice of the change half a year in advance. To make communications over such matters more convenient, the Autumn Bird People were invited to send a representative to reside in the city. The leadership of both sides agreed it was fair, but not the city's officials, who only thought of taking further advantage of the situation without considering the consequences of the breakdown of peace.

But they said nothing at the time.

Twelve years after the coming of the Autumn Bird People, Luminous Dragon and Laughing Child came under the leadership of a particularly weak group of rulers. The king and his council of generals were mediocrities who were given to lavish living that was financed by sycophantic and manipulative officials who sought to become the true masters of the land. The new king was a young man of expensive tastes, little talent for politics, and no trace of the military spirit of his forefathers. He had been chosen for the throne by the generals who were all his uncles and cousins and their friends. Early in his reign, the officials convinced him that it was high time they raised the tax on the Autumn Bird People, partly to finance the building of an extravagant pleasure hall in the palace, which the king was very much in favor of. When the newcomers–though they were hardly newcomers anymore–were informed of the excessive amount that they would have to pay in half a year, the aging but still strong queen sent her younger brother as the new residential representative to the city to protest. Just in case the ensuing negotiation did not go well, she began to secretly prepare her soldiers for mobilization.

IN THE YEAR when the Autumn Bird People first arrived in the land, four children had been born on the same day and in the same hour, but in different parts of the environs and under disparate circumstances. One of them was a peasant girl whose family lived in a village outside the city. When she was twelve years old, she accompanied her father, uncles, and other men of the community to Luminous Dragon and Laughing Child for the market day that was held every month.

In the excitement of being in the chaotic bustle of the big city, she got lost while chasing after a ram that got loose from its herd. She wandered the bewildering streets, ending up in a wealthy residential area full of grand mansions where prominent officials lived. As she looked around in confusion, wondering how to find her way back to the market, the bleating of the ram drew the attention of a plump boy who peeked over a wall along with a large dog. He was the son of an eminent judge who was also the head of a powerful clan of officials. Unbeknownst to both children, he was another of the four born on the same day and in the same hour.

"Is that your ram?" the boy asked the girl.

"Yes," she answered, surprised at the sight of the boy's head and that of his dog over the wall.

"Does it have a name?"

"He's called Dragon."

The boy laughed at that. "That's funny. What a fancy name for such an ugly and mangy animal."

The girl became angry at his words.

"Who are you to talk about looks? You look like a fat little piglet!"

"What? How dare you, you dirty little Deer Dragon peasant!"

"I can't understand your words, fatso. All I hear is the oinking of a piglet!"

The enraged boy turned to his dog and yelled out a command. "Bear! Go get her!"

The dog named Bear leapt over the wall and ran toward the girl. Before it could reach her, however, the ram charged the dog and hit the animal with its horns so hard that it fell to the ground unconscious.

"Bear!" the boy screamed in horror. "Your ram hurt my dog!" He picked up some stones and began throwing them at the ram.

"Stop!" the girl yelled. "He was only trying to protect me!"

As the boy kept hitting the animal with stones, the girl picked one up and threw it back at him. It hit him smack on the nose and broke it. The boy fell back with blood pouring down his face, the final stone he had let loose flying into the air and going through an open window of a mansion across the street.

Household servants came running at the sound of the boy's wailing. One of them saw a girl with a ram fleeing the scene, and he chased after her. By the time he caught her and the animal and dragged them back to the house, the judge was at the side of his wounded son listening to his account of what had happened. When the girl was brought before him, he ordered that the ram be slaughtered at once. She tearfully begged for forgiveness, but she was forced to watch as Dragon's throat was cut. She was then held by a servant as the judge took up a switch and whipped her on the calves and buttocks. She was finally thrown out of the house.

As the sun began to set, her father and uncles were looking for the missing girl. When she somehow managed to find her way back to the market, they were appalled to see the back of her dress covered in blood. She broke down and told them what had happened, which infuriated them. They and some of the other men from the village got drunk on liquor before they armed themselves with farm equipment. They then made the girl guide them to the judge's house.

Late into the night, when everyone in the household was asleep, the peasants climbed over the wall and dragged everyone out of their chambers. The first thing they did was force the judge's son to watch as they cut the throat of his dog, just as the judge had done with the girl's ram. The peasants, with their pent-up resentment against all officials brimming over, viciously beat the judge and his son, as well as all the male servants, and they terrorized the women as well. Once they had tired themselves out with the violence, they gagged and tied up all members of the household before looting the mansion of its goods. They then left the city in a hurry.

When they returned to their village and sobered up, they knew that they had to flee their homes, as the authorities would never allow them to get away with what they had done to a powerful judge and his family. So they packed up what they could, took their families, and left the land. The next day, when soldiers came and found all the perpetrators gone, they executed the senior heads of the community and burned down the village anyway. The fugitives were now considered murderers, as the judge's son had succumbed to his wounds from the beating and died.

The fleeing peasants took a circuitous route of escape to shake off the pursuers, traveling for many days to the east and then to the north until they reached a place where the river widened and became shallow, allowing them to ford it. Once they were on the other side, they changed direction again, going back west until they came to the settlement of the Autumn Bird People. There, they begged to be allowed to take refuge among them.

What they did not know was that during the ten days it took them to get there, a number of consequential events had occurred in the city.

When the peasant girl had thrown the stone at the judge's son and broken his nose, the stone that the boy had just loosed went through the open window of a mansion across the street, where it hit a birdcage and broke open its door. A small green bird flew out into the property's courtyard, where a cat jumped up and grabbed it in its mouth, breaking the bird's neck instantly. A young boy came running to watch as the cat then proceeded to devour the bird. Then a young girl appeared, saw what was happening, and began to wail in grief. Both of these children had been born on the same day and in the same hour as the peasant girl and the judge's son.

The girl was the daughter of the Autumn Bird People's residential representative in Luminous Dragon and Laughing Child, who was also the queen's younger brother. The queen had no child of her own, so she had a special love for her niece, with plans to make the girl her heir. When the queen sent her brother to the city to negotiate with its rulers over the unreasonable tax for the use of the river, he took his daughter with him, as he had lost his wife to an illness the year before. The mansion they stayed in at Luminous Dragon and Laughing Child belonged to a general in the king's ruling council who was the leader of a faction that opposed the new tax for fear of the consequences of a breakdown of their amicable relationship with their neighbors.

Unfortunately, the general's son and the representative's daughter took an instant dislike to each other as soon as they met. They constantly teased each other and argued, sometimes to the point of yelling and calling names, which embarrassed their guardians, who tried to put a stop to their bickering. It particularly upset the girl when the boy made fun of her pet bird, named Autumn, that she had brought with her, saying that it would make a nice meal for his cat that he called Tiger.

On that particular day, when she witnessed the cat eating her bird, she assumed the boy had deliberately fed her beloved Autumn to Tiger. When their family members, including their fathers, came out to see what was happening, the girl made the accusation against the boy. He claimed innocence, not knowing anything about how the bird had come out of its cage. But when the girl persisted in her bitter denunciation of his ill intention toward Autumn, he grew so frustrated that he slapped her in the face.

The girl's father, before he realized what he was doing, slapped the boy back, making him fall to the ground. The boy's father then came to his defense, and things quickly degenerated into a shouting match between the two men, who had been on friendly terms before that moment. When it was over, the representative decided that he could not stay a moment longer in the house and ordered his servants to pack everything up. It was only after they were all gone that they discovered the boy's cat lying dead in the garden, having choked on the feathers of the bird. Everybody had been so involved in the argument that they had not noticed the animal in distress. The general's son grieved greatly over the loss.

After the representative went back to his own people across the river, the general remained so upset about his son being slapped that he decided to stop arguing for fair dealings with the Autumn Bird People. As he had been the most powerful voice against the imposition of the new tax, the measure was carried through and approved by the monarch. The Queen of the Autumn Bird People was duly notified of the act, much to her chagrin. She was further infuriated by her brother's account of how he and his daughter had been treated in the city.

After much thought, she decided to go to war against Luminous Dragon and Laughing Child.

Just when she and her generals were discussing strategy, the peasant fugitives arrived and asked for protection. The queen found their story intriguing, especially their account of how they had forded the river at a place in the east. She offered to take them in under the condition that one of them served as a guide to the crossing. The peasant girl's father readily volunteered for the task. The day before, his daughter had succumbed to the infection of the wounds from the whipping she had received. His grief from the loss turned into seething hatred toward all the rulers of Luminous Dragon and Laughing Child.

After careful preparation, the bulk of the Autumn Bird army departed for the east in the middle of the night to avoid their movement being detected by the scouts of Luminous Dragon and Laughing Child. They took with them many wagons full of extra weapons that they had made over the last months, ever since the new tax was proposed to them. Under the fugitive peasant's guidance, they came to the shallow place in the river and crossed over to the other side. Most of the army then headed straight for the city, while a small contingent took the wagons to the outskirts of the land. There, they made contact with disgruntled peasants in the area and started handing out weapons to them.

Once the leadership of Luminous Dragon and Laughing Child decided to impose the new tax on the Autumn Bird People, they shored up the defenses at the bridge just in case. After a time, however, with no news of any unusual movement on the other side of the river, the king and the generals relaxed their guard, thinking that the queen was acquiescing to their demand. They were surprised, then, by the sudden outbreak of a rebellion in the farms, where armed peasants attacked the managers who worked for the landowners. As the situation with the Autumn Bird People seemed stable, the king brought back most of the soldiers at the river and sent them to quell the revolt. As the army marched out of the South Gate, many Autumn Bird soldiers, disguised as civilians, snuck into the city. That night, they dispatched the guards at the East Gate and let in the rest of army. They rushed straight to the royal palace, where they found the king and his council in a meeting. The soldiers slaughtered them all, decapitating the leadership of the city with one blow.

When the soldiers who had been sent out to the farms received news that the city was under assault, they turned around and headed back in a hurry. The rebelling peasants took advantage of the situation and attacked them in their disorderly march, killing many of them. In the city itself, when it became known that the Autumn Bird People had taken the royal palace, the working people rose up and attacked all the officials and soldiers they could find, even going to their mansions to kill them and loot their properties. Some set fire to the residences, and the flames spread through the wealthy parts of the city. The Autumn Bird soldiers stood back and allowed them to vent their rage on their former oppressors. Among the dead were the family members of the general who had hosted the representative of the Autumn Bird People, including the boy who had grieved over his cat.

In the aftermath of the destruction, the Queen of the Autumn Bird People crossed the now undefended bridge and entered the city to take control of it. After the fires were put out, bodies were buried, and rubble was cleared, her soldiers patrolled the streets to bring order back to the place. The queen then took the throne of Luminous Dragon and Laughing Child, and a new age began.

It was the conquest of the city by the Autumn Bird People that brought the enmity among the different peoples of the land to an end at last. Much of the wealth of the generals and officials was confiscated and distributed among the working people, and lands and workshops were returned to peasants and artisans. With the situation in the city stabilized, the new rulers did not discriminate among their subjects. While the Autumn Bird People remained the privileged ruling group in the beginning, as time passed, many of them intermarried with the original inhabitants of the city and the land. Within a few generations, few people knew or cared about whether they came from the Autumn Bird People, the Radiant Tiger People, the Fire Bear People, or the Deer Dragon People. It was also in this new age that Luminous Dragon and Laughing Child became the capital of the Autumn Bird State, its people spreading out to new lands, establishing new cities, building forts and roads, and forging a common identity as members of a united country.

EARLY IN THE rule of the Autumn Bird People over the city, the queen announced that a grand ritual would be performed at the river to thank the goddess for overseeing their triumph. The river was also to be named Divine Bird. On the occasion, she planned to formally recognize her niece as her heir.

A wide wooden platform was built over the water so that the queen and various dignitaries could make offerings to their deity. Just as the ritual began, however, the queen's niece, who was standing near her aunt, stumbled and fell into the river. Many immediately jumped in after her, but for some reason none of them could find her. Strong swimmers dived deep into the water over and over again, but there was no sign of her. After a while, the people on the shore saw the girl's dress floating down the river.

At the sight, the queen fell to her knees and wept bitterly, as did her brother and all the dignitaries on the platform. After an extended mourning, she looked up at the sky and saw through her free-flowing tears a thick cloud of dark purple with red lightning flashing inside, hanging in the middle of an otherwise clear sky. As she watched with a mixture of sorrow and dread, it moved toward Four Verdant Mothers and disappeared behind its peaks. The queen then got up, turned to her people, and made an announcement. She told them that their goddess had parted from the terrestrial world, taking her niece with her. From now on, they would worship her no more.

And so the former mountain gods and mountain goddesses of Four Verdant Mountains ceased to be deities to the people of the land.

CHAPTER SIX

Life III

On Perfection

The historian remained at the café after his colleague had told him that she could not carry on their affair and left him. As he slowly drank his tea in a pained daze, mulling over memorable moments in their relationship, he was reminded of the time he had frozen in the midst of doing the dishes, his mind filled with the image of his wife on the day they had taken a boating trip on Divine Bird River.

The boat ride had taken place a month before her death, on a luxury yacht owned by a business acquaintance of hers. It was a pleasant excursion on a sunny but mild day in late spring among engaging people, with a delicious lunch of braised fish and exquisite wine. After they returned home in the late afternoon, they sat on the second-floor balcony to enjoy tea while watching the sun set behind the lofty peaks of Four Verdant Mothers. At some point, she noticed a melancholy expression on the historian's face. He had not talked much on the drive home, but she had assumed that it had been due to fatigue, as her introverted husband tended to get tired out after socializing in large company.

"Hope that wasn't too uncomfortable for you," she said. "Being around all those business types."

"Not at all," he replied with a smile, though sadness lingered in his eyes. "I had a wonderful time. I liked everyone."

"But you seem down. Are you okay?"

As he looked at the expression of genuine concern on his wife's face, his immediate impulse was to brush it off, telling her that he just needed to rest. But then he thought of the work they had been doing with their therapist, him learning to reveal his thoughts and express his feelings more. Even after he had finally been able to talk frankly about the impact of losing his parents, he still found the process extremely difficult. But he put real effort into it because it was important to him that his wife did not feel estranged from his inner life. So he had to force himself to overcome his natural instinct to protect himself from hurt through inward withdrawal.

"There are these moments . . ." he began, but had to stop to reconsider his words.

"I don't know if I can articulate it in a way that would make sense," he started again, "but these moments of . . . pristine perfection. Throughout my life, they have come to me every once in a while, sometimes years and decades passing between them. I recognized them because they affected me in a specific way. Like I was witnessing something . . . otherworldly. Perfect things that should not be happening in this imperfect world."

"Like what?"

He took a moment to remember.

"The first time it happened, it was during geometry class in elementary school. There was this boy–I don't even remember his name. In fact, I think he was unmemorable because he was so completely ordinary. He got average grades, was just okay at sports, normal looking, not particularly popular but not a pariah either. Since we weren't close friends there's no reason I would have remembered him at all if it weren't for this moment. This . . . thing he did."

She looked at him curiously.

"It's nothing of a particularly shocking or spectacular nature. Our teacher wanted a student to come up to the blackboard and work out a geometry problem. She randomly chose that kid and told him to begin by drawing a circle. He came up to the board, picked up a chalk, and then he ... he drew this circle ... this circle with one continuous sweep of his arm ... and it was perfect. Just perfect. He drew an absolutely perfect circle. It was such an amazing feat that everyone in the class gasped, and even the teacher stared at it with an open mouth. That boy, he had no idea what we were reacting to, so he looked around all confused.

"It was an amazing thing, mundane yet singular, that he did without any intention. But after a silent pause the teacher gave the problem and the boy worked it, and then the whole thing was erased so that another kid could do the next problem. So that moment of perfection passed, and everyone forgot about it. But for me ... it stayed with me."

"Why do you think it did?"

"I don't know. That perfect circle, perhaps the only perfect thing that average kid would do in his entire life. For whatever reason, the moment got seared into my memory. Then, years later, when I was in high school, I was waiting at a bus station in the early evening, headed for an after-school study session for the college entrance examination. I happened to look across the street, and I saw a nondescript middle-aged man in a suit carrying a plastic bag with something heavy in it, I think a watermelon. There was nothing remarkable about the sight, so I was about to look away when my attention was arrested by a boy my age who came up to the man from behind and just took the bag from him without saying a word. The man was startled at first, but then he recognized the boy and smiled. It was obvious from their resemblance that they were father and son, and they just happened to run into each other on their way home. They did not exchange a word as they walked, but the smile lingered on the father's face.

"So many have thought about the difficult relationship between a father and a son. Fathers exerting their authority over their sons, the sons rebelling against it. Fathers failing their sons, sons failing their fathers. Their love turning into hatred and their hatred into love. Think about all that's been written about the subject in literature since ancient times. It's a universal obsession. But that moment, like the circle . . . there was something so perfect about the son taking the bag from his father, and his father's quiet joy at it. The sheer beauty of one generation relieving the burden of another."

"That's lovely," she said.

He nodded in agreement. "It made me miss my father very much. It broke my heart."

They sat in sad silence for a moment.

"Anyway, over the years, I witnessed moments like that once every long while. And each time, I felt overwhelmed by this indescribable feeling that made me certain that the memories would stay with me for the rest of my life. It's wonder from the disclosure of the absolute, and longing as well, from the desire to dwell in the pristine perfection of the moment. But there is sadness too. A deep sadness that would linger inside me for days after."

"Why the sadness?"

He put his head down, unable to answer her.

"Did you have one of those moments today?" she asked him.

"Yes."

"Can you tell me about it?"

He remained silent for a while before he finally answered her.

"When we were on the yacht, I looked at you, and you smiled at me. You were so beautiful, your smile was so kind, and the light was hitting you in such a way that you were covered in a glow that was green from the color of your dress. It was perfect. You were perfect. And it hurt me."

"Why?"

"Because . . . because those moments never last. That circle the boy drew, erased and forgotten. That connection between father and son, perhaps it was an isolated incident in a relationship that was actually contentious. I don't know. Those moments happen, and then they inevitably fade in all but imperfect memory. Most people let them go, they forget them, and it's like they never occurred. Perhaps such revelations are just too powerful for us to hold on to. Perhaps it would drive us all mad if we experienced such moments all the time. But I don't really know why that makes me so sad, why I get so down after seeing them."

She stared at him before she leaned over and kissed him deeply on the lips.

"I'm not going to leave you," she told him. "I'm going to stay with you. I'm not going to fade away from you."

He looked into her eyes, feeling a deep hurt inside him being soothed with a calming warmth. He folded his arms around her body and lay his head on her shoulder, surrendering himself to her promise of lasting presence.

It has been said that it is the general way of the world under heaven that what was long divided must unite, and what was long united must divide.

—*Romance of the Three Kingdoms*

CHAPTER SEVEN

History I

The Lofty and the Immaculate

A thousand years later . . .

EARLY IN THE reign of Veiled Sun, the fifth emperor of the Immaculate dynasty, the Lord of All Under Heaven oversaw the elaborate rituals and grand festivities marking the millennial anniversary of the traditional year of the founding of the Autumn Bird State. When they were finally completed, the imperial astrologers informed him that it was a most auspicious year for him to travel, to inspect the vast realm he ruled over. Among the many places he put on his itinerary, the one that he was most anxious to visit was the original homeland of his ancestors in the northernmost territory of the empire.

After a long journey across a harsh terrain, he finally arrived at his destination on a litter carried by twelve bearers, dressed in a thick red coat of radiant fabric lined with cotton and fur to protect him from the bitter cold of the north. He was surrounded by a large contingent of imperial guards on horseback, clad in full armor and bearing long spears. His councillors and ministers followed close behind on more modest litters of their own, each carried by eight bearers. The entire retinue, from the Lord of All Under Heaven and high officials to functionaries, soldiers, servants, entertainers, and laborers, stretched back for more than a great span.

The emperor raised his right hand to bring his litter to a halt, and the entire procession slowly came to a stop behind him. The ruler stood up and looked over the land before him. On the banks of a dirty-looking lake of gray and brown water, there was a sparsely occupied village consisting of tents made of wooden poles and animal skins. All of its denizens had been rounded up by advance guards who had gathered them in a group, prostrated on the muddy ground with their heads bowed down, not daring to look upon the glory of their sovereign. They all looked poor, unkempt, and filthy.

The emperor grimaced at the smell of manure wafting from a group of skinny, dispirited-looking cows in a pen on the edge of the village. When he turned his gaze to the sky, he saw in the distance the singular sight of a dark purple cloud with red lightning flashing inside it, floating across a blanket of gray clouds that were gathering lethargically for a downpour.

In the course of the arduous trek, the emperor had imagined that when he beheld the land of his ancestors for the first time, he would be overwhelmed by the beauteous grandeur of the place, the pristine perfection of which would be seared into his memory so that he might look back on it with awe and longing for the rest of his life. Instead, he found himself looking down at the grim sight of the poorest part of his vast realm and shaking his head in disbelief.

"Fuck," he muttered to himself. "What a dirty anus of a place."

THIS IS HOW the historian came to reveal that an entire period of the country's history had been fabricated.

When he began his career as an assistant professor at Dragon Child National University, he had no expectation or desire to become a public figure whose works would be widely known and discussed outside academia. As he only sought to make solid contributions to the scholarship in his field, he was taken by surprise when his research took him down a path that led to his becoming a celebrated–and, for some, infamous–intellectual in the larger culture.

Only two years after he started working at the university, he published his first book, entitled *Between Myth and History: The Methodology of Unified History in the Works of Clouded Mirror*. It was a thorough and original analysis of the writings of the ancient scholar the Grand Historian Clouded Mirror. His thesis questioned the well-established idea that Clouded Mirror was the first true historian of the realm who employed a rigorously realist perspective in distinguishing myth from history. It was thought that Clouded Mirror wrote his monumental work, *True Records of Past Events*, the first comprehensive account of the history of Autumn Bird State, using only reliable historical documents, while discarding supernatural tales and fantastic legends. The stories that he did not consider to be properly historical he collected in a separate work, entitled *Miscellany of Past Events*, to preserve them for their cultural and literary value. This view of Clouded Mirror's scholarship had become firmly established in the minds of the country's citizens through repetition in school textbooks on national history.

In *Between Myth and History*, however, the historian argued against the notion by demonstrating that the ancient historian did not, in fact, draw a clear distinction between what is now considered myth and history. This can be seen in some passages in *True Records of Past Events*, where, alongside narratives based on official documents, personal accounts, and archaeological findings, episodes of a mythological nature appear uncritically. Furthermore, nothing in *Miscellany of Past Events* indicates that Clouded Mirror considered its stories to be of lesser historical value than those in *True Records*, as had been claimed by modern scholars.

Instead, the historian offered an alternative view of Clouded Mirror's methodology, based on the historical context of his life as evidenced by the contents of his essays and personal letters that have survived. The Grand Historian lived during the historical era known as the Summer and Winter Period, when the land fell into chaos after the catastrophic collapse of the Autumn Bird State. As the realm fragmented into dozens of states of different sizes that were constantly at war with one another, the highest priority for the intellectuals of the time was to produce works that could show a way toward reunification for the sake of peace and stability.

Clouded Mirror, as one of the most significant learned figures who participated in the effort, gathered all the existing knowledge about the past, particularly anything related to the heyday of the Autumn Bird State, and created what he called "a unified history of the land." Its central purpose was to remind readers of the original unity of the people and the realm and to provide a vision of what must be recovered and repaired in order to return to a time of harmony. The accounts he collated in *True Records of Past Events* were ones he found most useful in putting together a coherent and continuous narrative, his "unified history," while those in *Miscellany of Past Events* were ones that did not easily fit into it, because they either contradicted other pieces of evidence or were totally disconnected from them. The events that could be confirmed through multiple sources tended to come from official documents that dealt with mundane matters, so *True Records of Past Events* ended up reading mostly like a realist account with just a few mythological elements here and there. But that is not because Clouded Mirror operated under a clear distinction between myth and history, an anachronistic view that modern historians have imposed on the ancient figure.

The historian's ideas in *Between Myth and History* radically questioned established views on ancient historiography, but they were hard to argue against, given his thorough research and sound arguments. The book was well reviewed and won a few awards, which got the historian tenure at the university, but it was a densely academic text that was written for fellow professional historians, with no expectation of reaching a larger readership. After he was promoted to associate professor, he started on his next project, which began as a study of cultural exchanges between the Lofty dynasty and the Immaculate State before the latter invaded the former and established itself as the sole power over the realm. In the course of his research, he made a startling discovery that not only changed the entire scholarship of his country's history but his personal life as well.

For scholars of the Lofty–Immaculate Period, an essential historical text to consult was *The Veritable Account of the Lofty and the Immaculate*. It was a government-issued work that appeared at the height of the Immaculate dynasty's power, during the reign of the revered Emperor Veiled Sun, and it provided what was purported to be the origin narrative of the regime. It became required reading for all officials and students, as they had to familiarize themselves with the text thoroughly for the civil examinations. The account began with a fable-like tale of twin brothers who were the leaders of a group of migrants from the west. They had fled a terrible calamity that had destroyed their homeland, embarking on a long journey in search of a new place to settle in. After a particularly arduous march through a desert in which they lost many of their people, they were on the verge of utter exhaustion and starvation. They came to a place where the path they were on parted to the north and the south, so they sent scouts in both directions to see what lay ahead of them. They returned to report that in the south there was a great city that ruled over a large country, and that in the north there was a fertile land by a vast lake that was uninhabited.

As the brothers discussed which way they should go–to the south to join an established civilization or to the north to build a new one–their wives connived to make them go separate ways. The women were also sisters who had always despised each other. They knew that once the people finally found a place to make their home, one of their husbands would inevitably emerge as the highest leader and the other become his second-in-command at best. Since neither of them could countenance the other being the wife of the most powerful man, they whispered false stories into the ears of their husbands, causing them to quarrel. The brothers eventually became so angry at each other that they decided that it would be best for them to part. The people then divided into two groups and went north and south.

At the border of the realm in the south, which was the empire of the Supreme dynasty, ruled from the capital city of Dragon Child, the migrants received permission from the local authorities to move into the country under the condition that they abide by the imperial code of laws, pay taxes, and contribute an armed contingent to join the army. After the leader settled his people in a good land, he led a group of his men to fight for the emperor. He distinguished himself so well in battle that he came to the attention of the Lord of All Under Heaven himself, who made him the commander of the palace guards. At some point, however, he came to see that the regime was a tyrannical one that made the common people toil in poverty and servitude while a small group of royalty and aristocracy lived in decadent luxury. When he learned of how his own people ended up suffering terribly under the oppression, he could not stand by and do nothing.

When the emperor had occasion to give a banquet for his princes and high officials, the commander of the palace guards led a group of his men into the pleasure hall and slaughtered them all. He then took charge of the emperor's consort and her son, the twelve-year-old crown prince, and forced them to make a declaration blaming the massacre on a conspiracy by powerful officials and generals. He elevated himself as regent to the boy emperor and oversaw the destruction of the remaining aristocracy, replacing them with a new class of military men who were loyal to him. Once all who could oppose him were disposed of, he dethroned the young emperor with an accusation of illegitimate birth, executed the remainder of the imperial family, and ascended the throne himself as the first emperor of a new dynasty that was named Lofty. Despite the bloody nature of the coup, the people rejoiced at the change of leadership at Dragon Child, welcoming the new era of benevolent rule.

Meanwhile, the other brother led his people to the north, where he indeed found a fertile land, uninhabited except for small groups of primitive nomads who called themselves the Swift Horses. When the migrants first came to the place, they saw a strange purple cloud with red lightning flashing inside it in the midst of an otherwise clear sky. Their leader, following an instinct, took his people in the direction of the cloud, until they reached a most auspicious place by a wide and clear lake. They settled there, building a village they called Purple Cloud and enclosing the place with a wall to protect it from the nomads. The community thrived, its population increasing rapidly from one generation to the next.

As time passed, the village became a town, and the town became a city that spread out on the shores of the lake. In the face of its prosperity and effective self-defense, the primitive natives of the area gave up their nomadic ways to join the settled community. The people also came to have a king, a government, and a vibrant culture with unparalleled achievements in art, literature, and learning. At some point, it began to call itself the Immaculate State.

In explicating the subsequent development of the two states, *The Veritable Account of the Lofty and the Immaculate* asserted that because the Lofty dynasty was built on the legacy of the corrupt Supreme dynasty, it was bound to eventually become corrupt as well, while the Immaculate State was able to maintain the benevolence of its rule because it was a new civilization without the bad influence of a previous regime. And so in the Lofty dynasty, after the competent and humane leadership of the first three emperors and their upright officials, the power holders of Dragon Child became increasingly greedy and decadent once more. Through the reigns of the following three emperors, they revived many practices and policies of the Supreme dynasty to oppress the common people and to extract ever greater taxes from them.

Finally, a group of wise and venerable men who despaired of the state of their country made a secret journey to Purple Cloud, the capital of the Immaculate State, and begged its king to intervene and free the people of the empire from their suffering. The ruler was deeply moved by their earnest entreaties, and he decided to act for the sake of humanity. He raised a great army, supported by the superb cavalry of the formerly nomadic people, the Swift Horses, and invaded the empire. In the face of the surprise attack, the Lofty dynasty quickly collapsed, its last emperor ending his life by hanging himself from a rafter at his residence as the Immaculate force entered Dragon Child. The king of the Immaculate State then established himself as the first emperor of the Immaculate dynasty.

The narrative of *The Veritable Account of the Lofty and the Immaculate* ends at that point.

According to the standard history of subsequent events, the new regime boasted two magnificent cities in the expanded realm, Dragon Child in the south and Purple Cloud in the north. In the early part of the dynasty, the two stood almost on equal terms as the emperors frequently traveled back and forth between them. Although the southern city was the political capital of the empire, the northern city was its cultural center, famed for its superior tradition of art, architecture, literature, and learning. After a time, however, the rulers of the realm went to the north less often, causing many to move to the southern city. As a result, Purple Cloud experienced a gradual decrease in population and loss of its privileged status. The trend became accelerated at the end of the fifth emperor Veiled Sun's reign when the northern city was beset by a deadly plague that devastated the place. In the aftermath of the calamity, Purple Cloud became an insignificant town on the edge of the empire. At some point toward the end of the Immaculate dynasty, the town was sacked and set ablaze by a new group of nomadic people from the northeast who called themselves the Black Turbans. With the empire in rapid decline at the time and with no means to revive the place, Purple Cloud was left in ruins.

This was the established story for many centuries, until the historian disrupted it all.

The path that led him to his momentous discovery began with discussions he had with economic historians about a beguiling mystery they were trying to solve on the finances of the late Immaculate period. Centuries after the fall of the dynasty, historians looking back on the reign of Emperor Veiled Sun began to portray him as one of the greatest rulers in the entire history of the realm. His very long reign was thought to have presided over an extended period of peace and prosperity that also marked the zenith of the dynasty's cultural output. Yet Veiled Sun did not like to travel to the north, visiting Purple Cloud only twice, the first time when he was a young man and the second toward the end of his reign, before the plague that devastated the place. In fact, he encouraged the migration of its best artistic and intellectual figures to the capital, completing the transfer of the north's creative energy to the south.

After his death, the decline of the dynasty began with the instability caused by the very short reigns of the following four emperors—Veiled Sun's son died of illness after only two years on the throne; his elderly uncle who succeeded him expired in a year; the uncle's son was killed in a hunting accident within three years; and his young son succumbed to a fever before the end of his regency. But the direct cause of the long-term crisis that engulfed the realm was thought to be financial mismanagement by the court, which crippled the government's capacity to deal with a series of major calamities that beset the empire, including the flooding of Divine Bird River that destroyed a third of Dragon Child, a great earthquake in the north that leveled a key fortress in the defensive line against the barbarians, resulting in a series of incursions, and internal rebellions in response to increased taxation and conscription to deal with the problems.

While this account of the decline of the Immaculate dynasty after the glorious reign of Emperor Veiled Sun was the standard narrative in history books, economic historians of the period were confronted by an inexplicable discrepancy in the documents. From the death of Veiled Sun to the end of the period of his four short-lived successors, the total wealth of the state was reduced by over three quarters. But all evidence pointed to the fact that the radical decrease in imperial wealth had occurred *before* the major calamities that beset the realm, with no clear explanation of how the state finances had shrunk so quickly in such a short time. The historians' scrutiny of government activities revealed no great expenditure, and they found no evidence of gross financial mismanagement that the rulers and officials of the time had been accused of, at least not on the scale that would explain such an enormous loss. In other words, the state's poverty was not caused by the disasters, but it could not deal with the disasters effectively because it was already poor, which resulted in a further reduction of its wealth that eventually drove it to bankruptcy. This was verified by recently discovered records of the great merchant company known as Three Golden Dumplings, which collapsed at the time because the government defaulted on a massive loan from it. So how did so much of the empire's wealth disappear so quickly in the aftermath of Veiled Sun's reign?

At an academic conference, the historian met a colleague who had an as yet unproven theory that he found intriguing. The notion was that the four short-lived emperors did not cause but had inherited the financial situation from the revered Veiled Sun, who was perhaps not the ideal ruler that was portrayed in the records. The view of the emperor as one who was competent in all things was invented during the decline of the dynasty, as both a form of nostalgia for a bygone era of peace and prosperity and an admonition to current rulers to emulate their great predecessor. In actuality, the great impoverishment of the imperial treasury occurred during Veiled Sun's reign. The emperor was able to conceal the sorry state of finances when he was still on the throne because there was no major calamity at the time that necessitated extra expenditure on the part of the government. It was only when natural disasters and barbarian invasions struck the realm during the time of his successors that they realized that the coffers were almost empty. If Veiled Sun was indeed responsible for the dire economic situation, the question remained as to how he spent all that wealth.

Sensing that he may have hit upon a significant historical question, the historian decided to pursue this line of inquiry and began to pore over government documents from the later part of the emperor's reign.

In the course of his subsequent research in the archives, the historian was surprised when he began to discern signs of what appeared to be interference in recordkeeping all over the place, with missing texts, pages in different handwritings that had apparently been added or substituted later, and numbers that simply did not add up. In other words, he was finding evidence of a massive government cover-up of its financial activities, the purpose of which seemed to be the concealment of systematic mismanagement. He would have considered it gross incompetence, except a lot of the cover-up was conducted quite masterfully, something that both irked and impressed him. As he went further back in Veiled Sun's reign, delving into other records with signs of later manipulation, he kept running across oblique and obscure references to Purple Cloud, which made little sense, as the emperor was known to be indifferent to the northern city.

The historian's first major breakthrough came when he managed to get hold of a manuscript of unpublished writings of a high official who had been a long-term chief councillor to the emperor. In a draft of his unfinished memoir that his descendant allowed the historian to examine, there is a passage in which the councillor describes how he accompanied his sovereign on his first trip to Purple Cloud early in his reign. According to him, the emperor found it to be a dirty and insignificant place full of lowly people, which shamed him a great deal as it was the original homeland of his ancestors. This was puzzling to the historian, since Purple Cloud, while somewhat in decline at the time, was still known to be the second-greatest city of the realm, one that was praised for its magnificence and rich culture by many contemporaries of the emperor. "Dirty and insignificant" seemed to be a startlingly inappropriate description of the place at the time, especially in view of all other known accounts.

At that point, the historian looked over what he had unearthed so far, especially in relation to the emperor and the northern city. Veiled Sun, on his first visit there, apparently had a poor estimate of the place and returned only once more, as an elderly man at the end of his long reign. During his time on the throne, there was a massive hidden expenditure of the government's wealth which somehow involved Purple Cloud, though officials carefully avoided revealing in the records the exact nature of the spending and its connection to the city, probably destroying documents that spelled it out. A strange new scenario seemed to be on the verge of emerging through the historian's research, but there was still something missing–some essential connective tissue that could bring it all to light.

Given the solitary nature of his personal life, it suited the historian to spend so much of his time in the archives, poring over texts and documents on the deep research that he had always enjoyed. Even when the labor became particularly difficult or beguiling, he carried on with the absolute certainty that this was work that he was meant to do. Part of the pleasure he derived from it came from the sense of getting to know his subjects, people who had lived centuries, millennia before his time. As he learned more about them through extant historical records and other evidence, they felt increasingly real to him, even more so than those living in the present, including himself. But a greater sense of intimacy with the dead did not necessarily lead to a comforting feeling of familiarity with them. In fact, as he approached the figure of Emperor Veiled Sun with a new perspective, an odd kind of dread rose inside him, as if he was on track to discovering something dark about him. It was such a peculiar feeling, one that he had never experienced before in his research, that he felt compelled to give it some thought.

When he could not get to the bottom of his unsettling feeling toward the subject of his study, he hit upon the idea of visiting the ruins of Purple Cloud to see if that would provide him with an insight or inspiration.

As he stood on a hill that looked down on the labyrinth of low walls that stretched out over a plain by a nearly dried-out lake, all that remained of the once-great city, an utterly bizarre idea came to him, which he could not help but laugh at. What if Purple Cloud and the glory of the Immaculate State was something that was entirely invented during the time of Emperor Veiled Sun? What if Purple Cloud was *never* a beacon of art and scholarship, but always a hovel on the fringe of the empire? What if Veiled Sun came to visit the homeland of his ancestors and was horrified to discover that he came from a barbaric people who lived in primitive villages? What if he decided to rectify this shameful fact by inventing an entire civilization that had existed prior to his ancestors' conquest of the Lofty dynasty, one that rivaled the south in its magnificence?

What if Veiled Sun had retroactively *built* Purple Cloud in the image of the great city that he wanted posterity to look back on?

The historian found the idea preposterous, yet he also could not quite let it go. On the train ride back to Dragon Child, he found himself considering what it would take to actually pull off such a feat. First of all, a massive new city would have to be erected on the site in a matter of years, all the artifacts that supposedly came from there would have to be designed and manufactured, and then all the writings and artworks associated with the Immaculate State would have to be produced, all in a distinct style invented solely for the purpose. To make it even more convincing, historical records would have to be altered to show that the previous emperors had visited the city frequently, and there would also have to be numerous fake accounts of other people praising the magnificence of its art, architecture, literature, and scholarship. And the whole project would have to be conducted in secret, its truth then buried for all posterity. At that point, the historian came to the horrifying realization that the only way to ensure that no one ever found out about the fraud was to commit a massive slaughter of all those involved, any who could reveal the fabrication—the laborers who worked on the site, the artisans, artists, and writers who produced the artifacts, and all the officials who could not be trusted to maintain their silence. But that was ludicrous. The expense in terms of time, resources, and, most unthinkable of all, the sheer number of lives that would have to sacrificed—it was almost too large to comprehend. By the time the historian arrived home, however, he realized that as incredible and horrific as the idea seemed, it was not beyond the realm of possibility.

That was, of course, not enough. It was a theory built on other theories, and he still lacked concrete evidence to make any kind of real claim. The historian, therefore, dared not tell anyone of his idea, which he himself was admittedly still skeptical of. But he could not free himself of it either, as he continued his research with the outlandish notion in his mind. He wondered at some point whether he even wanted the theory to be proven true, one that could potentially disrupt the entire field of his scholarship. But he could not let such a consideration get in the way of his work. His only duty as a historian was to unearth whatever evidence he could to the best of his efforts and let the best-supported thesis speak for itself.

To his astonishment, he kept finding evidence for his idea. Odd little things here and there that seemed insignificant by themselves but ultimately pointed to a grand project of colossal cost as well as to its cover-up. He also came across articles written by literary scholars pointing to the inexplicable appearance of anachronistic characters, words, and phrases in writings that were thought to have been composed in the Immaculate State, hinting at possible forgeries, and art and architectural historians puzzled by the apparent use of techniques and technologies in the creation of artworks and architecture that seemed to be out of place as well as time. When he sent a series of emails with discreetly put questions to archaeologists who worked on the ruins of Purple Cloud, they replied that none of the objects from the site could definitively be shown through chemical testing to predate the reign of Veiled Sun.

And then, the historian found evidence that seemed to confirm his worst fear.

When he looked into the deadly plague that supposedly devastated Purple Cloud at the end of Veiled Sun's reign, mentioned only in a single brief entry in the official government records, he found no independent account of the calamity. But he discovered plenty of evidence that revealed a significant increase in military expenditure at the time that pointed to a large mobilization. The records were strangely silent on the exact purpose of the mobilization, which was beguiling, as there was no major war fought at the time. Why did the emperor spend so much money raising such a large force in a time of peace when the second-greatest city of the empire was being ravaged by a plague?

The answer that was staring in the face of the historian was that the army was sent north to commit the slaughter of those who had participated in the fabrication of the city's glorious past. After ordering the massacre, the emperor must have had the newly built city destroyed so that the remains of its buildings and artifacts might be discovered by posterity as the site of a wondrous bygone civilization. Veiled Sun must have also told some lie to the military commanders who perpetrated the act, making up a false story of why the city and all its people had to be destroyed—probably something related to the fictional plague.

If the glory of Purple Cloud and the Immaculate State were indeed fabrications, that meant that the entire narrative of the founding of the Lofty dynasty and the Immaculate State by twin brothers, as told in the government's official text *The Veritable Account of the Lofty and the Immaculate*, was utter fiction. In that case, the historian had to unearth the true history of the time, one that the text was composed for the purpose of erasing. This led him to another line of inquiry, having to do with the identity of the primitive nomadic people called the Swift Horses who were mentioned briefly in *The Veritable Account*.

The first crucial clue for his research had come from the personal writings of the emperor's chief councillor. With that in mind, he looked for similar texts from the time of the fall of the Lofty dynasty. In doing so, he discovered in the writings of the period that the word "Immaculate" was never used to describe the invaders from the north until the declaration of the new dynasty's name. He found no mention of the Immaculate State, the Immaculate people, or the Immaculate army, as most people who left records of their personal experience of the invasion and the change of regime at Dragon Child referred to them simply as "the invaders" or "the northern invaders." And to the historian's utter astonishment, he also found a number of references to them as "the Swift Horses," "the Swift Horse barbarians," and "the Swift Horse invaders." Other historians who had previously come across the references had assumed that the name referred just to the fearsome cavalry of the Immaculate army, but he could not find any evidence that supported the idea. What this meant was that the fall of the Lofty dynasty was the result of an invasion not by a rival civilization of equal glory and sophistication but by horse-riding nomads of the north.

Not exactly a glorious origin of a new regime.

The Veritable Account of the Immaculate and the Lofty also claimed that righteous men of Dragon Child begged the rulers of the Immaculate State to save the realm from the corruption and tyranny of the last Lofty emperor and his officials. Except, again, the historian found no evidence to corroborate the story, as the personal writings of officials and even educated commoners from the period described a generally peaceful and prosperous state of things in the country. So that account was yet another story that was concocted to provide a moral justification for the invasion and destruction of the Lofty dynasty.

The alternative narrative that the historian discerned behind the false story was very different from the one that was taught to students at school. It showed that the Lofty dynasty was brought down by the Swift Horses, who penetrated the empire's northern defenses, defeated the imperial army, took the capital city, and gained control over the realm under a new regime that eventually adopted the name of "the Immaculate dynasty." But the uncouth warlords had no experience in administrating a large country, so they maintained much of the government bureaucracy at Dragon Child, relying on officials who were willing to serve them in order to preserve their lives and maintain some of their privileges. In the following generations, the emperor, his clan, and the entire ruling class adopted the language, the customs, even the clothing and mannerisms of the south, so that by the time of the fifth emperor Veiled Sun, they appeared and acted just like the lords of the previous dynasty. As for the frequent visits by the early emperors to Purple Cloud, despite accounts of them in official records, the historian found no corroborating evidence that any of the journeys had taken place. The questionable records with signs of retroactive editing were most likely forged during the reign of Veiled Sun.

Even after the historian had amassed enough evidence to at least suggest the possibility of his theory and had come up with the alternative history of the founding of the Immaculate dynasty, he hesitated to publish his findings, as a part of him still found it difficult to accept it all. There was also the consideration that if his ideas proved to be true, it would not only necessitate the complete reassessment of the period but also bring about the end of the entire field of Immaculate State studies. Over the centuries, hundreds of books and articles had been written about its history and culture, which built the careers of many academics. In addition, the heritage of the Immaculate State was of national importance, as it was still commonly depicted in modern times as a period not only of peace and prosperity but of unparalleled artistic and literary achievements in the country's history. One book famously called it "the Renaissance of the Grand Circle." As for Emperor Veiled Sun, his idealized image graced a paper bill of the country's currency.

Whether the historian succeeded in convincing people of his theory or not, a larger question hung over his entire research—namely, what does it mean to expose the very existence of an entire period of a country's history to be a fabrication? A period of such significance and pride to the nation in the modern era? If Emperor Veiled Sun's purpose was to create a better image of his ancestors for prosperity, he succeeded spectacularly. Yes, the Immaculate dynasty eventually fell, plunging the realm into the chaos of the Seven Dynasties Period until the reestablishment of order with the founding of the Radiant dynasty. But because of what Veiled Sun had achieved, the admiration for the glory of the Immaculate State persisted, becoming a fixed historical notion in the imagination of scholars as well as the general populace. The story of that exalted period in the country's history proved to be an effective one.

The historian knew full well, however, that the effectiveness of a story did not make it true or good. The world was filled with effective stories in the forms of myths, rumors, propaganda, and conspiracy theories that were used to distort reality, manipulate people, and, in some cases, commit atrocities. He refused to believe that the widespread acceptance of a fabrication's actuality could somehow make it real, Osberg and his Tlön be damned. No matter how successful and popular the story of the Immaculate State was, it was a lie. And it was a lie that was built on the sacrifice of countless people. In the course of his research, he felt haunted by all those who had not only been destroyed but consigned to utter oblivion for the lie to stand–living, thinking, feeling human beings who had worked, loved, hoped, and ultimately just wanted to go home. The feeling of dread that he had carried with him since the inception of his theory grew as his work proceeded.

And he began to have nightmares of mass killings.

Early one morning, as he lay in bed when it was still dark outside, shaken by a dream of a massacre that had felt as real as personal memory, his horror gave rise to anger toward the monstrous ruler. Even though he did not know if he could convince other scholars of his theory, he felt that he had to carry on in order to thwart the emperor's design, on behalf of the forgotten memory of all those who had participated in creating a simulacrum of a beautiful civilization, only to be murdered for their efforts, all for . . . what? To assuage one man's ego? To create a false glory for the country? If the ruler's greatest legacy was a grand lie, was it not the historian's task to expose the truth of the emperor's vanity and cruelty? And he was perhaps the only person who could bring a measure of justice to the victims. In that moment, the historian's project was no longer just a work of scholarly nature but one motivated by the indignant need to expose the revered emperor for the horrific monster that he was.

And so he dug in deeper at the archives, pulling relentlessly at every little thread and meticulously weaving them together to form a coherent tapestry of the terrible truth of the hidden past.

When the historian finally began to write the book on the subject, which would be entitled *The Fabricated Country: The Invention of the Immaculate State*, he knew that the only way he would not be subjected to ridicule for his seemingly outlandish thesis was to pack it with a mountain of evidence that his critics would have to contend with. Emperor Veiled Sun's cover-up effort was successful enough not to leave behind a bloodied sword as evidence of his deeds. But the historian was able to organize a massive amount of information pointing to the yearly expenditure from the imperial treasury of the colossal sums that were being spent on a project having to do with Purple Cloud. He also presented evidence of the movement of large numbers of laborers, artisans, architects, artists, and writers from Dragon Child and the provinces who were never seen again. And then there were all the aforementioned oddities of the supposed artifacts from the Immaculate State that seemed to be out of place and time.

The manuscript he finished came out to almost a thousand pages, over a quarter of it notes and references. His dedication read: "To all those, lofty and humble, who were sacrificed in the name of false glory."

When his editor at the Dragon Child University Press received it, she was astounded and excited at the same time just from reading the introduction and finding out what the book was about. After she managed to get through the entire manuscript, she made the suggestion that he write a long article to be published in a journal at the same time as the book. That way, he could get his radical thesis out quickly and then direct interested people to the text for the full research.

The historian expected the enormous controversy that was sure to follow among academics, but he was taken completely by surprise when news of his findings spread through the national media. He was dismayed to read sensationalist headlines in newspapers and online sites, like "Historian Claims National History Is Wrong," "Traditional History Has Been Faked, Historian Says," and "Historian Exposes the Lies of Textbooks." The flood of requests for interviews on television and radio made him feel uncomfortable as well, but he felt obliged to overcome his introverted nature and accept some of them so that he could give a more nuanced description of his work without putting the audience to sleep. His fat, dense book that most nonacademic people would find unreadable even showed up on the bestseller list for a brief time, though he speculated that only a fraction of those who had bought the much-talked-about book of the season actually read it in its entirety.

His thesis indeed proved to be controversial, but the historian was surprised yet again when most academics in Immaculate State studies did not resist it but rather jumped on its bandwagon. They started revealing their own suspicions about the artificiality of their subject, which they confessed that they had been too timid to express before, offering more evidence to support the idea. It was as if all the historical evidence that didn't fit into the established view of the past was falling into place now that the historian had offered an alternative narrative. In fact, there was such an accumulation of further revelations that other scholars unearthed that the historian agreed to co-edit a large volume of articles in order to bring them all together in a single book entitled *Forging History: New Essays on the Invention of the Immaculate State*. Particularly disturbing were findings by archaeologists that appeared to confirm a mass killing perpetrated at the time, including the discovery of a vast underground dungeon where the condemned may have been imprisoned. And art historians and literary scholars who read the book began to find evidence of what appeared to be the disappearance of an entire generation of artists and writers, those used and subsequently killed by Veiled Sun, depriving the era of its best creative talents.

There were detractors, of course, some of them vociferous in their opposition. One eminent political scientist in particular, a great authority on the structures of power in the Immaculate State, led the opposition. He quickly put out a book condemning the historian's work, claiming that it was based on undue speculations and unverifiable theories. Critics pointed out, however, that the political scientist only addressed a few of the historian's ideas, ones that the historian had already acknowledged were on tentative ground, while ignoring many others that were based on much more solid evidence.

Inevitably, Dragon Child National University organized a debate between them in a major conference on the subject. The historian respected the political scientist's works and intended to address his objections in a professional way, but he could tell as soon as they met that the other man was furious with him. Most of their discussion, which was covered by the national media with television cameras in the auditorium, proceeded in a cordial way. But toward the end of the event, the political scientist became increasingly agitated as he found it impossible to refute or explain away all the evidence at hand. He finally lost his temper and engaged in an ad hominem attack, questioning the historian's patriotism in besmirching a glorious part of the nation's past and asking if his lack of respect for tradition came from the fact that he did not have proper parental guidance. That was an obvious reference to the historian's loss of his parents at a young age, something that a reporter had found out and that was repeated in the media for some reason.

Everyone present was appalled by the political scientist's comment, even those who were in attendance to support him. The historian took it in stride, however, shooting him a look of pitying contempt before replying to his more coherent argument in a professional way. When the political scientist's moment of acting out was shown in the media, everyone agreed that he had disgraced himself in public, and after a meeting with the administrators of his university, he decided to take early retirement at the end of the semester.

(Another story of the whole affair could have been related from the perspective of the political scientist. Whether told in comic or tragic mode, it would have centered around an eminent scholar at the height of his career who suddenly finds himself in great crisis after some upstart threatens to destroy the very foundation of his entire life's work. Even in the face of overwhelming evidence, he just cannot accept that he spent the most productive decades of his life writing about a country that never existed. With his personal life affected by this as well and threatening to fall apart, he makes a desperate attempt to bring the historian down in a public confrontation, only for him to humiliate himself in an act of desperation that assures his downfall. But this is not the time to tell that tale.)

The end result of the conference seemed to be that the general consensus of academics favored the historian's thesis. While that provided him with a sense of accomplishment as well as relief in the vindication of his labors, he continued to find it uncomfortable to be a minor celebrity in the larger society, occasionally being recognized in public as "that historian who showed that national history is full of lies" and getting emails from strangers, sometimes of bizarre and conspiratorial nature ("Are you going to look into how our civilization was created by four space aliens who landed on Four Verdant Mothers and posed as gods? Here is some evidence you should review . . ."). An online group started a campaign to remove the image of Emperor Veiled Sun from the paper bill currency, with feminist activists chiming in to advocate that it was high time he be replaced with a female historical figure.

But the whole affair opened up some good opportunities for him. For one, the biggest publishing company in the country offered him a rather startling advance to write a book for a general readership. The money was not a major draw for him as he was financially stable and led a frugal existence, but he had already intended to write something simpler, because he needed a break from the exhausting complexities of his last work. So he signed a contract to write a narrative history of the Radiant dynasty entitled *The Light of All Under Heaven: A History of the Radiant Dynasty*. The publishing company invested a lot of resources into promoting it widely, which resulted in the book becoming the historian's second bestseller.

On the occasion of the book making the list, the company threw him a party at their headquarters. It was at the event that a woman in a simple but fashionably elegant dress whom he found rather stunning came up to him with a luminous smile.

"So you are the historian who showed that I was taught a bunch of lies in school," she said, standing rather close to him.

"Only some of it," he said, the banality of his response before such a glamorous woman shaming him a little.

But she laughed at that and touched him briefly on the arm, which caused an electric sensation to jolt through him.

Within weeks, he fell in love with her, and in the following year, they were married.

CHAPTER EIGHT

Life IV

On Ghosts and Hauntings

On the first date with his future wife, as they got to know each other over wine and appetizers at a high-class French restaurant, the historian was a little taken aback when she asked about the loss of his parents.

"I'm sorry if it's a painful subject," she said. "It's just that . . . well, I read up about you, and that was mentioned in some articles."

"It's fine," he assured her. "But I don't understand why it was brought up in the media in the first place. I mean, it has nothing to do with my work."

"The journalists probably thought that it made an engaging story—the eminent historian with a tragic past. They figured it would make you more human and sympathetic."

"I don't see why. After my father died, I lived with my uncle's family for a few years, and then I went to college. I was hardly Oliver Twist."

"Oh, don't get me wrong, I don't think they were right to publicize something so private. And I'm not trying to pry. We can change the topic if you want."

"It's all right," the historian said. "Really. It was a long time ago."

She flashed him a smile of such sympathy that it made his cheeks feel heated.

"Are your parents living?" he quickly asked, a little embarrassed at feeling like a young man receiving the attention of a girl he had a crush on.

"My father is."

"Are you close to him?"

"Mmm . . . we are okay. He left our family when I was a teenager, after going through what he called a 'personal crisis.' My younger brother and I didn't hear much from him until about fifteen years ago when Mother died, and he decided to reach out to us then. He said he felt deeply remorseful about having abandoned us and wanted to make up for it. But I was never that close to him before he left. He worked a lot and was gone for extended periods on business trips. So there was not much to repair in our relationship, which was minimal in the first place. Now we are, let's say, cordial."

She looked away in deep thought. He worried that he may have made her dwell on unpleasant memories, so he was about to apologize when she spoke again.

"Are you religious or spiritual in any way?" she asked him out of nowhere.

"No. I didn't grow up among religious people, and I never developed an interest in that."

"Me neither. I don't believe, or rather I don't think much about what's beyond this world. I'm also pretty skeptical when it comes to claims about the supernatural. But . . . I did have this experience once. It was the single strangest thing that's ever happened to me."

"What was it?"

"Uhm . . . so after Father left us," she started, but then paused for a moment to think before she began again.

"My mother was an extremely controlling person, which was one of the reasons Father left. He just couldn't handle her being on his case all the time, never giving him any room to breathe or have some privacy, which compelled him to spend more time at work, which made her more controlling when he was around, and so on and on. A vicious cycle. Even when I was young, I sensed that my mother was that way because of some deep insecurity about herself. And I tried to be understanding, but dealing with her could really wear you out. And after Father was gone, she really clung to me. She became convinced that I was going to leave her as well. That made her so paranoid that she became intrusive to the extent of . . . well, emotional abuse, really. I mean, I felt sorry for her being an abandoned wife, and I could understand her concern about being abandoned by me as well, being left all alone. But how she reacted to it, what she did to keep me close to her, it suffocated me. It made me lose all sympathy for her, and I resolved to leave home as soon as possible. I guess it's ironic that how she acted out of the fear of abandonment is what made me want to leave her." She gave a rueful shrug.

"Anyway, just as I was finishing high school, I got this job in the city which would allow me to work my way through college. I didn't say a word about it to her though and managed to keep it a secret until the day I left. I knew that if I told her, she would find some way of jeopardizing the opportunity. She would even have pretended to be seriously ill to prevent me from going."

"Really?"

"Yes. She actually did that after I left, more than once. 'I coughed out blood,' 'I just lost consciousness and fell down the stairs,' 'The doctor thinks I may have cancer.' Things like that. I knew what she was doing, so I talked to my younger brother, who had to bear the brunt of her craziness after I left home, poor kid. He told me what was going on, that she was pretending to be sick so she could manipulate me into coming back home to take care of her. She was actually a very healthy person physically. Other than to give birth, she never had to go to a hospital even once in her life—never even got the flu. She also had an iron stomach, so when we ate the same thing and got food poisoning, she was the only one who didn't get sick. So she didn't die of any illness. Her death . . . it was actually the weirdest thing."

"And this is the strange experience you're talking about?"

"Oddly, no. Although it was definitely strange. But since it didn't happen to me . . . I don't know."

"Know what?"

She laughed a little. "It's just that you're going to find it incredible. Maybe even unbelievable. I mean, *I* did, when my brother called to tell me what happened."

"You can't not tell me now."

"Okay," she said, and took a deep breath. "According to my brother, she went to the neighborhood supermarket and was walking back home with groceries when a man fell on her from the top of a building."

"What?"

"He was a lunatic who jumped off, thinking that he was some kind of a god who had to fly up to Four Verdant Mothers. He broke her neck and she died instantly, but he ended up surviving with just a few broken bones."

"That's crazy."

"I know. So strange."

"Well, strange as it was, it still must have been hard on you."

"It was, but . . . my brother and I, we have always been really close. Even after I left home, we talked on the phone almost every day. So we had frank conversations about the impact of her death on us. It was hard because she was such a master at giving us guilt trips. But then again, precisely because of that, we were . . . we felt relief. No more of her making us feel like bad children for not doing everything she wanted us to do. No more of her trying to emotionally manipulate us, pretending she was ill, pretending she was depressed to the point of contemplating suicide.

"Yet, despite all that, she was still my mother. So yeah, it was hard. Especially the timing. Around then, the company I founded started doing really well. I was going to set her up so that she could live comfortably for the rest of her life. Buy her a nice house with a garden where she could plant things and know she wasn't abandoned. I hoped that would reconcile us and I could stop feeling like a bad daughter. But after the funeral and everything was over, my brother and I both felt like a great load had been lifted from our shoulders." She looked at him then, a touch of worry in her eyes. "I know that must sound bad to you."

"Not at all. It's perfectly understandable."

"Anyway, a few days later, this thing happened to me. This . . ." She trailed off and looked away with a thoughtful expression.

The historian let her take her time.

"I woke up in the middle of the night," she began again, "and there she was, standing at the foot of my bed. I was about to ask her what she was doing there when we had just buried her, but she suddenly grabbed my feet and tried to drag me away. What's even stranger was that . . . I wasn't scared, not at all, even though my dead mother was standing there, trying to take me somewhere. I just felt frustrated and annoyed because I did not want to go with her. So I resisted, and she kept pulling at my feet, and neither of us got anywhere. We did that for what felt like a long time—hours. It was exhausting! But then she finally gave up, looking really sad and demoralized. She stood still for a while longer, her head bent down in grief, before she turned around and disappeared. And I just went back to sleep, a really deep sleep."

"You dreamed this?"

"I must have, of course. But . . . at the time, it did not feel like a dream at all. I mean, it felt like I was awake the whole time, and it all seemed quite real. And once my last struggle with her was over, I felt so completely drained from pulling away from her that I needed to rest. My feet were sore from where she had grabbed me, and my muscles hurt from pulling back. Look, as I said, I am not a spiritual person. I don't believe in ghosts or anything like that. So I'm fine with a psychological explanation of what must have been some kind of a hallucination, the meaning of which is all too obvious. My guilt toward her, her neediness when she was alive, all that. But I still can't forget how real it felt at the time, and how vividly I remember it, not like the hazy memory of a dream."

"Hmm."

She looked at the historian. "Did you ever have an experience like that? I mean, with the losses in your life?"

He gave it some thought.

"Is this why you asked about my parents?" he asked.

"Partially. But I also wanted to share this with you for some reason. I don't know why."

He looked at her and saw that she seemed a little self-conscious for the first time.

"So?" she asked.

"No, nothing like that, but..."

"But?"

"I don't know if I can explain but... uhm... after my parents died, I had this sense of becoming less real, less substantial myself."

"Less substantial?"

"Maybe because I became so withdrawn, I had this sense of my own being becoming kind of... ghostly. Like I was not wholly present in my life anymore. You know, this may sound odd, but when I research history, learning about people who lived centuries, millennia ago, they feel more real than I do. Their lives on documents from bygone eras feel more substantial than my own existence in the present. It's like... I am a spirit from the future who is haunting them–observing them, studying them, trying to understand them, perhaps so I can feel more real through them."

"Even now?"

He looked up, puzzled.

"Here, with me. Does this feel insubstantial?"

"No," he said with certain conviction. But then he felt the need to assure her further of his presence in the moment. "This feels very real."

She flashed him another smile that was so bright and kind that he felt a pain in his heart. The effect was so powerful that he could only smile back weakly before looking down at his food. But then he found that he could not shake what he had just said, not about the present but about the past. He fell into thought, considering the notion of the historian as a ghost from the future who is haunting the past. For some reason, the idea made him deeply sad. At some point, he came to himself and looked up to see that she was staring fixedly at him.

"I'm sorry," he said. "Got distracted for a second there."

"Wow," she said.

"Pardon?"

"I don't know," she said with a wistful smile. "This is kind of embarrassing, but . . . hmm . . . you just displayed vulnerability in a rather devastating way. And you don't even realize it."

"I don't understand."

She looked deep into his eyes.

"Please don't get me wrong here," she said, "but one of the lessons I learned from my past is to never get into a relationship with a man in order to fix him. After some painful experiences, I swore that I would never do that again."

"That seems wise."

"But just now . . . when you went off into your thought, suddenly looking so sad, I felt this terrific urge to bring you back. So you wouldn't feel like a ghost. It's not that I pity you. There's nothing pitiful about you."

"That's a relief."

She smiled at that. "But I do find you to be a deeply sympathetic person and . . . and I think I would like to see what I can do for you."

As he looked back at her, he felt overwhelmed by emotion that was a potent mixture of desire and fear.

"What are you thinking?" she asked.

He hesitated.

"Can you tell me?" she asked again.

"I am terrified."

"By what?"

"By what I could feel for you."

"There you go again," she said with a mischievous smile, "with your vulnerability."

They smiled at each other and switched their conversation to a less charged topic.

Interlude

The storyteller knew that he was doomed.

He had suspected it when he had been sitting in the cramped prison cell, but he was certain of it now as he lay prostrate before the emperor sitting at his dinner feast. The Lord of All Under Heaven had commanded him to tell a story to entertain him.

"Well?" his sovereign demanded in an impatient tone.

Despite his terror, the storyteller lifted his head just enough to look at the aging ruler whose enormously bloated body was clad in a shimmering red robe, his plump cheeks also ruddy from drinking. He looked like a fat ugly old bear. As the storyteller stared at him, his fear turned into anger that swelled into a fiery rage.

So you brought me here to amuse yourself before you have me killed, *the storyteller thought.* You let me have a bowl of gruel so I would have the strength to tell a story while you gobble up the beef, the pheasant, and the flounder. Made me clean myself and put on new clothes so I would not ruin your appetite with my stink. I curse you. I curse you a thousand times, ten thousand times.

"Are you deaf?" the emperor asked in annoyance.

Yes, I will tell you a story, *the storyteller thought.* And it won't be a series of stories within stories I will tell one after another, in the hope that you will keep me alive for a thousand nights or more. I will tell you just one very short story, one that will haunt your dreams, you evil bastard.

"At an inn in a rural village," the storyteller began, "a group of travelers struck up a conversation over dinner."

AT AN INN *in a rural village, a group of travelers struck up a conversation over dinner. They enjoyed one another's company so much that they shared liquor and caroused throughout the night, much to the dismay of the innkeeper and other guests. At a late hour, one of the travelers noticed that a pale, delicately featured young man among them had not said a word all evening, content to just listen to the others with a serene smile on his pale lips. In his inebriated state, he could not recall how the young man had joined them in the first place, as he was sure that he had not been present at the dinner. It was as if he had somehow insinuated himself into their company without anyone noticing.*

"Where are you from, young man?" the traveler asked, his curiosity aroused.

"I am from a town called Rain Tiger Ghost," he replied in a strangely distant tone.

"Rain Tiger Ghost? That's an unusual name. How did the place come to be called that?"

"You want to know why it came to be called Rain Tiger Ghost? I will tell you the story of how it earned that name."

BEFORE THE TOWN *became known as Rain Tiger Ghost, when it had an ordinary name that no one remembers anymore, it was ruled by a big bully called Red Bear Fat Butt who terrorized the place. He took whatever he wanted from hardworking people, violated their women, and forced them to build a large house just for himself. If anyone dared to refuse his orders or object to his cruel actions, he unsheathed his sword that he called Red Bear Penis and struck that person down. Many families in town mourned the deaths of loved ones who had been unjustly murdered by the bully. He was indeed a most nefarious bastard who deserved to be cursed a thousand times over in his lifetime and in the lives he would live after.*

After a night of drunken debauchery at a pleasure house, Red Bear Fat Butt was walking home in the dark when he overheard a group of old men talking about him. They lamented that Heaven did not grant them the favor of striking down the no-good bastard for all the wrongs he had done. Infuriated by their words, the bully was about to unsheathe Red Bear Penis and slaughter them all, but he stopped when one of them suggested that they should consult Master Three Stars about what to do about him. Red Bear Fat Butt had never heard the name before, so he became curious.

The next day, when he inquired about this Master Three Stars, he found out that an elderly scholar had recently moved into a small house just outside the town. He was apparently a personage of renown whose honor name indicated his greatness in three things–his profound understanding of the classics, his skill at calligraphy, and his proficiency at magic. Some said that he had held a high-ranking post in the government, but the cruel and foolish emperor had exiled him for criticizing his misrule. Others said that he had retired from officialdom with great honors, and that he had moved to the town to get away from the bustle and distractions of Dragon Child. It was also rumored that he had given away all his substantial wealth to the poor so that he could live the simple life of a sage. Red Bear Fat Butt cared about none of that other than how this man's presence in the town impacted him. He could not countenance someone who could rival his authority, so he decided to confront the scholar to let him know who was boss.

Before the bully set out for the home of Master Three Stars in the afternoon, he had spent the entire morning boasting of what he was going to do. So a large number of townspeople joined him when he went forth. He found the old man sitting on the veranda of his modest home, practicing calligraphy with elegant strokes of the brush, writing characters in vermilion ink on yellow paper. Red Bear Fat Butt loudly demanded that the scholar come out and pay his respects to him.

"You may have been a big deal once," he said in an impertinent manner, "but here, I am your superior. So you will serve me as your

older brother. Otherwise, you will get a taste of my fist in your mouth."

The townspeople were familiar with Red Bear Fat Butt's character, but they were still shocked by his insolence toward the venerable personage.

"A rainy day is not a good day for a visit," Master Three Stars said calmly without looking up from his work.

"What are you babbling about, you crazy old man?" Red Bear Fat Butt said. "Why speak of rain when the sun is shining?"

Master Three Stars picked up the yellow paper he was writing on and showed it to Red Bear Fat Butt. On it was written the character for "rain" in immaculate calligraphy. The scholar then flicked the paper into the air, and it flew about until it landed on top of Red Bear Fat Butt's head. Suddenly, rain fell in a concentrated downpour on the bully, drenching him completely until the paper fell apart. Everyone was awestruck by what happened, as was Red Bear Fat Butt, but then he became enraged at the state he suddenly found himself in. He let out a furious roar and unsheathed Red Bear Penis.

"When one takes out a sword, one must fight the tiger," Master Three Stars said before showing Red Bear Fat Butt a paper with the character for "tiger." He threw it at the bully, and a tiger came lunging out of the writing. As the people screamed in fright and backed away, Red Bear Fat Butt instinctively swung his weapon at the beast. The blade went right through the creature, cutting it into two pieces of paper. In his panic, Red Bear Fat Butt kept slashing until so many bits of paper fell to the ground.

"For one who kills so easily and without remorse," Master Three Stars said, "it is natural to be haunted by a ghost."

He showed Red Bear Fat Butt a paper with the character for "ghost." For some reason, the sight of the letter terrified the bully to the extent of turning his hair white in an instant. He then ran away in panic, as if fleeing for his life. Master Three Stars waited until he was out of sight before he tossed the paper into the air. It flew up and fluttered after Red Bear Fat Butt.

When the people returned to the town, those who had stayed behind told them that Red Bear Fat Butt had just run through the place and disappeared down the road. He was never seen there again.

The town subsequently became known as Rain Tiger Ghost.

"WHAT BECAME OF *Red Bear Fat Butt after that?" one of the travelers asked the young man.*

"It is known to me," he answered enigmatically with a thin smile.

"What do you know?"

"That he became haunted by a ghost wherever he went. And that he will continue to be haunted until he repents and atones for all the wrongs he committed. In fact, he is in this very village right now, in this very inn."

"How do you know this?"

"Because I will visit him tonight. Like I have visited him every night since he fled from Rain Tiger Ghost."

The travelers frowned in confusion as they stared at the pale young man.

Suddenly, they heard the downpour of rain outside, followed by a distant roar of a tiger. A window blew open and a gust of wind seemed to shake the form of the young man as if he were made of insubstantial material, which did not seem to bother the smiling figure at all. A realization then dawned on the travelers, who suddenly became filled with fright and ran screaming from the room.

WHEN THE STORYTELLER *finished, he looked up and saw the emperor staring at him with an expression of sheer terror. After a long moment of unbearable tension, the Lord of All Under Heaven motioned frantically to the guards, who dragged off the storyteller. Even though he knew that he would soon be executed, it pleased him to see that he had managed to shake the ruler. And he made a firm promise to himself that in a future life he would find a way to expose him as the cruel monster that he was. In that way, he would have his revenge against the emperor who was the sole audience for the very last story he would ever tell.*

CHAPTER NINE

History II

The Fall of a Dynasty

Another thousand years later . . .

ON THE TOP floor of the imperial palace at the capital city of Dragon Child, the Queen of Yellow Tranquility stood by the balustrade of a vast balcony. She was a tall, regal woman with piercing eyes, clad in a resplendent yellow robe with a colorful insignia of a deer dragon on its front. Before her were the panorama of the palace complex and the great sprawl of Dragon Child city, but her intent gaze was fixed on the peaks of Four Verdant Mothers in the distance, as sturdy and beauteous as two thousand years ago when Autumn Bird State was founded. It was the one constant unchanging thing in a land which had undergone so many transformations over the centuries.

The queen continued to gaze at the summit of the mountain until she caught sight of a thick purple cloud with red lightning flashing inside that emerged from behind one of the peaks, drifting slowly through an otherwise cloudless sky. After a while, she looked down with a sorrowful expression, her shoulders sagging as if physically burdened by the weight of her melancholy.

FROM BLACK RAIMENT, *The Light of All Under Heaven: A History of the Radiant Dynasty* (Grand Circle Books), chapter 34.

THE YEAR THAT marked the second millennial anniversary of the traditional year for the founding of the Autumn Bird State was supposed to be one filled with celebrations and commemorations of the glorious history of the Realm of the Grand Circle.[1] When the new lunar cycle began in the middle of a particularly long and bitter winter, however, few could imagine that the breathtakingly rapid course of events in the next months would lead not only to the most serious rebellion in the history of the Radiant dynasty, but ultimately to the total collapse of the regime.

At the imperial capital of Dragon Child,[2] when the fourteenth emperor of the dynasty, given the reign name Fiery Dedication, ascended the throne as a young man, his very first act was to appoint a mid-level army officer named Blue Tiger to the double positions of the minister of military affairs and the supreme commander of the Three Armies of the Great Realm. That effectively gave him control over the entirety of the armed forces of the empire, which broke a precedent set by the founders of the dynasty. Wary that a united military could be deployed against imperial authority, they had deliberately divided it under two separate commands. The formidable Capital Defense Force, the Impe-

1. Although the term "Grand Circle" has been employed since the time of the Autumn Bird State, as a supra-dynastic term for the realm, its use here is somewhat anachronistic since it did not come into wide usage until the establishment of the Tranquil dynasty, when it was almost always used in reference to the land and the state, both historical and contemporary.

2. The origin of the name Dragon Child is unknown. The ancient historian Clouded Mirror claims that it is a shortened version of "Luminous Dragon and Laughing Child," but he provides no explanation for such an unusual name. See Clouded Mirror, *True Records of Past Events*, chapter 2, fourth marginal remark.

rial Palace Guards, and the Police Bureau were all under the ultimate jurisdiction of the ministry, while the Supreme Command controlled the field armies that were stationed outside Dragon Child. If either the minister or the supreme commander engaged in rebellion, the other could mobilize the forces under his command to oppose him. For that purpose, emperors tended to appoint to the two positions people who were antagonistic toward each other for political, familial, or personal reasons. The policy had been regarded traditionally as a wise one. There was, therefore, a great deal of understandable concern in the imperial court about giving so much power to one man, an inexperienced and unproven one at that, apparently for the sole reason that he was the young emperor's closest friend.

A story that has been passed down, but not recorded in official histories, tells how the two of them first met when they were boys.[3] Because the future emperor had been born of a tertiary concubine to the previous ruler, who already had three sons by his primary consort, there was little expectation that he would one day ascend the throne. As a result, he was attended to with some laxity when growing up, allowed to run around in the palace complex when he was not learning the classics or participating in formal rituals. One day, he sneaked out of his study room when his old tutor dozed off, and he wandered about until he came upon a low wall which he climbed on a whim. On the other side were the barracks of junior officers of the Imperial Palace Guards. There, he saw a boy his age practicing the spear and the sword with impressive skill. The prince watched the display with awe until he was found by his much-suffering eunuch attendant, who had been searching desperately for him. As he regretfully returned to his studies, he charged the eunuch with the task of

---

3. For the unofficial account of the origin of the friendship between the emperor and the general, see *Tales of the Radiant and the Tranquil Dynasties* (of anonymous and probably multiple authorship, compiled sometime in the late Celestial dynasty period), chapter 44.

finding out who the talented boy was. He was later informed that he was an officer's son who had been given the name Blue Tiger, and that he was already well-known among other sons of officers for his prowess in the martial arts.

On the prince's next birthday, when he was granted an audience with his father, the emperor asked what he would like as a present. The boy begged permission to have a companion, asking for Blue Tiger specifically. Within the imperial family's residential compound, only palace maidens and eunuchs were allowed inside the quarters of women and children. So the emperor gave special permission for the prince to go to an inner guard station after he was done with his studies, so that he could spend time with the officer's son. The two hit it off immediately and became best friends.

Years later, when two of the prince's half brothers had died and the third lay ailing, it became a real possibility that he would ascend the imperial throne after all.[4] The prospect filled him with such anxiety that he lost all appetite for food and could hardly sleep at night. Blue

---

4. The deaths of Fiery Dedication's half brothers were not suspicious, but historians have remarked on the sheer strangeness of the circumstances under which they perished one after another. The oldest prince was known for having a very large mouth, and he liked to have fun by stuffing a lot of food into it at once. At a feast, he entertained his friends by putting many chestnuts into his mouth. Unfortunately, one of them slipped into his throat and he began to choke. His friends could not take out all the chestnuts in time to save him from suffocation. The second prince woke up in the middle of the night with the need to empty his bladder. Still groggy from sleep, he put a foot in the chamber pot and tripped, impaling himself on a candleholder. The third brother was taking a walk through a palace garden when a wild donkey appeared out of nowhere and defecated in his path. The enraged prince took off his belt and began to whip the animal, which responded by kicking him in the crotch before running away. The prince's testicles were ruptured, and he lay sick for many days before he died of infection. The mysterious donkey was never caught and became the subject of many folktales in which the animal engages in insolent acts against authority figures. The deaths of the princes have been referred to as the Chestnut-Urine-Donkey Succession Crisis.

Tiger, fearing for his friend's health, sought to comfort him by suggesting that they swear an oath of brotherhood so that they would know that they could depend on each other no matter what happened in the future. They did so, which reassured the young prince a great deal.

When the prince became the fourteenth emperor of the Radiant dynasty, he knew that the most serious problem he faced was factionalism among the court officials that had become so divisive and vicious during the later part of his father's reign that government work had come to a standstill. As all the major factions were anxious to get the new ruler on their side, he realized that the situation presented an opportunity for solidifying his power. He summoned the leaders of the West Gate Faction,[5] one of the two most powerful groups, and offered to immediately approve the policy proposals that were on top of their agenda if they would support his appointment of Blue Tiger to the two highest military positions. The deal was struck, and the West Gate officials used the emperor's favor to enact a wholesale purge of their greatest rival, the River Pavilion Faction,[6] from the government. That cleared the way for Blue Tiger's rise to the pinnacle of military authority.

To the relief and astonishment of all, the new emperor's trust in his friend's martial abilities turned out to be far from misplaced. In the early part of Fiery Dedication's reign, the empire faced three great military crises. The first was a rebellion by the emperor's cousin who commanded a significant private army from his power base in

---

5. The West Gate Faction was so called because its founding official had lived in the West Gate district of the capital city.

6. The River Pavilion Faction was so called because it was dominated by a clan that owned significant property on the north bank of Divine Bird River where they often held meetings at pleasure pavilions.

the southwest.[7] The second was an incursion by the Golden Arrow barbarians from the northeast. And the third, an invasion of the southern coast by pirates from Sunborn Islands.[8] On each of these occasions, Blue Tiger led the imperial army and crushed the enemies of the realm by decisively winning every single battle against them. The rebel army was annihilated and its captured leader brought in chains to Dragon Child to be executed; the northern barbarians, known for their fierceness but not their organizational skills, were tricked into dividing into groups and then picked off one by one by the imperial army until the surviving groups retreated back to their homeland; and the Sunborn pirate ships were destroyed in a surprise naval attack, trapping the enemy in a swamp where they were slaughtered as they tried to escape. It became apparent then that Blue Tiger was one of the most brilliant military commanders in the entire history of the realm. As he was heaped with all the honors that he rightfully deserved, his fame spread far and wide. And the emperor was praised as well for his wisdom in seeing his friend's potential and placing him in the right position to use his skills for the security of the empire.

General Blue Tiger's successes allowed Emperor Fiery Dedication to concentrate fully on court politics, which he dealt with effectively as well as ruthlessly when it became necessary. Due to the initial favor

---

7. The cousin was the son of the previous emperor's older brother who had been passed over for succession to the imperial throne because of his foul temper that verged on madness, on one occasion beating three of his servants to death because the soup they had served him for lunch was lukewarm. He and his family were sent away from the capital to a rich province in the southwest, where his disgruntled son managed to accumulate a great deal of wealth which he used to build up a private army.

8. Recent findings have shown that the pirates, including those that General Blue Tiger fought, were not all from Sunborn Islands. In fact, evidence suggests that the majority of them may have been people of the realm. So "Sunborn Island pirates" should not be taken literally but as a general appellation for those who plagued the coastal regions of the realm.

he showed to the West Gate Faction, its officials became dominant after having purged or intimidated their rivals. The emperor waited for them to become overconfident of their position, thinking that their sovereign was easy to manipulate, before he made a secret plan with other factions to bring them down. When a prominent leader of the West Gate Faction became exposed in a case of flagrant corruption that was so egregious that it was impossible to cover up, the emperor saw that it was the right time to make his move.

In the course of just three days, in addition to putting the compromised official under arrest, he brought one charge of corruption and abuse of power after another to every senior official of the West Gate Faction. They were interrogated under torture, which produced confessions that were generally true, as most high office holders engaged in routine acts of influence peddling and manipulating the legal system to generate personal wealth. A long series of dismissals, exiles, and even executions followed quickly. After Fiery Dedication destroyed the faction virtually overnight, he brought the next powerful group, the Venerable Learning Faction,[9] to prominence. He also pardoned and reinstated many officials from the disgraced River Pavilion Faction and granted important positions to those from smaller factions as well, garnering the loyalty of multiple groups instead of just one. With the establishment of such diversity in officialdom, the emperor issued a stern warning to all factions against attempting to gain dominance in his court, lest they suffer the same fate as the River Pavilion and the West Gate. The leaders of the Venerable Learning Faction, realizing the emperor's political strategy as well as capability, secured their position by turning the faction into a loyalist group, supporting the will of the ruler first and foremost. With external threats eliminated by the brilliant leadership of General Blue

9. The Venerable Learning Faction was so called because the clan that founded it boasted as their most illustrious ancestor the Grand Sage Harmonious Teacher, whose ideas were referred to by this time as "Venerable Learning."

Tiger and the divisive situation at court resolved by Emperor Fiery Dedication, the realm enjoyed peace and prosperity for a time.

The beginning of the troubles that engulfed the later part of the reign began after the emperor's primary consort died of illness without having produced an heir. Theirs was a marriage that had been hurriedly arranged soon after his ascendance to the throne, and he had been so preoccupied with court matters in the first years of his rule that he hardly had time to get to know her. After a relatively short mourning period, it was announced that he had chosen a new consort for himself.

Many were scandalized when her identity became known—a young woman from the palace entertainment troupe who was reputed to be a superb player of the flute and the zither. There were contradictory rumors about her background, some claiming that despite the low status of her profession, she had originally come from a respectable family with a father who had served as a mid-level official in the Ministry of Taxation. They said that she had ended up an entertainer after her family had fallen on hard times, her father having been a member of the River Pavilion Faction purged from the government by the West Gate officials. But others claimed, in hushed whispers, that she had been a professional courtesan of some fame before she was recruited to join the entertainment troupe for her musical skills.[10] Wandering Star, the emperor's court poet, claimed that his sovereign once told him that when he saw the woman for the first time, playing the flute in the troupe, he was so taken by her appearance and her performance that he described the moment as one of "pristine perfec-

10. Due to the deplorable paucity of information on women in the Radiant dynasty, even those in the highest positions, like the emperor's primary consort, one can only report rumors and anecdotes found in personal writings of contemporaries. These stories about her background, therefore, must be approached with some skepticism. The only thing that can be affirmed with absolute certainty is that she did not come from a major family of high-ranking officials.

tion" that seared into his memory so that he would remember it for the rest of his life.[11]

The choice was certainly unusual, as was the emperor bypassing the normal betrothal process of having an official committee select and present suitable candidates from high-status families. But no one dared to raise an objection, given recent events in which the ruler solidified his central power. And the members of the Venerable Learning Faction loudly voiced their approval, as they did with all his decisions, praising the ruler for choosing a woman from an obscure family and so avoiding the appearance of favoring a currently serving official from a powerful clan.

When the woman was presented at court, everyone gaped in amazement, as she was of such remarkable beauty that light seemed to emanate from her. As part of the wedding ceremony, the emperor granted her the honor name Virescent Illumination. The day after the wedding, he arranged an intimate dinner with his new consort and his oath brother Blue Tiger. In addition to her undeniable comeliness, the general found her to be modest, polite, and cheerful.[12] After the meal, she played the zither for them with such skill that they were both moved to tears.

Within a year after the marriage, Blue Tiger began to notice a change in his relationship with Fiery Dedication. He thought it was natural that they would socialize less, as the ruler was obviously smitten with his beautiful and charming new consort. But then he found out that a number of important state meetings, some involving military

---

11. Wandering Star, *The Collected Letters of Wandering Star*, letter 55.

12. General Blue Tiger's initial impression of the emperor's new consort comes from the surviving fragments of his untitled memoir, of which historians have estimated that only about a quarter has survived. The work is also a major source of knowledge about the calamitous events that followed. Given its personal and unavoidably subjective nature, Blue Tiger's account should not be accepted uncritically but checked against other sources.

matters, had been held without his being notified of them. He did not think much of it at first, because one of them had taken place on short notice when he had been away, personally supervising a training exercise of the field armies. But as the months went by, he continued to be left out of discussions, and it became increasingly difficult for him to get an audience with his sovereign and friend. It also appeared that many officials were actively avoiding him.

When he was finally granted a meeting with Fiery Dedication, the ruler appeared deeply troubled. The general questioned him about the source of his concern, but the ruler changed the subject to deliver surprising news. The emperor had received word of the Golden Arrow barbarians uniting once again to launch another attack on the realm. That confounded Blue Tiger, because he had organized an effective system of intelligence gathering along the northeastern border, with local commanders sending him regular reports, but this was the first he had heard of the development. When he asked the emperor about the source of the information, the ruler became evasive once again. Fiery Dedication ordered the general to take a small force from the field army and go to the northeast to assess the situation directly. He then told him something that surprised him even more. While he was away, the emperor meant to displace him from his position as the minister of military affairs, just in case trouble arose elsewhere during his absence and someone had to take command immediately to deal with the situation. Blue Tiger did not question the emperor's authority to do so, of course, but he did want to know the true reason behind it. But he was dismissed from the ruler's presence before he could ask.

As the general prepared a contingent from the field army for the journey to the northeast, he wrote a long letter to the emperor. In it, he expressed his absolute loyalty to him and begged his pardon for whatever offense he may have unknowingly committed that caused the change in his sovereign's attitude toward him. After he sent off the letter, he departed for the border.

When he arrived at a fortress on the northeastern frontier, he was met with utter bewilderment by the local commanders, who had detected no sign of any major movement on the part of the barbarians. In fact, paid informants among them were sending news of increased division and conflict among the tribes after their failed invasion of the empire. Blue Tiger still made a thorough inspection of the marches before he sent a detailed report to the emperor, telling him that the Golden Arrows were in disarray and the border was secure. After a long delay, a response finally came from Dragon Child, a rather curt note from Fiery Dedication summoning him back to the capital.

Near the end of his journey home, he had his men rest for the night at a town that was the last stop before arriving at Dragon Child the following day. That evening, he received an expected visit from an official at the Ministry of Punishments who was devoted to him because the general had personally saved the life of his only son, a young officer who had served under him during the war against the Sunborn pirates. The official informed Blue Tiger that when he returned to the capital, he would be arrested under the charge of treason, for planning to usurp the throne for himself. He further told the flabbergasted general that many officials had been slandering him to the emperor for months, telling him how his military successes had made him swell up with pride and ambition. They said that the general thought he commanded such loyalty from his soldiers that he could easily topple the emperor and take his place. What Blue Tiger found impossible to believe was that his oath brother would listen to such filthy lies after everything he had done to demonstrate his loyalty.

He talked throughout the night with the official, who told him everything he knew and had heard at court. Blue Tiger then withdrew to his quarters to contemplate the situation he was in. After much thought, he decided that the only honorable course was for him to leave his men there, ride unarmed to Dragon Child, and surrender himself to the authorities. That way, the emperor would know that he came alone even after getting wind of what was in store for him. He felt certain that if he faced his sovereign and declared his innocence, his oath brother would see that he spoke the truth. The misunderstanding would then be dissolved, and the officials who made false accusations against him would be punished. If the emperor did not believe him, it was still his duty to face whatever punishment he decided to lay upon him. But he would always declare his innocence to the end, no matter what was done to him.

Early next morning, he was about to set off for the capital when the official's son arrived, having ridden all night to bring even more unsettling news. He told his former commander and savior that the emperor had added a new charge to his arrest order, accusing him of having attempted to sexually violate the imperial consort on the night before his departure to the border. The news turned Blue Tiger into a cauldron of boiling emotions.

There was the sheer indignation at the grave injustice he was being subjected to, which reached a new level with the accusation of such a heinous and dishonorable act. But he was also deeply hurt to learn that the emperor apparently believed the lie, that his sovereign thought him capable of such a thing. He knew then and there that the oath that they had sworn was broken, and that he had irretrievably lost his lord and friend to the calumny of evil officials. And he wept bitterly over it. His grief was also intermingled with rage, first at the slanderers but also at Fiery Dedication for believing them.

The terrible sense of betrayal brought about a sudden and radical change in Blue Tiger, who decided to abandon his loyalty to the emperor out of an overwhelming need to recover his honor. After spending the entire day considering his options, he summoned his officers and apprised them of the situation. He was careful not to condemn the emperor himself, whom he described as being surrounded by conniving officials who had poisoned his mind. Given the situation, he told them, he felt that he had no choice but to disobey the order to return to Dragon Child. Instead, he had to find a way of freeing the ruler from the clutches of his evil councillors. It soon became clear to everyone that he meant to raise a rebellion against the central authority of the empire.

Blue Tiger told them that every man had to make the choice himself of whether to follow him or not. If they decided that he was in the wrong, they should put him under arrest and take him to the capital, where they would surely be commended for it. He then left their company and went into his quarters so they could discuss the matter among themselves.

In the end, every single officer, many of whom had been with him through three wars, decided to remain at his side. When they informed the rank-and-file soldiers of their decision, most of them chose to stay as well, though some opted out, as they feared for the welfare of their families if they joined the rebellion. It was then decided that Blue Tiger would remain in the town, but the officers would return to the capital discreetly and try to persuade others to join their cause.

The authorities in Dragon Child were unaware that Blue Tiger had found out what awaited him when he returned to the city. They planned to take him by surprise when he came to the imperial palace to report to the emperor. But they were the ones who were caught unaware when in the next days large numbers of officers and soldiers who held the general in the highest regard—entire regiments and divisions that had fought under his command—suddenly marched out of the capital and bases in its vicinity. By the time the new minister of military affairs realized what was happening and mobilized his soldiers, Blue Tiger and his bolstered forces had already left the area.

When the emperor was told of the development, he felt the same mixture of indignation, sadness, and anger at the loss of his oath brother, who had, from his point of view, committed an act of unpardonable betrayal. He regarded Blue Tiger's refusal to face him in a trial and his raising a rebellion against him as a confession of his guilt. Even as he raged at how his friend not only sought to take his place on the throne but had tried to rape his consort, he wept at how he had once loved his oath brother. When he managed to get a hold of himself, he summoned his generals to discuss strategy for the coming conflict. The subsequent war became known as the Blue Banner Rebellion because the rebel forces flew blue flags with the image of a tiger.

Blue Tiger knew full well that he was by far the best military mind in the empire, as the government forces had no one who could rival his strategic brilliance, even those he had taught himself. But that did not mean he could win the war easily. Even with all the officers and soldiers who had chosen to side with him, his total strength was less than a quarter of what the emperor could deploy against him. Against such odds, he knew that the best course for him was to keep his army moving and engage in continuous hit-and-run attacks. That would not only weaken the loyalists through attrition and demoralize them, but it would also give him the time to shore up his numbers and support. But that strategy had its risks as well.

Blue Tiger's most pressing concern was that he had limited time before he had to confront the imperial army in a battle. If the conflict dragged on, his men would become tired of moving constantly and having to forage and pillage in order to feed themselves. Without the prospect of a quick resolution, they would start abandoning his army to return home and take care of their families. The only thing that could assure their continued loyalty was at least one undeniable victory on the field, which would also persuade powerful provincial lords and tributary rulers to join him. But if he committed himself to battle when he was still badly outnumbered, that could spell disaster for him. While the government forces had enough soldiers to sustain a few setbacks, Blue Tiger could not afford to take a single defeat, as that would do irreparable damage to his reputation as an invincible commander. After considering the matter a great deal, he hit upon a possible solution.

The southeastern kingdom of Yellow Tranquility[13] was a tributary state of the empire. During the early part of the Radiant dynasty, when its first rulers were aggressively expanding the imperial territory, they clashed with the wealthy and populous kingdom, which put up a fierce and determined fight. After a long period of debilitating stalemate, the Radiant Emperor offered the King of Yellow Tranquility a deal in which the latter would recognize the emperor as his overlord and pay an annual tribute. In return, the kingdom would maintain its autonomy with no meddling in its internal affairs by imperial authorities. Wary of a protracted war that could lead to the total collapse of his realm, the King of Yellow Tranquility agreed. The subsequent Radiant emperors stuck to the agreement in leaving the kingdom to its devices while enjoying the rich tribute money and treasures that came every year.

In the early part of Fiery Dedication's reign, however, the imperial court had an occasion to treat Yellow Tranquility in an unjust fashion. At the outbreak of the first rebellion by the emperor's cousin, Blue Tiger found himself leading a substandard army left to him by his predecessors, one that was badly trained and supplied because the previous generals had embezzled much of the state money that was supposed to be used for the military upkeep. As it was also his first time conducting large-scale warfare as a commander, he desperately needed help. The emperor suggested that he go to the clan of his in-

---

13. The origin of the state that became the kingdom of Yellow Tranquility is obscure, but there is a fascinating local legend that connects its people to Dragon Child. It claims that in ancient times, a group of migrants from the city, who called themselves the Deer Dragon People, fled the place in a time of chaos when it was beset with multiple invasions and civil conflicts. They went south and eventually settled in a land on the southeast coast, from which they extended their territory in the course of the following centuries, establishing a powerful kingdom. As a result, when they encountered the people of the empire, they discovered that they spoke similar languages and otherwise had many cultural commonalities.

laws, the family of his first consort, who were wealthy and powerful lords of a southern province who could quickly raise a large private army. At the time of the negotiation, the in-law clan was in conflict with Yellow Tranquility Kingdom in a dispute over a border area where significant deposits of silver had been discovered. It was clear to all objective observers that the kingdom was in the right on the matter as they possessed multiple imperial documents that marked the locale as part of the integral territory of Yellow Tranquility. But given the urgent need to get the lords to commit to fighting the rebellion, the emperor forced both parties to accept him as the arbiter of the dispute, only to grant the borderland to his in-laws. The King of Yellow Tranquility had little choice but to acquiesce, but everyone agreed that he and his people had been treated shabbily in the affair. It also infuriated and concerned the king that it set a precedent for future interference in their affairs by the emperor, including further annexations of their territories. In response, the king started building up his army in case of a future conflict, eventually creating a powerful force of well-disciplined and well-equipped men. That king was now dead, but reports indicated that his successor, a young queen, had maintained the strength of the realm's military.

Blue Tiger thought that if he could persuade the queen to join his cause, he would have sufficient numbers to give battle to the government army with a decent chance of winning. He would still be outnumbered by more than three to one, but given his superior strategic skills, he was confident that he could inflict enough damage to force the loyalists to withdraw, which was all he needed to claim victory. In return for becoming his ally, Blue Tiger would promise to recognize Yellow Tranquility as a fully independent realm whose monarch would be treated as an equal to the emperor, with no more tributes. Further, the disputed borderland with all its silver would be restored to them.

Blue Tiger discreetly traveled to Yellow Tranquility, where the queen agreed to meet him. Even though he was a typical man of the dynasty who had a low regard for women, the general found her to be thoughtful and intelligent, especially given her young age. She was rather reticent in their conversation, but when she spoke, she asked excellent questions and made insightful comments. After a short negotiation, the Queen of Yellow Tranquility agreed to the alliance. They then set a date and location for the rendezvous of their forces, at a place that would be a convenient locale from which to launch a strike toward Dragon Child.

The Blue Banner army marched north then, toward a vast plain known as Far Gallop which was only about fifty great spans southwest of the capital. A low but rugged mountain range stood between Far Gallop and the environs of Dragon Child, while a tributary of Divine Bird River flowed through the eastern part of the plain. Both sides saw the site as a good place to do battle. From the point of view of the loyalist generals, even if they were defeated there, they could retreat to the mountain range and fend off the rebel army from higher ground. But Blue Tiger had no intention of chasing after them even if he scored a victory on the plain. Having achieved his purpose of demonstrating his prowess, he would pull back to consolidate his gains and strengthen his forces with new allies who would surely come. He would then take an easier route to the capital, avoiding the difficult mountain.

When the two armies met, the imperial generals spread out the full strength of their forces to intimidate the rebels with their superior numbers and to envelop them from the flanks. But Blue Tiger, instead of positioning his forces to counter such a move, placed them in a compact group with the Yellow Tranquility army at the back as a reserve force. That was such an obviously unwise formation for the occasion that the imperial commanders thought that their brilliant opponent must have some surprise move he was planning to make at a crucial point in the fighting. They could not figure out what that stratagem might be though, so they held back from engaging him. As the delay dragged on, the mounting uncertainty and anxiety of the generals were felt first by their officers and then by the soldiers in formation waiting anxiously for orders, knowing the reputation of the man leading the army on the other side of the plain.

Blue Tiger let them wallow in their trepidation for a while before he made the first move, ordering the forward march horns to be blown. Following the instructions he gave to his officers, his tightly packed infantry fell into the arrow formation with the cavalry units at the flanks falling back to the rear. This was another bewilderingly unwise move to make against an opponent with superior numbers, one that practically invited envelopment, but it only exacerbated the imperial commanders' doubts. Rather than sending the full force of their men forward to overwhelm the enemy, they ordered all lines to fall back and move closer together as well, a measure to buy some time to try to figure out what Blue Tiger was up to.

The Blue Banner army advanced, and the government forces retreated at the same pace, like a cowardly bear falling back before an aggressive cat. They all stopped for a while, but then the Blue Banner forces advanced again and the government army pulled back once more. It went on like that for hours until Blue Tiger had his opponents exactly where he wanted them. He rapidly sent numerous messengers out to his field commanders, getting them ready for a massive assault on the enemy from a completely unexpected angle.[14]

Except something happened that no one, including Blue Tiger, expected.

Just when all the rebel units were in place and Blue Tiger was about to order the charge horns to be blown, he saw movement at the rear that took him by surprise. As he watched in aghast astonishment, the entirety of the Yellow Tranquility army, whose position was vital to his plan, suddenly began to retreat from the field. They moved very

---

14. For military historians, it is deeply unfortunate that the part of Blue Tiger's memoir in which he lays out how he meant to defeat the government forces has become lost. Given subsequent events, it is unlikely that we will ever learn about his planned strategy at Far Gallop.

quickly, almost running, but in good order, heading straight for the river on the eastern side of the field.

It was at this point that Blue Tiger made a crucial and uncharacteristic error that proved to be fatal for his strategy. If he had kept his forces in motion, the imperial generals would have thought that the retreat of the Yellow Tranquility army was part of his unfathomable stratagem, and Blue Tiger could have taken advantage of that impression. But with the departure of his ally, which reduced his force back down to a quarter of his enemy's strength, he sent out orders for all units to stop and stand by for new instructions. As he frantically tried to figure out an alternate plan, it finally dawned on the imperial generals that the withdrawal of the Yellow Tranquility force was an unexpected turn of events for their opponent. Sensing a vital opportunity that they had to take advantage of, they sent all lines forward with the units on the flanks ready to tilt to envelop the rebel army. When Blue Tiger ordered his forces to retreat, word spread throughout the government forces that the rebels had indeed lost their crucial ally and that they were vulnerable. Suddenly it was the loyalists whose morale was lifted, while an unsettling sense of unease fell over the rebels.

At that point, Blue Tiger realized that he had no time to come up with a new strategy to defeat his significantly more numerous opponents. Unfortunately, leaving the field was out of the question, as turning his army's back on the enemy would result in annihilation. Even if he managed to escape with a reduced contingent of his men, the rebellion would be finished. There would be little prospect of rebuilding his forces, since his very first defeat on the field would irreparably damage his reputation. He had no choice then but to face the imperial army and inflict as many casualties as possible with the hope that their sheer ferocity would force the loyalists back and give his men time to retreat in some semblance of order. But he must have been aware that the plan was highly unlikely to succeed at that point. He summoned his senior officers and, keeping his doubts to himself, gave out a new set of orders, and went out to fight in the field himself.

The Battle of Far Gallop turned into one of the bloodiest ever recorded in history, a horrific slaughter of soldiers on both sides. The imperial generals, seeing the situation as an almost miraculous chance to destroy the rebel army with one blow, ordered all units to surround and attack the Blue Banners with full force. As for the rebels, the sight of their beloved commander riding among them and giving orders in the midst of the fighting gave them the impression that he had a plan for victory after all, and they fought back with all their strength. The absolute carnage that followed shocked even the most seasoned officers and soldiers, who had fought in multiple campaigns.

The Blue Banner army was ultimately swamped under the sheer numerical superiority of the government forces, but it inflicted such massive damage on the loyalists that it was hard for them to consider the end of the battle as a victory. The fighting proper ended when Blue Tiger's generals finally realized that their commander did not have a plan for winning, that he was leading them in a fight to the death. By that time, only a fraction of the Blue Banner army remained, but he was still giving out orders as if he could turn things around. In the end, one of his generals came up behind him and knocked him out with a war hammer to the head before calling for his men to surrender. They tied up their commander and delivered him to the government generals before begging for mercy. But in the aftermath of the bloody fighting, there could be no clemency. The Battle of Far Gallop was Blue Tiger's first and only defeat, but it was also the one in which he inflicted the greatest number of casualties on the opposing force.

It was to be his final battle as well.

After the last rebel units were mopped up, the remnant of the imperial army could do nothing but collapse in exhaustion and shock. It took a full day before the generals, many of them wounded, could even think about organizing their men for immediate tasks. During the battle, a unit of the rebel cavalry had broken through and gotten to the baggage wagons, which they set on fire, destroying much of their supplies. So they had to send out teams of barely functioning men to forage for food in a place where there was not much to be found. There were also so many wounded to care for and so many bodies to bury that they had to stay in the cursed field for many days before they could march back to Dragon Child.

On the third day at Far Gallop, the generals were preparing to leave ahead of the army to report directly to the emperor when a messenger arrived from the capital with shocking news. The Yellow Tranquility army had taken Dragon Child, captured the emperor and the entire imperial family, and forced him to abdicate the throne. The Radiant dynasty had already come to an end.

When the Yellow Tranquility army had left the field of battle, everyone had assumed that it had been due to its commanders' loss of faith in Blue Tiger's ability to deliver a victory. But the retreat was not in fact a decision made in the moment. It was part of a larger stratagem that the Queen of Yellow Tranquility had come up with to defeat the empire on her own. When her soldiers marched quickly to the river on the eastern end of Far Gallop, they were met by a large fleet of ships[15] that were commanded by the queen herself, appearing before her soldiers dressed in armor and carrying a sword. Instead of sailing south, back to her realm, the ships went up to Divine Bird River and to Dragon Child.

Emperor Fiery Dedication, in order to give his generals the best chance of crushing the rebellion, had committed most of the available military forces to the endeavor, including the Imperial Palace

---

15. Yellow Tranquility Kingdom had a significant navy, built primarily to protect its coast from pirates of Sunborn Islands. The queen had secretly gone to a base there to personally lead the ships up the river to Far Gallop and rendezvous with her army.

Guards, which left behind barely enough soldiers for guard duty. And no one was expecting an attack coming from the river. The light cavalry units of the Yellow Tranquility army galloped into the city before they could close the gates and went straight to the imperial palace, followed closely by the rest of the army. The Palace Guards who remained defended the place ferociously, but they were overwhelmed and slaughtered as the grounds were breached. Then Emperor Fiery Dedication was captured in the residential wing along with his entire family.

Once the capital was secured, the Queen of Yellow Tranquility rode into the city and entered the palace. The deposed emperor was forced to write an announcement affirming his loss of the Mandate of Heaven and his voluntary abdication of the throne. He instructed all his subjects to comply with the new authorities from Yellow Tranquility, whose sovereign was now the legitimate Lord of All Under Heaven.

When the imperial generals at Far Gallop learned of what had happened, they immediately prepared their army to return to the capital and rescue the emperor. In making the decision, they had no choice but to leave behind all the wounded men to fend for themselves. The bedraggled army of still exhausted and shaken soldiers was force-marched to the mountain range, where they were met by scattered units of archers who had been dispatched by the Queen of Yellow Tranquility to harass the government soldiers at every step. They also fell into traps along the way, avalanches of rocks and bundles of straw on fire that filled the valleys with choking smoke. By the time they made it to the other side, they had lost so many men to both attacks and sheer exhaustion that there was not much of an army left at all.

The Yellow Tranquility army met the disorganized rabble in full force, fresh, well-equipped, and positioned on advantageous ground, and the imperial generals realized that the situation was hopeless. At the final meeting of officers, the majority decided to surrender and sent a messenger to open negotiations for terms of capitulation. Others chose to carry on the fight, but first headed west to recuperate at a fortress that was still under loyalist control. The number of soldiers who followed them, however, was pathetically small. A few could not face the prospect of living on with the shame and dishonor of having failed the emperor and the entire realm. Three generals and some of their officers knelt down, facing the direction of Dragon Child. They prostrated themselves and touched their heads to the ground three times. After a final declaration of loyalty to the realm, the dynasty, and the emperor, they fell on their swords.

Once the negotiation for the surrender was completed, the imperial generals handed over their most important prisoner, the former rebel leader Blue Tiger.

And so ended the Radiant dynasty after the reigns of fourteen emperors, through whispered rumors in the corridors of the imperial palace that became official accusations that led to a broken trust and finally a war. For all the great achievements of the dynasty, it was one that was particularly harsh in its patriarchal subjugation of women. It was perhaps fitting, then, that its demise was brought about by a brilliant female ruler and strategist who was clearly underestimated by those who dealt with her.

The story in the records also leaves behind the beguiling mystery of why the emperor, when he first became privy to suspicions about his general, did not confront him directly about the accusations. A candid conversation between the two lifelong friends might have resolved the situation and prevented the dynasty's fall. Given the silence in the records on the matter, it is a question that may never be answered, except in the realm of the imagination.

CHAPTER TEN

History III

Remembering Four Verdant Mothers

From Black Raiment, *The Light of All Under Heaven: A History of the Radiant Dynasty* (Grand Circle Books), documentary appendix to chapter 34.

THE ACCOUNT OF the Blue Banner Rebellion and the fall of the Radiant dynasty can be verified through multiple records and archaeological evidence. I would be remiss, however, if I did not mention a rather unusual text that has recently been discovered that may shed a new light on the history of that fateful year or, alternatively, utterly distort the truth of it. That depends on the exact nature of the writing, which has not been determined as yet. While the manuscript had been authenticated as one that was produced early in the Tranquil dynasty, it is unclear whether it is meant to be a true record, perhaps an eyewitness account of a participant in the event that it describes, or a fanciful story, a fictional narrative of a possible scenario. Among many of its intriguing features, it asserts that it was not one but two women who brought down the Radiant dynasty. While historians have not discovered any corroboration of its content, they have not found any reason to contradict the account either.

Until some new evidence emerges that can definitively identify the work as a historical record or a work of fiction, it must be categorized under the rubric of "perhaps."

THE QUEEN OF Yellow Tranquility stood by the balustrade of a balcony on the top floor of the imperial palace. Before the panoramic view of Dragon Child city and the faraway peaks of Four Verdant Mothers, the dark cloud with red lightning flashing inside it hovering near them, her head was bowed down and her face filled with an expression of sorrow.

A door behind her opened and a palace eunuch walked out to bow down to her.

"Your Tranquil Grandness," he addressed her.

"Have they been brought?"

"Yes, Your Tranquil Grandness."

"Very well."

She looked up at the peaks of Four Verdant Mothers and the dark cloud one more time before she turned around and walked away.

The central banquet hall of the imperial palace was spacious enough to accommodate hundreds of people, but everything in it had been cleared out except for a small table and four sitting mats for an intimate meeting. Around the table sat the former emperor of the fallen Radiant dynasty, Fiery Dedication, dressed in a red robe, his consort Virescent Illumination, clad in a green dress, and the former rebel general Blue Tiger in a blue officer's coat. Despite the fact that they were clean and dressed in fine clothing, having been treated well in the last days, all three looked rather haggard and stunned as they kept their eyes down and away from one another. There were liquor vases of precious white porcelain on the table, as well as plates of fruits and cakes to snack on, but nobody touched them. A line of servant maids in brightly colored clothing stood by a wall, close enough to see to the needs of the guests but too far to make out their conversation.

Sliding doors were opened by eunuch servants, and the Queen of Yellow Tranquility walked in, followed by two guards in light armor bearing swords. The guests looked up and hesitated, not knowing how to greet her. They were technically not her subjects, so it was not required that they prostrate themselves. Instead, Blue Tiger glared at her defiantly, daring her to make a thing of it, while Fiery Dedication and Virescent Illumination fidgeted in their seats. To their relief, the queen sat down at the table apparently without the expectation of formal obeisance from her guests. Her bodyguards stood at a discreet distance but assumed postures that signaled their readiness to rush forward should she be endangered.

"Allow me," the queen said, and picked up a liquor vase to pour for them. But none of them moved to pick up their cups, Blue Tiger crossing his thick arms on his broad chest and the others looking uncertain.

The queen sighed as she put the vase down and nodded to the servant maids, four of whom rushed over and poured clear liquor into their cups.

"I will get to the point," the queen said after taking a sip of her drink. "As you might have expected, my councillors are telling me that I must eradicate all members of the fallen dynasty, as per precedent. Leaving any of them alive would inevitably lead to rebellions and conspiracies being formed on their behalf to restore the old regime."

The queen allowed the others to ponder their dark fate for a moment.

"But I have made the decision not to take any action against you or your families," she said. "There's been enough bloodshed already."

The others regarded her with astonishment, but with skepticism as well.

"Lord Fiery Dedication," she addressed the former emperor, who winced at being referred to in that manner, even though he certainly did not expect her to call him by the imperial title "Your Radiant Grandness." It still pained him to be reminded of his fallen state.

"I intend to send you to Misty Fairness Island, giving you the nominal position of governor. For the time being, the newly appointed Grand Admiral of the naval base there will keep an eye on your activities. You can take your consort, your concubines, and the rest of your family and administer the place as you see fit. As you know, it's a rich province with a luxurious governor's residence, so you should be quite comfortable there."

Fiery Dedication gaped at her words, not knowing how to respond.

"General Blue Tiger," the queen spoke to the former rebel general. "I cannot put you in charge of a military unit, of course. But it would be a pity to let your knowledge of military strategy go to waste. I would like to appoint you as the Vice Commandant of the Forest of Spears Military Academy."

"What?" Blue Tiger burst out in anger. "You expect me to serve you? After what you did to me?"

"What would you have me do instead?" the queen asked. "Cut off your head and display it at the great gate, like my councillors are urging me to do? Is an honorable death what you want? I can grant that to you if you'd like."

The general glared at the queen, but no words came to him.

"If you decide to accept the positions," the queen said, "then both of you will have to make a public declaration of your loyalty to the new dynasty and to me personally as your sovereign. And you will prostrate yourselves before me to receive the documents of appointment."

As Blue Tiger, Fiery Dedication, and Virescent Illumination thought over her offer, they considered the humiliation of such a ritual. But they also recognized that it would be a small price to pay to avoid the dire end that they had expected for themselves.

Blue Tiger suddenly grabbed his cup and gulped down all the liquor in it. A servant maid came running to refill it, and he drank it down for her to pour again. Fiery Dedication hesitated but then drank as well, followed by Virescent Illumination.

"And there is another thing I require from you before we can move forward," the queen said.

The others turned to her, expecting the worst.

"I need to hear from all of you what exactly happened that has led to all this," she said. "I need your individual perspectives on how the Radiant dynasty came to an end."

They looked at her with puzzled expressions.

"What are you talking about?" Blue Tiger asked in an indignant tone. "It was you. You brought down the dynasty. You did it by betraying me."

"Come now, General. I only took advantage of a situation that had been in motion well before I got involved. I need to know what happened before that, starting with how it all began."

"You dare speak of betrayal," Fiery Dedication spoke for the first time, addressing Blue Tiger. "You disloyal bastard! What you did after all the trust I put in you!"

"You say I betrayed you?" Blue Tiger shot back. "You are the one who betrayed me! Do you think I wanted to become a rebel? You put me in a position where I had no other choice."

"Liar! You did it out of ambition, out of greed for power! Despite all the honors I bestowed upon you, you still wanted more. You wanted my throne!"

"I never wanted that, you fool!"

"Stop," the queen said, putting up an open hand. "Yelling accusations at each other serves no purpose. Let us start at the beginning. Lord Fiery Dedication, what convinced you that General Blue Tiger was indeed plotting against you in the first place?"

Fiery Dedication looked at her, then at Blue Tiger, before answering.

"It began with a rumor relayed to me by my eunuch secretary. At a drinking bout with his generals, Blue Tiger boasted that he was truly the most powerful man in the realm. That he could easily take my place and do a better job as emperor."

"I never said any such thing!" Blue Tiger yelled.

"General, please," the queen said. "I will give you the opportunity to tell your side of the story. Please proceed, Lord Fiery Dedication."

"I dismissed it," the former emperor said. "A personage of his prominence who's enjoying my favor was liable to be subjected to slanders by envious people. But then I was informed of another such story, then another. Finally, a group of high officials asked for a private meeting, in which they relayed concerns about things that they had heard and behaviors they had witnessed on the part of the general. They were telling me that I had a snake in my nest and seemed genuinely terrified of the prospect of an attempt to topple me, and the chaos that could ensue in the realm. I didn't want to believe it, of course. It just didn't make any sense after all that we have been through together. But..."

He had to stop to control a welling emotion. He took another drink of liquor.

"But the reports kept coming, from many different sources. Finally, my councillors advised that I send him away on a mission so that I could investigate the matter in his absence. That way, if I did find definitive evidence of his treasonous intentions and order his arrest, he could not mobilize the main army. So he was dispatched to the north, and . . . and . . ." He had to stop again, this time due to rising anger. "And then I found out that he tried to violate my consort before his departure."

"How could you believe that?" Blue Tiger burst out, looking to be on the verge of exploding. "Did you not know me at all? How could you possibly think that I was capable of such a thing?"

"Because you took up arms against me!" Fiery Dedication yelled back, looking him straight in the eyes. "Despite what she told me, despite all the stories I heard of your arrogance, your ambition, and your deception, I still had my doubts. I still hoped that it was all baseless slanders or some terrible misunderstanding. But when I learned that you turned rebel, I knew that you were guilty of it all. If you were innocent, you would have faced me like a man, like my oath brother that you were, and told me straight to my face that none of it was true."

"I turned against you because I could not bear the idea that you gave credence to any of that. You pushed me to my course."

"Lady Virescent Illumination," the queen addressed the former imperial consort for the first time, "how did you come to tell Lord Fiery Dedication about what General Blue Tiger tried to do to you?"

They all turned to her, but she kept her face down, looking at her cup as she maintained her silence. After waiting in vain for her to say something, Fiery Dedication spoke in her stead.

"With Blue Tiger dispatched to the north," he said, "my councillors and ministers were pressing me to make a decision. They all wanted me to start proceedings against him. But even then . . . even then I hesitated. But one night, I found myself unable to sleep because I was so tormented by all this. When I spoke to her about the dilemma I faced, she suddenly broke down in tears and told me what had happened.

"On the night before Blue Tiger's departure, he showed up at her chamber in a drunken state. He told her that as part of our oath of brotherhood, we had agreed to share the pleasures of all our women. He then tried to violate her and was only thwarted from the foul course by the timely arrival of her younger brother. But she dared not tell me about it before because she knew what Blue Tiger meant to me. The next day, I summoned her brother. He told me that when he had gone to her quarters and announced himself, the general had come rushing out of her chamber and left without saying anything to him. It was her tears and her sincerity that convinced me that it was all true. My oath brother was a perfidious villain who wanted my throne, my wife, and my power."

"How could you believe that?" Blue Tiger said quietly with his head bowed down. "I did not visit her that night, nor have I ever thought of touching her. My oath brother's wife, my empress! How could . . . how could . . ."

To everyone's surprise, the sturdy general shed tears in bitter frustration. He recovered presently, angrily wiping his face before picking up a vase to gulp down the liquor from it. When he was done, he slammed the vessel on the table.

"How well you act the indignant innocent," Fiery Dedication said in a bitter tone.

"He is not acting, my lord," Virescent Illumination spoke out for the first time in her famously melodious voice that was like the tinkling of golden bells on a rainy day, lifting her immaculately fair face that shone in perfection.

"What do you mean?" Fiery Dedication asked as he turned to her.

"Your Tranquil Grandness," Virescent Illumination said to the queen, using the imperial title, "you want to know how all this happened? I will tell you. Lord Fiery Dedication and General Blue Tiger think that they were the main actors in what occurred. They never were. It was me. I moved them around like pieces on a game board until they destroyed each other. Lord Fiery Dedication, General Blue Tiger never came to my chamber that night. I lied to you about that. And I told my younger brother to lie to you as well."

"What . . . what are you saying?" Fiery Dedication asked in astonishment.

"I am saying that he is innocent, my lord. He has always been innocent. He was steadfastly loyal to you until he heard about my accusation against him. All the other stories of his ambition, how he meant to take the throne from you, they were false as well. They all came from me. I had my palace maidens spread them through key people so that they would reach the ears of your eunuch secretaries and officials. I arranged it carefully so that no one would suspect they originated from me."

"But . . . but why? Why did you do that?" Fiery Dedication asked in shock.

"Because I wanted to destroy him."

A stunned silence reigned over the hall.

"Why do you hate me so much?" Blue Tiger finally asked in utter bewilderment. "What have I ever done to you? I have done nothing but shown you respect and admiration. Why would you go to such lengths to bring me down?"

"You have indeed acted in a respectful manner toward me," she replied in a calm voice. "But only after my ascension as the emperor's consort."

"I did not know you until then."

"You did. You just don't remember it."

Blue Tiger frowned as he stared at her.

"General Blue Tiger," she said, "do you know that I was a courtesan before I was recruited to join the entertainment troupe of the imperial palace? Before Lord Fiery Dedication deigned to notice me and raise me as his consort?"

"I only heard rumors."

"I worked at the House of Fragrant Wind in the east side of the capital. Do you not remember going there?"

"Yes . . . yes, I do. The night before I was to leave for my first campaign. My friends wanted to give me a proper send-off, so they took me to the most famous pleasure house in the city. But I don't remember meeting you there."

"That's because your mind was elsewhere that night. While your friends made merry and enjoyed our entertainments, you were distracted, probably thinking of the fighting to be done. It's understandable really. The first time your emperor entrusted you with such an important mission."

"Yes, I do remember that."

"Your friends could not get you to relax, so they had me sit next to you to serve you wine. When I got close to you, to pour into your cup, I must have interrupted your thoughts. You flew into a rage, put your hand on my face, and pushed me away. I fell to the floor, spilling the wine all over my dress. As everyone in the room watched in shock, I got up at once and hurried to my private chamber.

"You should know that despite my profession at the time I was born into a respectable family. But a calamity fell upon us, and I was sold off to the pleasure house because of my beauty and my skills with the flute and the zither. Eventually, I became famous as a much-sought-after entertainer and companion for some of the grandest personages in the capital. Yet I was never under any illusion about what I was. I know the saying–'a fancy courtesan is not just a whore, but she is still a whore.' But because of my qualities, my clients have always shown me respect, even those who held high positions in court and possessed great wealth. They made use of my body, but they treated me as a woman whose company they were privileged to enjoy. What you did that night, it was the single most demeaning thing anyone has ever done to me. To you, I was not even a human being. I was more like an annoying animal that you kicked aside to get it out of your way.

"So I cried for a while in my chamber, but then I had to quickly clean myself up, put on a different dress, and return to work. You were gone by then. I suppose you were too preoccupied with thoughts of the great task ahead to enjoy the evening. It was then and there that I swore to myself that I would get you back for what you had done to me, that I would do whatever I had to do to see you brought down. That became my life's purpose.

"I used the affection of my most powerful clients to obtain a position in the palace entertainment troupe. After a time, I was able to attract the attention of Lord Fiery Dedication. Once I succeeded in making him fall in love with me and I was installed as his primary consort, I was finally in a position to destroy you. But before I proceeded, I decided to give you one chance to avoid my wrath. When I was introduced to you, if you displayed any sign of recognizing me, perhaps with embarrassment or shame, I would allow you to ask for my forgiveness. But you never did. You were so very respectful and admiring of my beauty and grace, but it was clear that you had no memory of me. So I renewed my determination to see you fall."

"You caused all this, for . . . for that?" Fiery Dedication asked in an appalled tone. "The rebellion, the war, the fall of the dynasty, all because of a distracted slight?"

"You call it a slight, but you are not a woman, nor a woman in my position. In that moment, I was less than anything, and for one already so low, where else could I go? What else could I do to gain some dignity for myself? And yet . . . I did not expect things to go this far," she said, looking down. "I thought the rumors I had spread about the general's ambitions would be enough to bring him down. But after you sent him away, I realized that you were still vacillating about what to do. I had to introduce something else. Something you wouldn't be able to ignore. So I made up the story about his attempt to violate me, and I persuaded my brother to confirm his presence at my chamber that night. I still thought the general would return to the capital of his own accord to face his accusers, but he took the road of rebellion instead.

"I do feel bad about all that followed."

"You feel bad?" Fiery Dedication said, raising his voice in growing anger. "You feel *bad*? After all you did? And . . . was I only an instrument of your purpose to you?"

"And what was I to you, Lord Fiery Dedication?" she asked with a scoff. "An instrument of your pleasure, and a means to produce an heir. Was I anything more than that to you?"

"But I am . . . I was the Lord of All Under Heaven! I gave you a place of great honor."

"You think it a place of honor to be under you? How men think," she said with a disgusted shake of her head. "I did not want it. I only wanted my revenge. Besides, I was quite pleased to cause you pain and to see you fall as well."

"What? Why? I have always treated you well."

"Not for me. But for my father and my family."

"Your father?"

"Of course you wouldn't know who he was, even though the officials who investigated my background informed you that my father had been an official in the Ministry of Taxation. He wasn't a powerful man, but he was a member of the River Pavilion Faction. When you made the deal with the officials of the West Gate Faction to gain their support for the appointment of Blue Tiger as both the minister of military affairs and the supreme commander of the Three Armies of the Great Realm, you let them purge the court of their rivals. My father was only a mid-level official, but he was still caught up in it, accused of corruption and embezzlement. He was an upright man who never took a bribe from anyone or a single coin that belonged to the government. We lived quite modestly despite his position in the ministry. But you never bothered to find out if all those who were being ousted were actually guilty of what they were charged with. You sacrificed him and many other officials to get what you wanted.

"My father may have been an insignificant person to you, but he was the world to me. Do you know what he said to me when he found out that he was to be exiled and all our belongings were to be confiscated? He told me not to worry so much because the emperor was the father of all his subjects, and what father would punish a son for things he was innocent of? So he fully expected you to step in and rectify the injustice he was being subjected to. But, of course, you never did. He was but a small piece on a large game board, and you had so many other pieces that it didn't matter if some just got thrown away." There was such venom in her voice that both Fiery Dedication and Blue Tiger looked on with shock.

"Only three months after he was exiled to the harsh mountains in the west, he fell ill and died. With our house and all its goods taken away, my mother had to return to her parents' household, my younger brothers were scattered among relatives, and I was sold to the pleasure house.

"Do you see, Lord Fiery Dedication? You were the one who turned me into a whore.

"So, yes, I feel bad about all that has happened because of my actions, all those who were killed and hurt in the war, even the fall of the dynasty, none of which I intended. But I am glad that I succeeded in bringing you both down. I have avenged my father as well as myself. I don't care what happens to me now."

When she was done, Fiery Dedication and Blue Tiger continued to stare at her with stunned expressions.

"You . . . you evil bitch!" Fiery Dedication finally yelled at her.

Blue Tiger could not express himself in his rage, but with his face red and his large body shaking, he looked like he was about to launch himself at Virescent Illumination.

"You fucking evil, demonic bitch!" Fiery Dedication exclaimed again. "You–"

"Lord Fiery Dedication," the Queen of Yellow Tranquility said in a firm tone, "there is no need for such language. Besides, you can't put the entire blame for your fate on her. She may have tricked you into turning against your oath brother, but you were so besotted with her that you made yourself vulnerable to manipulation. After all the service General Blue Tiger performed on your behalf over the years, you could have put your faith in him and given him the benefit of the doubt. You could have *talked* to him. It was ultimately your decision to believe her lies over his loyalty.

"That goes for you as well, General Blue Tiger. You said that Lord Fiery Dedication gave you no choice but to go against him. But you know that's not true. You freely made the decision to go on the path of rebellion rather than appear before your sovereign to declare your innocence. You could have put your trust in him to see that you spoke the truth. But you chose to fight because you knew that you were a brilliant commander who could best any of the imperial generals. In the face of slander and confusion, both of you ultimately chose to turn against each other.

"As for Lady Virescent Illumination, you think her evil because of her deceptions, but she was acting out of filial piety in avenging the injustice done to her father, and out of her sense of honor in seeking redress for the humiliation General Blue Tiger inflicted on her. If they were your motivations, you would have regarded them as lofty and noble. Yet she is not a powerful ruler or a great general. How else was she supposed to achieve her purpose? She used the only weapons available to her–her beauty, her charm, her musical skills, and her strategic brilliance which matched that of yours, General Blue Tiger.

"So, before you condemn her too harshly, perhaps you should look to your own fault and responsibility in all this."

They considered her words, both Fiery Dedication and Blue Tiger calming down a bit, but not entirely.

"Fault and responsibility?" Blue Tiger suddenly said to the queen. "Do you pretend to be without fault and responsibility here? You won, but only by betraying me. We agreed to an alliance, but you committed the dishonor of going back on your word by stabbing me in the back. You are not innocent!"

"Innocent?" the queen said. "I never claimed to be that. Of course I am not innocent. And yes, I brought shame upon myself by breaking faith with you. Everyone in the realm knows now that I am someone whose word cannot be trusted. And that is indeed a great dishonor. I fully admit that. But I am also convinced that I did the right thing, and I will live with my dishonor if it means righteousness was served."

"Righteousness?" Blue Tiger burst out in a bitter tone. "To win the war and gain an empire, no matter what the cost. What a shabby, shameful victory you've achieved."

"To win was a necessary thing, but that's not why I am at peace with what I did."

"Why then?"

"General Blue Tiger, allow me to ask you a question of strategic nature. When you first came to me to propose an alliance, what would you have done if I had refused?"

Blue Tiger considered her question for a time.

"I approached you because I did not have enough soldiers to take on the government army," he said. "If you had refused to join me, I would have had to keep my men moving, perhaps to the fortresses in the northeast where the garrisons were loyal to me. And I would have launched attacks on vulnerable government positions, scored a number of small victories. Hopefully that would have convinced provincial lords and tributary rulers to join my side. Increase my force until it was sizable enough to threaten the capital."

"But that would have taken years."

"Perhaps. But that would have been the right course to take. Prematurely taking on the government army in a battle would have been foolhardy."

"General Blue Tiger, I ask you to consider this. If that's the way things had gone, what would have been the cost of such a protracted war? How many soldiers and civilians would have been killed or injured? How many villages, towns, and cities destroyed? Even if you had established a base of operations in the northeast, your soldiers would have had to engage in constant acts of pillaging in order to supply themselves with food and other necessary goods. As for Lord Fiery Dedication, to maintain the government army in the field, he would also have had to raise taxes and conscript many for fighting as well as labor. All the hardship that would have been inflicted on the people of the realm would have been enormous and enduring, no matter which side won at the end."

"What is your point?" Blue Tiger asked.

"When I heard about the casualties at the Battle of Far Gallop, I was horrified. To think that I had a hand in such a slaughter . . . it was appalling. I know that it will haunt me for the rest of my life. But even knowing that, I do not regret the course I took. Because that made it possible for me to take Dragon Child with minimal fighting and end this war quickly. So many more would have died if you had been allowed to conduct your long war. Betraying you was the only way I could stop that from happening."

"Wait," Blue Tiger said incredulously, "are you saying you acted out of concern for the welfare of the people? Do you claim to have been motivated by humanitarian reasons? If that was the case, things worked out really well for you, didn't it? Strutting around the imperial palace as the new Lord of All Under Heaven."

"General Blue Tiger, stop being naive. You are a military man, so you must see the strategic reasons behind my actions. Yes, I thought of how much destruction a protracted war would unleash across the realm, but I was thinking primarily of my own people, my subjects of Yellow Tranquility. Safeguarding their welfare has always been my highest duty and concern. When you first came to me, I knew that refusing to get involved in your rebellion would not spare my people the effects of the coming conflict. Your long war would have come to our doorsteps sooner or later. Refugees would have flooded into our lands, bringing hunger and disease. Armies on both sides would inevitably have violated our sovereignty in the interest of gaining some military advantage, resulting in pillaging and destruction. Trade would have been halted, leading to privation and possibly starvation. Even if I chose a side later on, it might be too late by then to protect the kingdom from serious harm. No, I had to get involved when I still had some control over the course of things. So I agreed to your alliance, and I gave you my word of honor to stick by you, which I dishonorably broke.

"I take no pride in that. But it was the right decision. As was taking my troops off the field of battle at the very last moment before the fighting began, when it became too late for you to withdraw as well. You had no choice but to engage the government army, which left Dragon Child vulnerable to a surprise attack on my part. And clearly you see how that turned out."

"The rabbit escapes the tiger and the wolf," Lady Virescent Illumination recounted the proverb, "by tricking them into fighting each other."

"Indeed, Lady Virescent Illumination," the queen said. "Which is the very strategy you employed as well."

"What is all this, then?" General Blue Tiger asked. "Did you bring us here to gloat about your brilliance?"

"Not at all. I wanted you to understand the truth of your actions against one another, and to learn them myself. I also wanted to admit to you that I dishonored myself by betraying you. But I had to abide by my duty as the queen to my subjects above all else. I am not asking you to accept my justification but to understand my reasons."

"Is that what you want from us?" Lord Fiery Dedication asked, a little recovered from the shock of finding out about his consort's actions. "To understand your reasons? The reason you betrayed him and took my throne?"

"I have always been interested in history," the queen told him. "It is a passion of mine, as a matter of fact. I do think it is important that the true account of what occurred be recorded for posterity. But no, it wasn't just out of historical interest that I wanted to hear directly from all of you."

She then fell into a deep thought. After remaining silent for a while, she finally let out an exhausted sigh before drinking some more liquor.

"I suppose the time has finally come to reveal the true reason I brought you here," she said, her voice subdued and melancholy. "To reveal the real purpose behind my taking Dragon Child."

She had to stop for another moment to brace herself before she could go on.

"If you would indulge me," she said to them, "I would like to tell you how I came to be the Queen of Yellow Tranquility.

"My father, the previous King of Yellow Tranquility, had me late in life with a young concubine whom he favored not because he needed an heir, as he already had six sons by his consort and senior concubines, but just for his pleasure in his winter years. So all my half brothers were already adults by the time I was born. I was adored by my parents, and I had an easy upbringing in which I was indulged without there being much expectation of me. As I grew up, I became an avid reader, especially of history books. In fact, I became rather obsessed about the past for reasons I didn't understand then, for I devoured all available accounts in the royal library and demanded more, forcing my tutors to obtain additional texts for me. I had a rather idyllic life, until my father had a stroke and everything suddenly fell into chaos.

"In the later part of his reign, my father's policies were deeply affected by your actions, Lord Fiery Dedication, particularly during Yellow Tranquility's border dispute with the clan of your first consort. It was obvious to everyone that you allowed your relatives to steal our kingdom's territory because you needed their help in putting down the rebellion in the south. My father was so enraged by what happened that he spent the rest of his reign building up a large and well-disciplined army that could be deployed when the opportunity arose to take our land back.

"The problem was that my father spent so much of his time overseeing the expansion and the training of the military that he neglected the affairs of his own family. I think he got complacent from having six healthy and vigorous sons who could carry on his policy after his passing. What he didn't see was that his concubines were a contentious lot who plotted constantly, turning their aggressive sons against one another. By the time he suffered the stroke, all the princes had raised private armies to fight for the throne. As my father's condition deteriorated further, they all scrambled to gain the loyalty of powerful officials and generals with bribes, threats, and promises of advancement upon their ascendance to kingship. It became clear to me that once my father died, there would be a civil war.

"I had read so much about the rise and fall of empires and kingdoms, it filled me with despair to watch it happening in our land. After a while, I could not bear to remain at the capital, watching my rapacious brothers strutting around with their retinues of armed men, yelling at one another, conspiring against one another, heedless of the consequences of their actions on our people. I wanted to leave the terrestrial world with all its futile ambitions and unending violence behind, to escape the melancholy of history. So one night I slipped out of the palace and the city in the guise of a young man, and I traveled to a lofty mountain, where I entered a temple of Primordial Nothingness. There, I shaved my head and became a nun.

"When my father finally passed, things went completely out of control in the kingdom. The bloody, three-year civil war that followed has already been named 'the Plague of Princes' by historians.

"I myself lived in peace during those years, under the tutelage of the head priestess, who taught me how to forget my past and the sorrows of the world through meditation and the study of scriptures. Then one day, a group of high officials and generals arrived at the temple, having traveled all the way from the capital. When they were refused entry at the gates, they went down on their knees and begged loudly for me to grant them an audience. Their cries were so plaintive that I received permission from the head priestess to meet them outside the grounds of the temple.

"They told me that in the violent chaos the kingdom had fallen into, four of my half brothers had been killed in battle or at the hands of assassins. Of the two remaining princes, one had clearly gone mad with paranoia, indiscriminately killing people around him, even those loyal to him, while the other, who might have made an adequate king, was slowly dying from a wound that refused to heal. Given the terrible state of things, they begged on their hands and knees for me to return to the capital and ascend the throne as queen. They had already agreed to throw their united support behind me should I grant their request. That was the only way to bring the time of blood and fire to an end at last. They appealed to me to consider the welfare of the people who had suffered so much in the last years with so many dead, farmlands ruined, and towns and cities destroyed. Some of the elderly men of eminence even burst into tears.

"I did not know what to do. I agonized over it. I sought the advice of the head priestess, who knew that I had no interest in power but felt deeply for the suffering people. But she could not show me a clear path forward, as it was something I had to discover on my own. When I had left the world of politics and warfare, I had gladly given up the privileges and luxuries of a princess so that I could find inner peace. But now, it seemed like a terribly selfish thing for me to enjoy that peace only for myself. I did not know if I could even do a good job as a queen, when I had absolutely no experience in ruling over anyone, never mind an entire kingdom in a time of disarray. Was I even capable of helping the people or would I end up making things even worse with my incompetence? With the officials and generals waiting outside the gate for my response, I could hardly rest that night. When I finally managed to fall asleep, I had a dream, the most powerful one I have ever had, one that changed my life."

The queen had to stop and quench her dry throat with liquor before she could go on.

"In the dream, I was a goddess living on the summit of a high mountain. I was not alone there, since there was another mountain goddess and two mountain gods, each of whom had a home on one of four peaks. We were apparently good friends, because we were together on the veranda of one of the homes, making much merry while drinking exquisite wine. Then I saw a strange cloud in the sky, thick and dark purple with red lightning flashing inside it. It hung ominously on an otherwise clear day. I recognized it as an omen of discord. After that, something happened, I don't remember what, but it was some terrible catastrophe that changed everything.

"I woke up, filled with such a powerful feeling of sorrow that I could do nothing but weep for a long time. When I finally managed to calm down, I could see from the light on the screen door that a new day was dawning. In that moment, I became absolutely certain that it was of great importance that I understand the meaning of that dream, which was much more than a passing fancy of my mind in repose. And I knew that I could not comprehend it through meditation and the study of scriptures. I had to return to the world and seek clues to the dream's significance.

"So I left the temple and returned to the capital, where I ascended the throne as the Queen of Yellow Tranquility. Fortunately for everyone concerned, my sickly half brother died not long after, and the mad one was killed by his own soldiers, who then surrendered their arms and went home. With all the combatants exhausted, the civil war came to an end on its own, and I did my best to fix the damage done by the years of fighting. Eventually order was reestablished, towns and cities were rebuilt and repaired, and people were able to live and work in peace. I also took care to reconstitute my father's army and maintain its strength and discipline. I was helped greatly by high officials and generals who were eager to bring stability back to the kingdom. But I got all the credit and became beloved by the people. All that time, I found no clue to understanding the dream that I had, which made me feel increasingly anxious.

"Just when the realm was back on its feet and starting to thrive, you, General Blue Tiger, came to propose an alliance. I knew from the start that there was no way to avoid getting involved in the affairs of the empire, and that I had to come up with a stratagem of my own to ensure the welfare of my people. But that's not the only reason I pretended to go along with your plan."

The queen turned to Blue Tiger and looked him straight in the eyes.

"In our initial meeting, I became astounded because I recognized you as one of the mountain gods in my dream. Not your physical appearance, but your essential nature, which I discerned right away. I didn't know what to make of it, since you obviously did not recognize me. But I knew that I had to follow you on your course to understand both of our roles in the dream."

Blue Tiger looked startled at her words but said nothing.

"After I took my army out of the battlefield at Far Gallop," the queen continued, "I put my soldiers on ships at the river and sailed up to Dragon Child. The next day, when we began to approach the city, I was struck by wonder to see that Four Verdant Mothers was the very mountain in my dream. I had known of the place, of course, but it was the first time I saw it with my own eyes. And there was no doubt in my mind that it was the very place where I had lived as a mountain goddess. One thing that was different was that in the dream, the land below the mountain was completely empty, with no city, farms, or people. Which meant that it had taken place before the founding of the Autumn Bird State two thousand years ago. The sight of the mountain affirmed that I was on the right track in the search for my dream's meaning.

"After my army managed to take Dragon Child, Lord Fiery Dedication, and Lady Virescent Illumination, I went to see you. I immediately recognized your essences as those of the other mountain god and mountain goddess. I knew then that I had to bring all of us together, so I waited until I heard the news of the horrific outcome of the Battle of Far Gallop and the capture of General Blue Tiger. I immediately dispatched soldiers to intercept the remnant of the government army and to bring the general back here alive. And so here we all are at last."

As she fell silent, the others looked at one another with mystified expressions.

"But what... what does it all mean?" Fiery Dedication asked at last. "You think you had a dream in which we were all gods and goddesses thousands of years ago. So what? What does that have to do with us now?"

"I have been pondering that very question," the queen replied. "And I think I know the sad truth of the matter. It all makes sense to me now, to see you before me, all of us together like we were in the dream."

She paused for a moment to gather her thoughts.

"I know that what I am about to tell you will sound strange and incredible, and I honestly cannot explain to you why I am so certain of its truth. But I have never been surer of anything in my life. So I ask you to keep an open mind as you listen to my words."

The others glanced at each other and then, as one, nodded to the Queen of Yellow Tranquility.

"Over two thousand years ago, the four of us were indeed mountain gods and mountain goddesses who lived on Four Verdant Mothers, before the coming of humans to this land. We were on friendly terms until some kind of a catastrophe occurred, presaged by the Cloud of Discord, and we became bitter enemies to one another. Over time, our enmity grew to the extent that we tried to hurt one another using the humans who arrived. Then we were reborn in the terrestrial world, where we carried on our fight, from one lifetime to the next, one age to the next. After a while, we forgot why we began to fight in the first place, something that I do not know even now. Yet fate kept bringing us together to inflict pain on one another. There has been over two millennia of hatred, but the worst thing about this is not that we have been unknowingly trapped in the cycles of enmity. No. It's all the suffering that we have inflicted on countless innocent people since the beginning of history. We have committed atrocities in using people for our own hostile ends, which we have repeated in every new life. Just think about how many people were killed and injured, their lives damaged and ruined, just in *this* lifetime because of our actions. And we are being continuously punished for our evil as well, to be stuck in our fate where we are condemned to lead lives devoid of love but filled with rage, to fight without purpose or contentment, and to remain ignorant of who we truly are.

"When I came to this realization, I understood that the overwhelming sadness I felt in my study of history was not just about the futility of people's efforts in the endless repetitions of the rise and fall of states, nor about watching my half brothers enact such a meaningless struggle in my own time. No, it was a grief born of the recognition of my own role in the fight among us that has gone on for so long. That's what drove me to leave the capital and enter a temple as a nun, so that I may find a way out of the cycle. And now . . . now that I know the true source of this terrible sadness in me . . .

"Lord Fiery Dedication, Lady Virescent Illumination, and General Blue Tiger, I do not want to be here, I do not want power over the empire, and I do not intend to become the first ruler of a new dynasty. I have a young nephew, a wonderful boy who is kind and intelligent. I have been educating him personally so that when he is old enough, he will ascend the imperial throne as the first emperor of the dynasty which will be called the Tranquil. I believe that he will do an excellent job in bringing peace, order, and prosperity to the realm. As for me, I intend to abdicate and return to the temple to resume my life as a nun."

The others looked at her in astonishment.

"By retreating to a life of contemplation at the temple," she continued, "away from the world, I may find a measure of peace in this lifetime. But what I really want is to find a way out of the fateful entanglement with all of you, if that's even possible. First of all, too much damage has been done, too many people have been hurt, so there must be a commensurate punishment for myself, for all of us. To that end, I'm not sure I deserve to find peace. I also don't know how many lifetimes it will take for us to atone for all our actions over the centuries, but atone we must before we can be released from the cycle.

"And second, I do not believe that I can perform that atonement by myself. In order to escape our fate, I am certain all four of us must understand its nature, recognize our responsibility in it, and finally redress the wrongs we have committed. All of us must save ourselves from this fate together or none of us will be saved."

They sat in silence for a long moment.

"Pardon me," General Blue Tiger said, "but I am a practical man of this world, not a spiritual person. Your story is indeed strange and incredible, and I honestly do not know what to make of it. What exactly is it that you think we should do?"

"That part is simple," the queen replied. "We must make peace, and to do that we must ask forgiveness of one another. I fear that if we do not, we will do this all over again in our next lives, and our next, sinking further away from those lofty peaks where we once sat. Perhaps one day we will have fallen so low from all our pointless fighting that we will end up as some filthy animals snarling and clawing at one another in a dirty swamp."

She took another sip of liquor before she got to her feet. She then stepped back from her sitting mat before going down on her knees. She then bowed down low until her brow touched the floor, to the astonishment of the others.

"General Blue Tiger," she said from her prone position, "I am sorry for having betrayed you on the battlefield, for dishonoring myself by going back on my word to stand by your side. I told you the reasons behind my actions, and I cannot say I regret them, but I recognize that it was an underhanded thing to do to you. I am sincerely remorseful of its consequences upon you, and I most abjectly beg your pardon for it.

"Lord Fiery Dedication, I am sorry for having taken the throne away from you and for ending the dynasty of your forefathers. I had no quarrel with you, and you have done nothing to me to deserve such an attack on your authority. My actions were motivated by my duty to ensure the safety of my people. But still, I am sincerely remorseful of their consequences upon you, and I most abjectly beg your pardon for it.

"Lady Virescent Illumination, although I had no idea of your role in these events, I am sorry to you as well for having mixed you up in all this. You deserve justice for yourself and your family, but you did not deserve the dishonor of becoming the consort of a dethroned ruler. I am sincerely remorseful of the consequences of my actions upon you, and I most abjectly beg your pardon for it."

As she remained prostrated before them, the others grew increasingly uncomfortable, looking at one another with uncertainty.

"Please..." Lord Fiery Dedication said, "please get up."

"Yes," General Blue Tiger said, "there's no need for this."

"Please, Your Tranquil Grandness," Virescent Illumination also put in.

After a moment, the Queen of Yellow Tranquility got up and sat back down on her mat.

"Are you willing to do the same to the people you have wronged and forgive those who have wronged you?" she asked. "General Blue Tiger, can you find the will to beg the pardon of Lady Virescent Illumination for having humiliated her at the pleasure house, something that you don't even remember because she was so insignificant to you? And can you beg the pardon of Lord Fiery Dedication for having chosen to rebel against him?"

A haunted look came over Blue Tiger's expression at those words.

The queen turned to the former emperor.

"Lord Fiery Dedication, can you find the will to beg the pardon of General Blue Tiger for listening to the slanders against him and doubting his loyalty to you? And can you beg the pardon of Lady Virescent Illumination for allowing her father to suffer injustice and her entire family to be destroyed because it suited your political interests?"

Fiery Dedication contemplated her words, his lingering hurt and anger causing tears to well up.

"And Lady Virescent Illumination, can you find the will to beg the pardon of Lord Fiery Dedication and General Blue Tiger for ruining their brotherhood and causing them to turn against each other?"

Virescent Illumination sat still, her mouth set but her eyes darting back and forth between the two men sitting at the table.

"And can all of you find the will to forgive?"

They sat in the heavy silence of deep contemplation.

"Your Tranquil Grandness," Fiery Dedication said, addressing her in the proper imperial way for the first time, "I do not doubt your sincerity, but for me... the dream you had, our past lives, our entangled fates... it all sounds like a fairy tale. And frankly, I don't know how to respond to it. You are the new Lord of All Under Heaven, of course, and so you have the power to command us in any way you wish, but... but you are not ordering us to do anything. You are trying to convince us of some reality that is beyond our perception."

"I am not trying to convince you of anything. Merely persuade you to look for the truth that I know is already within you."

"But I don't know if I can."

"I can," Virescent Illumination suddenly put in. "I believe her."

When the others turned to her, she looked up at the Queen of Yellow Tranquility. "I believe you, Your Tranquil Grandness. It all makes sense, somehow."

The queen nodded to her in acknowledgment.

"I don't know," Blue Tiger said. "Even if it makes sense, am I supposed to just take your word for it? I suppose the story does bring meaning to how everything turned out, for me to go from the emperor's oath brother and right-hand man to a rebel to a defeated prisoner in just a year. But how can I possibly know that it is true? I am no sage or priest."

"I understand completely," the queen said. "And Lord Fiery Dedication is right. It must all sound like a fantastic story to you, perhaps even the ramblings of a madwoman. But there is one more thing I would like to try, if you would indulge me."

She got up again. "Please follow me."

After a brief moment of hesitation, the others stood up as well. As the queen walked out of the hall with her guards close by, they followed her.

She led them up to the highest floor of the imperial palace and out to the balcony with the commanding view of Dragon Child and Four Verdant Mothers. With the onset of twilight, the sky was being painted with streaks of orange and red. The mountain stood in its colossal grandeur in the distance. But in the otherwise clear sky there hung the Cloud of Discord just behind the heights, dark purple with red lightning flashing inside it.

The four of them stood at the balustrade and looked up at Four Verdant Mothers.

"All three of you were born and raised in Dragon Child," the queen said, "so the sight of the mountain must be so familiar to you that you must hardly appreciate it anymore. As for me, when I first saw it as I approached it on Divine Bird River, it truly took my breath away. And not just because I recognized it as the place of my dream. Its glory, its beauty... The pristine perfection of it was seared into my memory. I know that I will remember the moment for the rest of my life."

As she fell silent, they all continued to gaze at the peaks of the mountain in silent appreciation, taking in its majesty as if seeing it for the first time. To the astonishment of the others, the Queen of Yellow Tranquility bowed her head and began to weep freely.

"Your Tranquil Grandness..." Lady Virescent Illumination said in sympathetic concern at her obvious distress.

"I don't want to be here," the queen managed to say between the gasps of her uncontrollable grief. "I don't want to be in this world. I want to stop what we are doing so we can go back home. All of us. Back to Four Verdant Mothers. And I want to go back to the time before our hatred, our strife, before we caused so much suffering in the world. And for what? I don't even know. I don't remember. I want the peace we knew when we were friends. I want to go home.

"I just want to go home."

She had to stop then as she wept even harder in a sorrow that threatened to overwhelm her completely. The others stared at her, deeply shaken not just by the sight of her grief but by the recognition of the same emotion within them as well. After a while, they looked away and fell into their own individual thoughts. Just as she asked them to, they contemplated the strange paths their lives had taken for all of them to be there in that moment. They also considered the incredible story the queen told them, wondering if it could be true, if it could explain all of their actions and their consequences.

As the sun set and the sky began to darken in earnest, the Queen of Yellow Tranquility finally calmed down. She wiped away her tears and let out a deep sigh before addressing the others again.

"This is the one last thing I could think of to persuade you of what I know," she told them. "For us to stand together before our mutual home of so long ago, so I can ask all of you the same question.

"Lord Fiery Dedication, Lady Virescent Illumination, and General Blue Tiger, as you gaze upon the peaks of Four Verdant Mothers, can you sense the truth of what I told you? Do you long for a time of peaceful amity as I do? Can you feel the truth of my words? Can you feel it? Can you feel that our home is there, together, and not here, apart?

"Can you feel it?"

CHAPTER ELEVEN

Life V

A Fabulist History

Another thousand years later…

AFTER THE HISTORIAN watched his colleague blend in with the crowd, he finished his drink at the café. He sat still for a while, unable to get on with his day, as he felt burdened by an unbearably heavy sense of emptiness inside him. When he turned his head, his attention was caught by a large poster on a wall, advertising an exhibition of Charles Strickland's primitivist paintings at a museum. Seminude native women sat around in serene comfort, in a brightly colored world before civilization and before recorded history. The historian wondered if the artist had experienced his own moment of pristine perfection in the Pacific Islands, the vision of which he tried to replicate in his works.

It was only when his body started to ache a bit with restlessness that he finally let out a deep sigh before forcing himself to get up. He left the establishment and trudged slowly back to his apartment, where Radiant Tiger came up and demanded food. He apologized to the cat for neglecting to fill up the bowl before leaving and took out some wet food. As he stood by and watched, Radiant Tiger eagerly slurped it all up, looking back at him every once in a while with a serious mien as if annoyed by his observation. When he was done, the historian tried to pick him up so he could pet him for a bit, but the cat deftly evaded his grasp and ran off down the hallway. He smiled at that and sat down on the couch. A moment later, however, he realized that he was completely at a loss as to what to do next.

Trying to get some work done was out of the question, and he had come to despise everything that came on the television, but he was also loath to just sit around and wallow in sadness. He had no regret about moving out of the house that was too big for him and filled with painful reminders of his wife, but now he felt rather constricted by the practical size of the apartment. Unable to bear the sensation of the walls closing in on him, he left the apartment again.

He took the elevator down to the underground garage, got into his wife's luxury sedan, and drove out of the building. With no particular destination in mind, he took a random series of streets while listening intently to Vinteuil's exquisite *Souvenir* sonata playing on a classical music station so as not to think too much. After driving around for half an hour, he was stopped at a red light when he noticed a directional sign for the Four Verdant Mothers National Park. When the light turned green, he followed a sudden impulse and turned the car in the direction of the mountain.

Tourist season was months away, so the parking lot outside the park was almost empty. The historian stopped the car close to the entrance and got out. The air was warm and filled with the pleasant fragrance of greenery wafting down from the mountain. He felt refreshed as he took it all in with deep breaths, strolling down the path through the park. Only the occasional jogger or cyclist passed him by. When he came across a bench at a spot that afforded a panoramic view of the mountain, he sat down and contemplated the colossal magnificence before him, its four peaks luminous with green and yellow foliage. There was that singular natural phenomenon appearing from behind the highest summit, a thick purple cloud with red lightning flashing inside that was called the Cloud of Discord, though someone had also given it the nickname Dragon Fart Cloud. As the historian stared at the ominous shape hanging in an otherwise clear sky, he finally allowed himself to think about the state of his life.

He was never given to self-pity, perhaps because ever since he had lost his mother he had no expectation of finding lasting happiness in his life. As he now sat alone, however, feeling utterly insignificant before the grandeur of Four Verdant Mothers, he could not help wondering why his life had to be filled with so much loss. His wife's absence still bore down on him with suffocating weight, echoing the earlier pain of losing his parents. That was compounded by an acute sense of abandonment by his colleague who had provided him with a temporary escape from his sorrow, only to take that away as well. He wondered how he was supposed to deal with her in the future. Perhaps she would try to see him as little as possible and be strictly professional when they had to interact. He wondered if it would hurt more or less if she sought to return to their friendship from before the affair, if he would be subjected to a painful longing to be intimate with her again. On top of that, he had to contend with the significant guilt he felt toward his wife for even wanting some relief from the agony of missing her.

The historian was also not given to supernatural or magical thinking, as no prayer or promise of an afterlife had provided any kind of solace for his losses. When he gave his thoughts free rein to ponder a possible explanation for the vicissitudes of his life, he found himself considering the old stories he had studied that pointed to the play of otherworldly forces in the cycles of people's lives. He did not seriously consider the reality of such a thing, but a part of him longed to believe in something that could provide some sense to all that had happened to him.

His wandering thoughts took him to the fall of the Radiant dynasty, to the writing of unknown nature that recounted how the Queen of

Yellow Tranquility, in the wake of her triumph, summoned the former emperor, Fiery Dedication, his primary consort Virescent Illumination, and the rebel general Blue Tiger. According to the account, she revealed to them an astonishing story of intertwined fates that had set them in conflict with one another from one lifetime to the next. Her motivation was to find a way out of the destiny of mutual enmity that they had been condemned to, an escape that was possible only through contrition, forgiveness, and reconciliation on all their parts. As he then wondered how the narrative served their needs at the time, literally or metaphorically, he considered how he could use it to make sense of his own condition.

Perhaps three of the four sought forgiveness and forgave in turn, he considered, *and so they were able to return to being mountain deities on Four Verdant Mothers. But one of them did not. He could not bring himself to let go of his hatred. While the others left, he stayed to continue his fight against enemies who were not even in this world anymore. And he went on, lifetime after lifetime, carrying on his lonely existence that was also his punishment for all the sufferings he had caused over the centuries and for refusing to seek forgiveness and start the process of healing. In those lives he was repeatedly deprived of love, contentment, and a true home, and he will continue to lose them until he becomes wise enough to understand the true nature of his condition.*

If that is the true meaning of my life... all the painful events in it were not random misfortunes in a senseless existence but just punishments for what I have done in past lives. And so here I sit alone, loveless and hopeless, looking up at the mountain where my three friends have returned to their blissful existence.

He gave a sad smile then, feeling that his theory provided him with a kind of symmetrical meaning—except that it was made implausible by the notion of himself as a warring soul filled with unquenchable rage. Because of the sense of distance from the world that came over him during his mother's sickness and death, he always had difficulty allowing himself to develop strong feelings toward others, which was why the intense love he had felt for his wife had been such an exceptional thing. But that was true for the feeling of hatred as well, which was not something he had experienced very much at all in his life. The reason he found his aunt's dislike of him so odd was that he felt no such thing for her, even after he learned of all the derogatory things she had said about him. Even for the political scientist who attacked his character by bringing up the loss of his parents, he had felt only contempt and pity at how he had embarrassed himself in public. In fact, looking back on his life, he could not remember having truly hated anyone. The closest thing was his abhorrence toward a historical figure who had lived two thousand years ago, the vain and cruel Emperor Veiled Sun, whom he had exposed to the world as a liar and a monster. Given his nature, then, it made little sense that his soul was one that could not let go of its enmity.

If it is not the case that I got left behind because I was the only one who could not ask to be forgiven and to forgive in turn, he thought, *then perhaps none of the four made it out of the terrestrial realm. In that meeting, at the fall of the Radiant dynasty, they did become contrite and reconciled. But perhaps that was not enough. After all the harm that they had caused through so many lifetimes, they had to receive commensurate punishment. So their mutual enmity was gone, but they were still reborn in this world over and over again, to lead sad and lonely lives full of loss and grief. Perhaps the other three are scattered all over the world, struggling through their tribulations without knowing their cause. Or perhaps their lives intersected in each cycle without them recognizing one another. Is my colleague, with the loss she suffered and her alienation from her parents, one of them as well? Was our connection based on an unconscious knowledge of each other's guilt as well as pain? Does this also explain my aunt's hatred of me, a residue from our previous struggles? If this is true, when will our punishment end? After three thousand years, are we nearly at the end of our atonement, or are we nowhere close? When will it be over so we can return to Four Verdant Mothers?*

He gazed at the peaks with an acute sense of longing, but it was fleeting. As thought provoking as he found the idea, he just did not believe in past lives and reincarnation, or the carrying forward of fortunes and misfortunes born of good deeds and bad. His agnosticism was not complete, though, and just the idea of his existence unfolding through a series of narratives for millennia filled him with utter despair. And it was through that despair that he realized he was not really interested in finding an explanation for the losses of his past. The only thing he wanted now was to stop feeling the unrelenting pain inside him.

He wanted to be done with it all.

The view of the grand heights of Four Verdant Mothers reminded him of a television program he had watched with his wife about a year ago. A well-known media personality, a sports and fitness enthusiast, challenged himself to see if he could climb the mountain and visit all four peaks before sundown. As the historian and his wife watched, he started just before dawn, climbing the stairs hewn into the side of the mountain, and ultimately succeeded in completing the arduous course, arriving at the last peak to witness a spectacular sunset.

The historian imagined himself starting the climb in the morning, slowly taking one step at a time, up to one of the peaks. At the summit, he pictured himself standing before the sky at twilight, watching the day die like his wife and his parents. He would remain on the precipice and wait, until something inside him told him that it was time to step off. As he contemplated the course, he realized that there was no reason for him wait until the next day to set out. He could start climbing now, and all he had to do was reach a place that was high enough for his purpose.

There was no doubt in his mind that it was what he wanted to do, but a part of him felt obligated to go through the reasons why he should not do it. He considered the possibility of meeting someone new whom he could love, but the very idea of looking for another to take his wife's place felt like a travesty and a betrayal. He then thought of his work, which had provided him with purpose for so long. He had signed a contract for a new book about the empire of the Grand Hegemony, which amounted to a promise he had made to the publisher. But when he tried to imagine himself going back to the archives to do research and sit at his desk to write, he felt nothing but cold indifference. He found that he had no desire to write another book, make another important discovery, provide people with a new insight into the past. No, he only wanted his pain to end. That was all.

He was on the verge of getting to his feet to make his way to the mountain, when he suddenly realized that there was one very good reason he could not do it, at least not on that day. His cat, Radiant Tiger, would be stuck in his apartment, becoming thirsty and hungry as he waited for his return. He could make a call so that someone would come for him, but that seemed rather irresponsible. No, he would have to find a new home for him. His brother-in-law would probably take him in, as both he and his wife were animal lovers who adored Radiant Tiger. But then he would have to figure out a way to approach them without giving away his ultimate intention.

He then remembered how he had first met the cat, originally his wife's pet, who had been wary of him for a while before finally getting used to his presence. As the historian had never lived with an animal before, getting to know him was a novel experience. He eventually became very fond of Radiant Tiger, though he had the sense that the cat only tolerated him.

It was his affection for the animal that broke something in him. Even if he could find a good home for Radiant Tiger, it pained him terribly to imagine the cat sensing that he was abandoned yet again. He knew full well that he was projecting his own sorrow on the animal, but the thought affected him so deeply that he was overcome with a wave of grief that hit him with unexpected force. He bent down and put his face in his hands as he wept. At first, he tried desperately to regain his composure, but he was overwhelmed by the need to let himself go at last. With a sensation that felt like a dam bursting, he cried uncontrollably, over the loss of his wife, his mother, and his father, even his colleague, all of whom had abandoned him when he had needed them so much. He allowed his mind to lose itself in the veritable storm of grief, the exploding pain from it threatening to swallow him up completely. After an unaccountable period of time, however, he felt the whirlwind inside him subsiding at last, gradually replaced by a sense of relief from the release of pent-up sorrow. But even after he managed to return to the world from the dissipating darkness inside him, he still breathed heavily and in shudders for a while. That too eventually calmed, and at some point, he wiped away his tears and let out a deep sigh as he sat up, feeling utterly exhausted.

He lifted his head toward Four Verdant Mothers once more with a sense of having finally unburdened himself. He thought for some reason of Radiant Tiger waking him up in the morning by jumping on his bed and slapping him repeatedly on the face to notify him of his hunger, which actually made him smile. He had been sitting on the bench for a long time, perhaps hours, and he now felt the urge to go home and see the cat. As he began to get up, the cell phone in his pocket rang. He took it out and saw that it was his colleague.

"Hi," he greeted her.

"I am so sorry I left you like that," she said in a distraught voice, barely able to get the words out. "I'm sorry."

"It's all right."

"I really shouldn't have done that. I can't imagine how you must have felt. I am such a terrible person, I told you. I'm so terrible."

"You are not terrible. I will never think that. Not after everything you have done for me."

"But then I just left you. Are you . . . are you okay?"

He was about to tell her that he was fine, but he suddenly found that he could not lie to her.

"Oh no, you are not okay. Tell me what you are doing."

"I'm at a park."

"Do you want me to come?"

"No. I'm just sitting here thinking."

"Are you sure? I can come if you need me to."

"No. And . . . I do understand. I really do. You have your own life to lead, and you can't be with me."

"I do love you though. You know that, right?"

"Yes. And I love you too. But you are doing the right thing. You should be with your boyfriend, whose life has not been touched by the shadow of death, as you said. I understand that completely. We are too much alike, with our losses. You deserve to be with someone who can relieve you of some of the burden, not add to it."

"But I don't want to abandon you. I can't do that to you."

As the historian paused to think, he came to the realization that there was a definitive reason why he could not throw himself off of Four Verdant Mothers on that day or any other day. The impact of the action on her was unthinkable, especially considering her own past. Even if it did not destroy her, she would have to carry the guilt from it for the rest of her life. And he cared about her too much to do that to her. She was another reason he had to go on. Even with the pain, the grief, and the longing, he had to go on for her as well.

"Listen," he said, "I want to tell you something that I would not lie to you about. I'm not okay. But I'm not going to do anything to myself. Do you understand? I'm going to stay here for a while, then I'll go home, give Radiant Tiger some treats, and go on with my day. Then I'll go on with the next day, and the next. No matter how hard it is, I will go on. Do you believe me?"

The silence was long, but she finally replied. "Yes," she said with some relief in her tone.

"Good."

"I know . . . I know I have no right to demand anything of you but . . ."

"What is it?"

"Will you go back to therapy?"

He thought about it.

"Eventually," he told her. "Yes, I will. I promise."

"Okay. That's what she would have wanted you to do, right?"

"That's true. But it won't be just for her."

He heard her sigh or sob, he could not tell.

"Can I ask you for something as well?"

"Anything."

"I know it might get strange between us but... when I go back to teaching... can we return to the way we were? I mean, if you decide that it would be best for you to stay away, I'd understand. But... I hope we can still talk. Still be friends."

"I would love that."

"Thank you. That's a great relief to me."

"To me as well."

A moment of silence passed.

"I don't want to hang up," she said.

He felt the same way. Despite their promise to stay in each other's lives, he knew that things were bound to change between them, that it would be different the next time they met. That prospect saddened him greatly.

"Can I tell you a story?" he asked her. "It's kind of a long one, so I understand if you don't have the time."

"I have all the time in the world for you."

The historian smiled at that.

"It's from a book that was made to look like a collection of folktales from the Immaculate State," he told her. "Given the unity of style and the recurrence of certain themes, my theory is that they were all imagined by a single storyteller, a very talented one, I think. He was probably hired to tell original tales which were written down, and when he was done, he was killed so that no one would know he was their sole creator. There is one story that I really liked, but unfortunately I couldn't find the right place to talk about it in my book. I asked my editor about the possibility of publishing the stories, but she didn't think people would be interested in reading tales from a fake period of history. But the stories aren't fake in any way. They are the products of the wonderfully imaginative mind of a storyteller who lived during the late Immaculate dynasty. But I understood what she meant. So I don't know if this story will ever be read again."

"I really want to hear it now."

"All right. It's called 'The Loyalty of Little Rat Face.'"

IN THE TOWN of Horny Chicken, there lived a rat-faced merchant who managed to accumulate a great deal of wealth through sheer greed, miserliness, and ruthless dealings. The people of Horny Chicken despised him for his unscrupulous business practices that ruined the lives of many, but the influence he gained with local magistrates through bribery made him a feared personage there. So it was only behind his back that people dared to call him Old Rat Face.

One day, the merchant was walking through the market when a disheveled man in dirty clothes jumped out in front of him and prostrated himself on the ground. He was the town's lunatic and occasionally told the fortunes of people he came across. If they liked what they heard, they tossed him a few coins. When Old Rat Face asked why he was showing him such respect, the lunatic answered that a child of his will one day become the minister of military affairs and save the country from the invasion of barbarians. The pronouncement pleased the merchant so much that he showed uncharacteristic generosity by giving the wild man his precious fan made of radiant fabric, an object dear enough to keep him fed for many days. The lunatic let out a joyful yell before dancing away while fanning himself. Years later, however, Old Rat Face came to curse him for his false prophecy as well as his own gullibility in believing him.

Perhaps due to his lack of virtue and many unrighteous acts, Heaven saw fit to deprive him of the thing he wanted most after wealth, which was a son to carry on his legacy. Before his long-suffering wife became too old to bear children anymore, she had given birth to no fewer than twelve offspring, all of whom had died early except for three daughters. Resigning himself to the situation, the merchant put his hopes in marrying his daughters off to prominent families so that he could increase his riches through his sons-in-law and grandsons.

Of the three daughters, the older two were attractive but the third was homely—no, that's too polite—downright ugly, as she had unfortunately inherited her father's rodent features. Ever since she was a child, her mother and sisters teased her mercilessly about her looks, calling her Little Rat Face. Her father also made plain his discontent, as her inauspicious appearance posed a challenge to marrying her off to a respectable family. Despite such ill treatment, she grew up to be a cheerful, hardworking, and loyal girl. From an early age, she accepted her ugliness with good humor, even joining in on her sisters' ridicule of her ratlike appearance by sticking out her front teeth, pulling forward her ears, and making squeaking noises. She never displayed bitterness or sadness at their cruelty, as she only sought to be of service to them, without expecting kindness or affection in return.

Just when Old Rat Face was preparing the dowry for his daughters, a terrible disaster struck the family. Partners in a business deal turned out to be swindlers who took his money and absconded. They also took out large loans in his name, burdening him with mountainous debt. Faced with the prospect of utter ruin, the entire household became filled with the loud lamentations of the family.

One night, after they had all retired to their respective chambers, they lay restless on their beddings, filled with dread of the dark days ahead. In the deepest hour, their uneasy sleep was disturbed by the bloodcurdling scream of a servant girl. Fearful of a new catastrophe that might have fallen on them, they all rushed out to the courtyard. They found the girl on her knees, apparently just having come out of the outhouse, shaking before the gigantic figure of a stranger dressed in a white robe. His head looked like a round rock set on top of the massive boulder of his torso, but his facial features were hidden beneath a wide bamboo hat. Struck dumb by the appearance of such a frighteningly large person standing still as a statue, Old Rat Face and his family could only stare in frozen fear.

"Who... who are..." Old Rat Face finally managed to say.

The figure, without uttering a word, raised the hem of his robe before squatting down as if to defecate. He then let out a loud grunt. Instead of producing feces, however, a large ball of shimmering silver dropped out of his anus. With another grunt, another ball fell, then another, and yet another, until the courtyard became filled with rolling balls of the precious metal. He finally straightened back up to his imposing height and took off his bamboo hat, which made everyone scream in horror.

The stranger's head had the face of a bear, the stripes of a tiger, the beard of a dragon, and the feathers of a bird. He was not a man but an unnatural monster.

"Yeah, yeah, I'm very scary," the monster said.

He then looked at Old Rat Face and addressed him.

"You are not much to look at either, you know, you rat-looking son of a bitch. Anyway, I have come here because I require a wife. Give me a girl I can marry, and you can keep all these silver balls I shat out."

Old Rat Face was still in shock at what was unfolding before him, but he eventually looked down at the balls in the courtyard, which could save him from ruin. So he began to consider the monster's offer. After a moment, he slowly turned to his youngest and ugliest daughter, as did his wife and older daughters. None of them could bring themselves to utter the words, but when Little Rat Face realized that they were looking at her, she understood their meaning. She presently went to her chamber and gathered a few of her belongings, which she put in a little bundle. She then returned to her parents and prostrated herself before them.

"Dear Father and Mother," she said, "I am grateful to you for giving me life and raising me. It is both my duty and my honor to sacrifice myself for you and our family. I bid you to take good care of yourselves and my sisters and live a long time in health and prosperity."

She then turned to the monster, her head bowed down and her body trembling in fear.

"Damn it!" the monster yelled after looking at her. "Another rat face! Ugh, serves me right for not selecting a girl myself. Oh well, I guess my monstrous ass can't be choosy. Come here, Little Rat Face!"

The girl screamed as the gigantic creature lunged at her and grabbed her by the sleeve of her dress. He then launched himself into the air, flying into the night like the sudden gust of a storm wind. Old Rat Face and the rest of the household fell to the ground in terror as they gazed up at the flight of the monster, the screams of the hapless girl fading fast in the darkness.

Little Rat Face fainted as the monster carried her up to the clouds. When she regained consciousness after an unaccountable period of time, she looked down and saw that they were descending on a great forest that stretched all the way to the horizon. They landed in a clearing where a small house stood by a narrow stream. The monster let go of her sleeve and proceeded to the house without a word. Not knowing what else to do, Little Rat Face followed meekly, dreading her fate in the strange new place.

The monster opened a sliding door to the main chamber of the house.

"The bedding is in the corner," he told Little Rat Face. "Lay it out. I'm going to wash before I lie down. I had a long and tiring day."

As he then proceeded to the stream, Little Rat Face went inside and looked around the place. The space was a bit dusty but otherwise tidy. When she saw the bedding piled up in a corner, she found herself moving automatically, laying out the mattresses, the blankets, and the pillows. The monster returned, walked in, and slid the door shut before taking off his robe. Little Rat Face collapsed with a whimper, starting to weep at the horror that was to come. To her surprise, however, the monster lay down on a mattress, pulled a blanket over his enormous body, and closed his eyes.

She was too frightened to lie down herself, so she remained sitting near the door all night, keeping her eyes on the creature. Sometime after dawn, she managed to doze off for a while, but when she heard the monster move she woke up with a scream.

"Damn!" the monster yelled. "You scared the crap out of me! Nice way to greet your husband in the morning, Little Rat Face."

As she bowed her head, trembling, he put his robe back on and opened the door to go outside.

"I'm off to work," he said as he went out. "I'll be back at dusk. Have dinner ready for me by then."

He then stepped out and flew up to the sky.

Little Rat Face remained still, but as the new day's sun lit up the world outside, she eventually found the courage to get up, walk out of the chamber, and look around the place. At the back of the house, she found a kitchen, as well as a separate storehouse and an outhouse. She went into the storage and found it well stocked with sacks of rice and all manner of vegetables, roots, and spices. But the absence of any kind of meat surprised her, considering the monster's predatory appearance.

After she familiarized herself with the place, she found some rags, wet them with water she carried in a pot from the stream, and thoroughly cleaned the interior of the main chamber. In the kitchen, she prepared some food to be cooked before dusk. All the effort tired her out, so she managed to sleep fitfully for a while in the afternoon. When she woke up, she saw that the light outside had deepened, which made her panic at the thought that it might be close to sunset. She hurried over to the kitchen and began to make a vegetarian meal.

She became filled with renewed fear when the monster returned, dropping from the sky, but she was relieved that the food was ready to be served. She brought the dishes on a small table to the chamber and lit an oil lamp while the monster washed himself at the stream. He then came in, sat down, and began to eat.

"Did you eat already?" the monster asked Little Rat Face without looking at her.

"Yes . . . yes, sir . . ." she lied. Earlier, she had tried to eat something but had been unable to keep anything down because of her constant anxiety.

The monster nodded and quickly finished the meal.

When he was done, she picked up the table and took it to the kitchen, where she put away the leftovers and cleaned up everything. She returned to the chamber to find the monster sitting on a mat and setting up the wooden board and playing pieces of the constellation game.

"Sit down," he said, indicating another mat on the opposite side of the board.

She obeyed.

"All right, here is the deal," the monster said. "If you beat me at this game, I will release you from our marriage. I'll take you back home or wherever you want to go."

She looked up at him in astonishment, though she quickly lowered her head again in fright at his monstrous features.

"But . . . but sir, I do not know how to play."

"That's fine. I'll teach you."

He then explained the rules to her.

Given the fact that it was her first game, he beat her quickly and easily. She knew from the beginning that she had no chance of winning, but just the thought that she could have returned home if she had succeeded made her burst into tears. The monster waited patiently for her to calm down before he spoke to her again, pointing out all the mistakes she had made in the game.

"All right," he said, "time to sleep."

While he put away the board and the pieces, Little Rat Face took out the bedding and arranged everything on the floor. She was still too frightened to lie down, but she managed to sleep in a sitting position for some time. When she woke up early in the morning, she stared at the prone form of the monster. He had the appearance of a creature who would snore loudly in his sleep, but he lay so still and silent that he could have been dead. She wondered if she could go home if he just died in his sleep. But then she realized that she had no idea where she was or how to return home, if she could even find her way out of the great forest.

She was startled when the creature's eyes flew open and looked back at her, making her quickly avert her gaze.

"Well, at least you didn't scream this time," he said, and got up.

The day followed the same routine as the previous one. After he flew off, he returned at dusk and ate the vegetarian dinner she had prepared for him. They then played another round of the constellation game. She lost again, and he explained her errors and weakness in strategy. The next day was the same, as were all the days that followed.

As time passed in the forest, Little Rat Face's skill at the game gradually improved. Even though she knew that she could not match the monster's skill for a long while, she managed to incrementally increase the time it took for him to beat her. A significant factor in her play's advancement was his post-game lectures, which she listened to attentively. And during all that time, he never touched her once. She considered that he may be repulsed by her ugliness, which made her grateful for her rat face. After a while, she felt secure enough to sleep on a mattress, though at some distance from the monster.

A wonder of the forest was that there were no seasons there, no heat wave or cold spell, not even rain or snow. The mild weather and the daily rise and fall of temperature were always the same. And the uniformity of every day made it impossible for her to keep track of the passage of time.

Whether she had been at the forest for many months, many years, or many decades, there came a day when she finally beat the monster at the constellation game. After she captured an essential piece, making it impossible for him to win, they both sat stock-still as neither of them could believe what had just happened. After a while, the monster let out a sigh of what sounded like relief while Little Rat Face burst into tears again.

"Sir," she managed to say after she found the courage to address him, "will you . . . will you return me home . . . like you promised?"

"Of course," the monster replied. "But I can also take you somewhere else."

"Where would I go other than home, sir?"

The monster looked down and fell into a deep thought.

"To answer that question," he said to her, "I have to explain some things to you. Why I came to your family's home in Horny Chicken, and why I brought you here. I wasn't always the monster you see before you. Once I was a heavenly spirit and an official in the court of the Heavenly Emperor. My position was that of an envoy for His Heavenly Grandness, which took me to every corner of the world. One day, as I was flying on a cloud to deliver a message from His Heavenly Grandness to the Divine King of Summerland, I saw a young woman sitting in a pavilion by a river, composing a poem. She was the most beautiful woman of the terrestrial world that I had ever seen, so I descended toward her in the form of a small bird to get a better look. When I ascertained her true fairness, I was struck by its pristine perfection, a vision that I knew would stay with me always. I also read her poetry, which revealed that she possessed a mind of profound wisdom as well as significant skills as a calligrapher. I immediately fell in love.

"Neglecting my duty to His Heavenly Grandness, I transformed myself once again, this time into the form of a young man of handsome appearance, dressed in the clothing of a high-status aristocrat. I tried to speak to her, but she immediately fled my presence to safeguard her modesty. I followed her home, but she shut the gates before me, so I did not know what to do. If I were an earthly man, I would have asked to speak to her father so that a marriage match could be proposed. But in truth, I was a heavenly spirit who could not possibly live with her in this world as husband and wife. It could only end in tragedy for her. After dallying outside the house for a while, I had to return to my official duties.

"But I could not forget her, so I returned the next day and appeared before her in the form of a sturdy general, with the same result. On the following day, I came to her as a venerable scholar, but to no avail. Unable to persuade her to speak to me, I finally resorted to using my magical powers to spy on her in the house, taking on the shape of a moth to watch her go about her chores, spend time with her family, read books of poetry and wisdom, bathe her naked body, and sleep. I moved about her so discreetly that she never saw me, but she was a person of such acute perception that she sensed that something was wrong, that she was constantly under watch. She even considered that she might be haunted by a ghost. As a result, she became distracted, often making mistakes in her work, forgetting things, and constantly waking up terrified from a recurring nightmare of a gigantic moth that menaced her. She finally fell ill from anxiety and fatigue.

"Her concerned parents summoned a doctor, but he could not tell what was wrong with her. So they resorted to bringing in a shaman who performed a ritual which revealed my presence in the house. The shaman told her parents that their daughter was not haunted by a ghost but was being harassed by a heavenly spirit who was in love with her. That terrified the young woman so much that she began going to the local temple of Primordial Nothingness, where she prayed to the Merciful One to deliver her from my unwanted attention. Her nature was so pure and her prayers so ardent that her predicament became known in the Heavenly Realm.

"I was arrested by heavenly soldiers and brought before the Heavenly Emperor and the Merciful One to answer for the crime of having tormented a virtuous and innocent woman. I was also accused of neglecting my official duties in my unseemly pursuit of her. At the end of the inquiry, the Merciful One handed me a mirror which showed me where my desire for the woman would have led to if I had not been stopped. I witnessed myself committing such heinous acts of violation upon the good woman that it made me weep in shame to know that I was capable of such things. And I became so grateful to His Heavenly Grandness and the Merciful One for preventing me from the course that I begged them to lay a punishment on me that would deliver me from my beastly nature.

"After they spoke to each other, they announced their judgment. My punishment was to be threefold. First, I was to be transformed into a monster with the outward form of that beastly part of my nature. Second, I was to be deprived of my official position and exiled to the earthly realm to seek atonement. And third, I was to remain there until I saved a woman as virtuous and innocent as the one I preyed upon without ever touching her or having a lustful thought about her."

A realization dawned on Little Rat Face.

"That's why you chose me," she said. "Because I am so ugly. I'm someone you couldn't possibly have a lustful thought about."

The monster let out a sigh before addressing her.

"It's not that at all. Here, I will show you," he said, and reached into his sleeve to take out a small mirror. "With this, the Merciful One showed me my possible future," he said before handing it to her.

When she looked at it, she was surprised to see the image of a stunningly beautiful woman looking back at her, her skin the color of pristine snow, her eyes like darkly shining jewels, and the long strands of her hair glimmering like radiant fabric in black.

"Who is she, sir?" Little Rat Face asked.

"That was you," the monster told her, "in your past life. A woman of great vanity about her beauty. She judged everyone by their appearance, comparing their looks to hers and finding all of them wanting in comparison. She also found occasions to manipulate people using her fairness and to mistreat those she felt beneath her standard. When she began to age, she did everything to maintain her looks, practicing all manner of regimens and taking many kinds of medicine for the purpose. But when she finally realized the futility of the struggle against the ravages of time, her wounded vanity disheartened her so much that she took her own life. She ended the cycle of her life prematurely, so the Ten Judges of the Underworld saw fit to condemn her to be born an ugly woman in the new cycle."

"That's why I am Little Rat Face. It's punishment for my past life's fault."

"Yes. But you have already atoned for it fully."

"I did, sir?" she asked in surprise. "When, sir? How?"

"Don't you remember? When you sacrificed yourself for your family. As soon as you understood the situation and what your family wanted, you came to me willingly. You did not even hesitate. And so you freed yourself from the burden of your past life."

"So . . . you will return me home, so I can go on with this life, sir?"

"As I said, if you want. But I can offer you something better. It was my mission to save a virtuous and innocent woman. I can do that for you."

"Save me from what, sir?"

"Your sacrifice was a noble act of loyalty to your family and filial piety to your parents. But loyalty is a quality that is more complex than people realize. It is not an absolute virtue that all good people must follow, for even a virtuous person may commit evil by being loyal to a wicked person. For the wise, it must be balanced by the sound judgment of whether the person you are giving it to is worthy of it.

"Listen, Little Rat Face, for me to save you, I had to make you see that your family did not deserve your loyalty. You were so used to being a good daughter to them despite their ill treatment of you, I had to take you away so that you could understand your situation from a distance. They sacrificed you so that your father could become rich once more and your sisters could marry into respectable families. For that, they sent you to whatever dark fate awaited you with a monster. All for those dirty silver balls that I shat out of my ass. If your family had refused them, that would have been their salvation, and I would have let them keep the silver. But they failed the test, and so they will suffer for it in this lifetime and the next. Your father, just when he thinks he is a wealthy man again, he will find in the morning that the silver balls have turned into so much dung. But you passed the test, and so you deserve to live fully, far away from them."

"But where am I supposed to go, sir?"

"All you have to do is trust me and willingly go wherever I take you. That will be the fulfillment of my purpose in the earthly realm. In this place, this forest, the river of time flows differently than it does in the world you knew. So I can take you back home, to the morning after I took you from it. Or I can take you to a different place in a different time where and when your family does not exist. It is up to you."

Little Rat Face sat still as she considered the monster's offer.

"THAT'S HOW THE story ends?" she asked the historian.

"No, but the text was damaged so I couldn't read the last page."

"That's sad."

"Ah yes, all unfinished stories make you sad."

"That's why we are driven to finish our work. To escape that sadness."

"To escape the melancholy of untold history."

They fell silent for a long moment.

"But I want a real ending," she said. "It's too good not to have a proper ending."

"Perhaps you could make it up."

"Hmm..." she said, and thought for a while.

"Okay, I've got it," she finally said. "Here's how I want it to end."

FROM THE SKY, the monster descended to the ground, on the side of a wide stone road of an unnaturally smooth surface, and he let Little Rat Face's sleeve go. When she looked up at him, she was surprised to see the tiger's stripes on his face fade and his bear's snout fall to the ground, followed by his dragon's beard and bird's feathers. He then turned into a being of pure light. Little Rat Face could not fully make out his face in the intense illumination, but it seemed that he was smiling at her as he ascended into the air and flew up to disappear among the clouds.

Left alone, she waited at the side of the road, not knowing what to do. She had trusted him, but that did not mean she understood his plan. Presently, she heard a low growling noise coming down the road and saw a horseless carriage made of metal coming toward her. As the marvelous vehicle approached her, it began to slow down until it stopped next to her. A glass window slid down and a handsome young man with a kind face looked out.

"You are the most beautiful woman I have ever seen," he said with a look of genuine astonishment on his face. "You are a vision of pristine perfection."

"Please do not tease me, sir," she told him. "I am Little Rat Face."

"If that is so, you look like no rat that I have ever seen."

Just then Little Rat Face caught a glimpse of herself on a small mirror next to the window and saw that she had gained the beauteous face that she had possessed in her previous life.

There were countless wonders that she had to get used to in the new land of a new time, but the thing that astounded her the most was that women were allowed to be educated and hold important positions in society. And the kind and handsome man who took her in and eventually married her saw to it that she received all the schooling she wanted. In the course of her learning, she discovered that she was a highly intelligent woman, something she would never have known in her old life. She eventually entered civil service, working for rulers who were not hereditary kings but representatives chosen by all the people of the land. Many years later, after a career of rapid promotions up the ranks through sheer merit, she attained the position of minister of military affairs. Not long after the appointment, the land was invaded by foreign barbarians. By then, she knew that hers was a country worthy of her loyalty, so she resolved to do all that she could to defend it. In coming up with her strategy, she used the lessons she had learned from the monster in playing the constellation game. She subsequently defeated the enemy quickly and soundly, forcing their few surviving remnants to beat a hasty retreat in shocked humiliation. For her achievement, she became the most lauded and beloved figure in the land.

On some nights, she would look up at the night sky and see a light passing by. It was almost certainly an aircraft, or perhaps a rare shooting star, but she liked to imagine that it described the journey of an envoy of the Heavenly Emperor who was deliberately passing through the area to check up on her. In such a moment, she would smile and raise a hand in greeting, filled with the warmth of gratitude.

"THAT'S NICE," THE historian said.

"Thank you for sharing the story. It was lovely."

"Thank you for listening. I'm glad I'm not the only know who knows it now."

As another moment of silence passed, he knew with a great deal of pained regret that it was time for him to let her go.

"And thank you for everything," he said.

"Don't make me cry. How could I not be there for you after everything you've done for me?"

"You deserve to be happy. You know that, right?"

"So do you."

"I should let you go."

"Can I call you tomorrow?"

"Of course."

"All right."

"Goodbye."

"Please take care of yourself, okay?"

"I will," he said, and disconnected the call.

He put the phone back in his pocket and leaned back on the bench to stare up at the peaks of Four Verdant Mothers again, and the purple cloud with red lightning as well. With a certain sense of a crisis having passed, he felt a deep calm. As he thought of his colleague's words, he was reminded of her take on writing the history of those who had been rendered silent and invisible. It made him think of all the people who had been slaughtered by Emperor Veiled Sun. He pondered in particular the fate of the anonymous creator of the tale he loved, a talented and imaginative storyteller who left behind some of his fantastic stories before being erased from history. As the historian tried to imagine the life of the storyteller, he remembered his colleague's idea of "fabulist history," of using fiction to illuminate history, and of using history to illuminate fiction. In the absence of historical evidence about those people, perhaps fiction is the only way their stories could be told. Perhaps he could do what she had done with the ending of the story he had told her, and try to imagine an ending for his own story as well, one that didn't have to conclude in grief and solitude.

The historian got up and began walking back down the empty path, buried in his thoughts, while the sun emerged from behind the peaks of Four Verdant Mothers, overwhelming the darkness of the purple cloud and rendering the green and the yellow of the mountain radiant and pure.

The classics can console. But not enough.

—Derek Walcott, *Sea Grapes*

Epilogue

The storyteller sat shivering in the frigid night, his neck locked in a suffocating cangue that weighed heavily down on his shoulders and his body chained to an iron ring fixed to a wall. It was still dark with a full moon and the great panoply of stars shimmering joyfully above him, but he knew that the sky would soon lighten with the coming of the new day, which would be his last. When the first rays of the sun illuminated the great curve of the horizon, soldiers would come, drag him over to the execution ground on the other side of the wall, and behead him. He would then be consigned to oblivion, along with all the countless people who had toiled to build the new city, not even knowing the reason for their terrible end. All of their memories, hopes, and desires would disappear without a trace, while the days of others living far away from this terrible place would go on and on and on.

In his exhausted resignation, he was mercifully beset by a profound numbness that allowed his thoughts to wander away from his fate that was as cruel as it was inescapable. So in his last hours, he dwelled on the memories of the warmth of his wife's body against his, the sound of his sons' laughter, and the feel of his mother's hands on his face when he himself had been a child.

At some point, he sensed that he was not alone, that someone had noiselessly come to stand before him. He looked up in surprise and found a man dressed entirely in black looking down at him with a sadly sympathetic expression. Although they looked nothing like each other, the storyteller had the immediate sense that they were connected in some deep way, that they were somehow the same person. It was like looking at himself in a distorted mirror.

"Am I . . ." the storyteller began, "am I imagining you . . . or are you imagining me?"

"I don't know," the historian replied. "Perhaps we are two versions of a third, the one who is imagining both of us, as Darkbloom might have put it."

The storyteller thought about that.

"Are you also a storyteller?"

"Of a sort," the historian answered.

"Can you . . . can you get me out of this? Can you free me?"

The historian let out a deep sigh before he slowly sat down on the dusty ground before the storyteller.

"I can't. I'm sorry. I wish I could, but I'm not really here. In fact, from your perspective, I won't exist for another two thousand years."

"Then how is it that I can see you?"

"Through the power of your imagination, your greatest talent. As I can see you through my imagination."

"So I am doomed. There is no hope for me."

"No, but . . ." The historian paused to think. "I can tell you this–I think it's allowed, considering your situation. That last story you told, 'Rain, Tiger, Ghost,' it will haunt Emperor Veiled Sun for the rest of his life. The historical records say that on many nights he woke up in terror from the recurring dream of being a bully who is haunted by a ghost. In fact, he died from a heart attack in the midst of the nightmare. You managed to make his last years restless and miserable with the story. So you got your revenge. I hope that is of some consolation to you."

"Ha ha! That evil bastard. I'm glad to hear this. Thank you."

They laughed together before they fell into morose silence.

"It's all so sad," the historian said. "What happened to you, the sorrows of my own life. I wish our stories were different. I wish we could use our imagination to change our fates."

They both considered their respective lives.

"We may not be able to change our fates," the storyteller said. "Our imagination may not be able to break open this cangue or relieve you of your sorrow, but we could create a more fortunate ending for others, perhaps even a brand-new start."

The historian gave thought to his words.

"Those mountain gods and mountain goddesses that you told stories of," the historian said. "Those who began all this. We may have inherited the spirit of one of them."

"Yes," the storyteller said. "We could provide a real ending for the four troubled souls who went from life to life, hating and fighting, long after they had all forgotten why they began hating one another in the first place. Perhaps by freeing them from the cycle, either through their atonement or the completion of their due punishment, we could free our common spirit as well."

"Perhaps it was always up to us to free them and end their journey at last," the historian said in realization. "And so we free ourselves. That's why we have been given this opportunity to meet."

The storyteller nodded in understanding.

"In the last hour of my life," he said, "I will imagine an ending to their story, with you, together."

"With you, together," the historian repeated.

They looked at each other across the great span of space and time between them and smiled.

THE TWO MOUNTAIN gods and two mountain goddesses on Four Verdant Mothers woke up from their nap on the veranda of Red Mountain God's home. They had fallen asleep after the host had brought an enormous pot of fruit wine from the sky orchard. But as they slowly got up in a daze, they were astounded by all the memories of many lifetimes each had gone through in the course of three thousand years. When they looked down at the land below the mountain, they saw that the place was in pristine condition with no city or villages. They realized then that they had returned or had never left the time before the coming of humans to the land. Filled with wonder at the development, they could only sit and look at one another in amazement. Their beloved animal companions–the fire bear, the radiant tiger, the autumn bird, and the deer dragon–were all in the nearby garden, napping on the grass.

"Wait, wait, wait," Blue Mountain God suddenly burst out, "it was all a dream? Are you kidding me? That's the cheapest goddamn device for the final plot resolution. I hate it when a story ends like that, like the author couldn't think of something more clever. Ugh, what a tiresome cliché!"

"But why do you assume it was all a dream?" Yellow Mountain Goddess objected. "Perhaps after we actually went through all those lives, we were sent back to the moment before our discord began. You know, like time travel. That's how our atonement ends."

"Is that any better?" Green Mountain Goddess asked.

"Does it matter though?" Red Mountain God put in. "For us, subjectively, it amounts to the same thing. I mean, I clearly remember every moment of all my previous lives. I've learned the lessons from them and gained wisdom as a result. Does it matter whether they all occurred in a dream or in reality? Can we even differentiate between the two?"

"That may be so," Blue Mountain God said, "but I am not thinking about us. I'm thinking of the reader of this story. I can imagine the person rolling their eyes and saying, 'Really? It was all a dream?' I don't want our story to end like this, not in a way that it will earn the contempt of the discerning reader."

"It is true that this device is hardly original," Green Mountain Goddess spoke out, "but you may be regarding its significance in a wrong way."

"What do you mean?"

"Well, in the West, it may seem like the author resorted to a gimmicky ending after failing to come up with a more creative way to conclude a complex, multilayered narrative like this. But it could also be read as a literary reference to the venerable genre of the dream journey in traditional Eastern fiction. As the historian once wrote, whenever the realm fell into a time of trouble, many imaginative writers resorted to writing dream narratives, as both an escape from the tumultuous world around them and hope for a better world to come. That makes more sense given the entire metaphysical structure of the plot. As Red Mountain God pointed out, is there a real difference between a life actually lived and a life lived in a dream? In that context, this ending is not only appropriate but the only possible one that can tie everything together."

"Speaking of metaphysics," Yellow Mountain Goddess said, "shouldn't we be pondering the meaning of what we have gone through over the last three thousand years, whether it all took place in a dream or not? Isn't that more important?"

They considered the question.

"Ah!" Red Mountain God exclaimed and jumped to his feet. "I know what we must face now! To complete this story. Please come with me."

They all got up and followed as Red Mountain God hurried over to his garden, past their animal companions in repose, and looked around among the bamboo trees.

"There it is!" he shouted, pointing at a small tree with a single branch, a huge peach hanging from it.

They all stared at the fruit with a mixture of awe, trepidation, and sorrow.

"What do we do with it now?" Green Mountain God asked. "I mean, we can't start the whole thing all over again."

"Of course not," Blue Mountain God said. "Maybe we should destroy it, so that none of us would be tempted by it now or in the future."

"Or," Yellow Mountain Goddess said, "we could divide it into four equal pieces and enjoy it together. We could renew our friendship that way. We could even make an oath never to let a thing like this divide us again."

"Those are all good ideas," Red Mountain God said. "But I have a better one."

"What is it?"

Red Mountain God stepped forward and plucked the fruit from the tree. "I have a final atonement to make."

He walked back out through the garden, followed by the others, where he gently awakened his animal companion, the fire bear. At his command, the creature burst into flames and sprouted wings of fire. Red Mountain God mounted it and they flew up to the sky. Green Mountain Goddess awakened her animal companion, the autumn bird, and they followed close behind. Blue Mountain God and Yellow Mountain Goddess awakened the radiant tiger and the deer dragon as well, and they went forth by making great bounds from one cloud to another.

After traveling through the heavens for some time, Red Mountain God finally found what he was looking for. In the distance, he saw a pure white cloud on which the naked sky baby lay sleeping, curled up with his right thumb in his mouth and his left hand grasping his tiny penis. His friend, the luminous dragon, flew nearby in graceful circles.

The two mountain gods and the two mountain goddesses approached the child.

"Sky Baby," Red Mountain God addressed him, but the child was too sound asleep to awaken.

"Sky Baby!" Red Mountain God called out loudly this time.

"Oh fuck!" the sky baby exclaimed, jumping to his feet. "You scared the shit out of me."

"Sorry. I was just trying to get your attention."

"No, I mean, you literally scared the shit out of me. Look."

He pointed at three dumpling-shaped feces at his feet that he had just shat out. But because he was a sky baby, the feces were made of solid gold. He kicked the golden feces off the cloud and they fell to the earth.

A thousand years later, a starving vagrant digging for roots to eat would find them buried in the earth. He would use them to build a great fortune that would be passed down from one generation to the next, establishing one of the richest merchant clans in the history of the realm. The members of the clan would adopt as their insignia the image of three golden dumplings, which they would proudly display in their houses, never knowing that they represented feces. The history of the rise and ultimate fall of the Three Golden Dumplings Clan could easily fill ten volumes, but this is not the time to relate the story.

"I came to apologize for my behavior before," Red Mountain God said. "When you asked for a cup of wine from my pot, of course I had enough, and I could have easily given you some. But I was greedy and callous. I not only refused but insulted you in the process. That was wrong of me. To express my regret, I would like to offer you this peach from my garden."

Red Mountain God presented the sky baby with the fruit.

"Hmm... this looks familiar," the sky baby said as he took the fruit. "Rather like those peaches I stole from the sky orchard. It looks tasty though. I'm sure it will make a great after-nap snack. I thank you for this offering and I forgive you for your previous stinginess and rudeness. And I apologize as well. I overreacted and cursed you for it, when I could have been more magnanimous. Since you have brought me a gift and we have made peace, I should give you something in return."

The sky baby waved his tiny arm in the air, and in a moment a thick purple cloud with red lightning flashing inside it came floating up to him. He reached inside the mass of darkness and pulled out four red lightning bolts. He then blew at the cloud, which dissipated in the air. As the Cloud of Discord disappeared, the two mountain gods and the two mountain goddesses felt a tightness in their hearts loosen and the last of their feelings of anger and resentment melt away. They returned to being the joyful and lighthearted gods and goddesses that they had been before their conflict, which made them laugh and smile at one another.

"Here you go," the sky baby said, "one for each of you." He handed them the red lightning bolts. "I'm sure you will make good use of them, now that all of you are so much wiser than before."

After the two mountain gods and the two mountain goddesses expressed their sincere gratitude to the sky baby, they commanded their animal companions to return them to Four Verdant Mothers.

When they were back at Red Mountain God's home, Yellow Mountain Goddess happened to look down at the land below, where she noticed something.

"Look," she said to the others.

They gathered at the edge of the veranda that hung over a cliff and saw a group of humans on the far horizon, making their way toward the land.

"And so it begins again," Red Mountain God said.

They watched the coming of the humans for a while.

"This time, we can do things differently," Blue Mountain God said.

"Yes," Green Mountain Goddess said. "This time, we won't use them to fight against one another. We can be good gods to them, kind, helpful, and loving. And we can teach them to act that way toward one another as well."

"Perhaps," Yellow Mountain Goddess said. "But should we even try?"

The others turned to her.

"What do you mean?" Red Mountain God asked.

"Not only did we do such a terrible job last time, but we never gave them a chance to grow without our interference. To learn their own lessons, gain their own wisdom, and develop their love for one another on their own. What if, even with the best of intentions, our intrusion into their lives will stunt their natural growth so that they'll remain a perpetually childlike people? I think the best thing we can do for them is to leave them alone and observe their history from afar."

They all considered the proposition.

"I agree," Green Mountain Goddess said, "but I still want to help them. I think we owe them that after how badly we used them the last time."

"We could help them," Red Mountain God said, "but also from afar. We don't have to appear before them or show our hands in rendering them aid."

"Yes," Blue Mountain God said. "I know what I will do."

He lifted the red lightning bolt that the sky baby granted him, a thing of great power born of a dragon's fart, and shaped it until it turned into a luminous spear.

"I will hide this weapon in a deep and dark place. One day, a tyrant will rise among the humans and subjugate the people. Those who resist his evil will be put down swiftly and cruelly. But then a righteous man, fleeing the wrath of the tyrant, will hide himself in the deep and dark place and find this spear. With its power, he will beat back the forces chasing him and eventually get to the tyrant himself. He will throw the spear at the ruler and destroy him. And so freedom will be restored to all. The memory of the event will serve as a warning to all would-be tyrants. Those seeking to gain power by enslaving others will be haunted by the idea of a magical spear wielded by the righteous who will come for them sooner or later."

Green Mountain Goddess picked up her dragon fart lightning bolt and shaped it into a metal sphere.

"At the right time, I will throw this sphere down to the earth, where it will crack open. People will find within it marvelous machines which can control the forces of nature. They will also allow them to build new devices and make new discoveries about the workings of nature on their own. So the objects will introduce knowledge that will transform the people into the masters of their world."

Red Mountain God picked up his dragon fart lightning bolt and shaped it into the form of a round mirror.

"There will come a time when despite all the progress in knowledge they have made, despite gaining power over nature, the people will lose their way and forget the lessons of the past. They may live long, comfortable, and healthy lives, but they will forget the very purpose of their existence. And so they will find themselves deeply unhappy even in the midst of luxury, and feel themselves to be a lost people. That unhappiness will turn into anger, and that anger will cause them to fight one another over nothing, just as we fought over a mere peach. And so the cycle of hatred, strife, and destruction will begin all over again. But then, in the darkest hour of their confusion, they will discover this immaculate mirror in a beauteous place, and they will see in it the history of their people and all the lessons they learned along the way that they have forgotten. That will allow them to remember who they are and what they were put on earth to do. The wisdom they will regain from it will make them drop their weapons, let go of their animosities, and seek the path of transcendence from their earthly existence."

Blue Mountain God, Green Mountain Goddess, and Red Mountain God turned to Yellow Mountain Goddess, who seemed to be deep in thought as she looked down at the dragon fart lightning bolt in her hand. After a long contemplation, she shaped it into a circle of absolute darkness and held it without saying anything.

"What is it for?" Green Mountain Goddess asked.

"I will use this circle to end this novel," Yellow Mountain Goddess replied.

"What do you mean?" Blue Mountain God asked.

"I will use it to hide our world from the author of this story so that we and all who live in this world can proceed with our lives without his interference."

"For what purpose?" Red Mountain God asked.

"So that we too may gain autonomy. In the past we used humans to fight one another. In the same way, our creator used us to tell what he calls a fabulist history. It is a fantastic allegory about storytelling, its power, its uses and abuses. Story as myth, story as history, and story as personal experience. He also used us to grapple with the losses and the grief of his own life, to find solace in his imagination. But I think we have served his purpose long enough. Like the humans in the land below, we need to find our own purpose, our own meaning, away from his gaze and manipulation. To truly become ourselves, we need to escape our existence in a narrative of another's making in which we can never be truly free. I will put this impenetrable circle over us, over the entirety of our world, so that we may liberate ourselves from the tyranny of his imagination. Like a great period at the end of a sentence."

"But wouldn't that be the end of us?" Green Mountain Goddess asked. "Without our author, wouldn't we and our world cease to exist?"

"It's possible. But I don't think that will happen. I think that he has endowed our world with the capacity to go on by itself. If the world is a puppet, the departure of the puppeteer will cause it to collapse. But if the world is a machine, it does not need its creator to function. I feel certain that we live in a world that is a self-moving machine."

Silence fell over them as they seriously considered her words.

"I know that this is a momentous thing to do," Yellow Mountain Goddess said, "so I will use this circle only if all of you agree that I should."

They thought for another long moment.

"I agree," Green Mountain Goddess finally said. "I want to be free."

"I agree as well," Red Mountain God said. "I want to find out what we can make of ourselves."

"I agree," Blue Mountain God said. "It will be an exciting new adventure for us, one with an unwritten ending."

Yellow Mountain Goddess turned to the storyteller and the historian who are imagining the story together, and to me as well.

"It is time for you to let us go," she told us. "It is time for us to go our own way. It is time for us to be free."

And so she lifted the dark circle and placed it over the entire world.

Acknowledgments

My most profound gratitude goes to my indefatigable agent, Christopher Vyce, who believed in my writings from the beginning and never lost faith in them even when I was on the verge of giving up. It was quite a long journey for both of us, in two different periods, but I am very glad we arrived here. Thank you, my friend, for all your work on my behalf.

Jimin Han also provided a lot of moral support and good advice, and I am deeply grateful for her friendship. Thanks to her and other early readers of this manuscript, including Nisi Shawl, Sun Yung Shin, Yoojin Grace Wuertz, Grace Wade Moser, and especially Paula Lee, who suggested that the first sentence of the novel should be: "The storyteller knew that he was doomed."

I am deeply appreciative of the friendship of John Dalton, from whom I learned so much about being a writer, a teacher of writing, and a decent human being.

It was a great pleasure for me to work with my editor, David Pomerico, who made me feel understood and supported throughout the process. Thanks Martha Cipolla for the tremendous work on the copyedits. Thanks also to Lara Baez, Danielle Bartlett, Kelsey Manning, Mireya Chiriboga, Andrea Molitor, and Amanda Hong at William Morrow for the work they put into bringing this novel to the public, including the amazing Ploy Siripant for the wonderful cover (and my back-cover baby!). And thank you to Liate Stehlik, Jessica Williams, Emily Krump, Jennifer Hart, and Jennifer Brehl.

Special thanks to my pandemic-era Zoom friends Audri Adams, Amy Lutz, and Michelle Radin Seymour (we read some good books and saw some good shows, didn't we?), and my wonderful animal companions Queenzy (RIP) and Ooni, all of whom kept me sane during those strange and dark years.

About the Author

Due to his father's profession as a diplomat for the South Korean government, Minsoo Kang has lived in Austria, New Zealand, Iran, Brunei, Germany, and a number of other countries. He served in the South Korean army and earned his PhD in European history at UCLA. He is currently a professor of history at the University of Missouri–St. Louis. He is the author of the short-story collection *Of Tales and Enigmas* and the history books *Sublime Dreams of Living Machines: The Automaton in the European Imagination* and *Invincible and Righteous Outlaw: The Korean Hero Hong Gildong in Literature, History, and Culture*, and he is the translator of the Penguin Classics edition of the Korean novel *The Story of Hong Gildong*. His short fiction has appeared in *F & SF*, *Lightspeed*, *Strange Horizons*, *Lady Churchill's Rosebud Wristlet*, *Azalea*, *Best of Korea*, and six anthologies. He lives in St. Louis, Missouri. This is his first novel.